South African-born Jack Bennett began his writing career in 1957. He travelled the world as a journalist and was in Saigon in 1968 during the May Offensive by the Viet Cong. He worked for Reuters in London, and for newspapers in Tanzania and Hong Kong. Jack was at Australian Associated Press and the *New Zealand Herald* before joining the Australian Broadcasting Commission in 1974. Subsequently Jack worked for the Australian National Maritime Museum and the NSW Government's Waterways Authority. A prolific author, he wrote adult and children's fiction and non-fiction backgrounded by his special interest in military and maritime history and his experiences in Africa, Hong Kong and Australia. Jack Bennett died in March 2000.

Also by Jack Bennett

GALLIPOLI

JACK BENNETT

The classic story that captures the Anzac spirit

GALLIPOLI

The Novel

HARPER PERENNIAL

Harper*Perennial*
An imprint of HarperCollins*Publishers*

First published in Australia by Angus & Robertson 1981
This edition published in 2005
by HarperCollins*Publishers* Pty Limited
ABN 36 009 913 517
A member of the HarperCollins*Publishers* (Australia) Pty Limited Group
www.harpercollins.com.au

HarperCollins*Publishers*
25 Ryde Road, Pymble, Sydney, NSW 2073, Australia
31 View Road, Glenfield, Auckland 10, New Zealand
77–85 Fulham Palace Road, London W6 8JB, United Kingdom
2 Bloor Street East, 20th floor, Toronto, Ontario M4W 1A8, Canada
10 East 53rd Street, New York NY 10022, USA

National Library of Australia Cataloguing-in-Publication data:

Bennett, Jack.
  Gallipoli.
  Based on a screenplay by David Williamson
  ISBN 0 7322 8227 6.
  I. Williamson, David, 1942– . II. Title.
A823'.3

Cover design by Miriam Rosenbloom, Stomata
Cover image by Sidney Nolan, courtesy of Australian War Memorial
Typeset in English Times by Hedges & Bell Pty Ltd
Printed and bound in Australia by Griffin Press on 50gsm Bulky News

5 4 3 2 1   05 06 07 08

Contents

Chapter 1

BINDANA STATION
Western Australia, 1897

1

Archy Hamilton came into the world running. Scarcely had Dr Hedley Parker given him a slap on the bottom and a quick wash than he did two things: yelled until he was purple in the face, and flailed the air with his tiny feet as though he was running a mile.

Dr Hedley Parker, who had driven over from Figtree Crossing for the occasion, let Archibald Orlando Hamilton's feet brace against his wide palm, and nodded approvingly.

"You've got a real little athlete here, Mrs Hamilton," he said. "Strong little blighter."

Mrs Hamilton, her face wet with sweat and as creased as her son's, smiled weakly, and Dr Hedley Parker wrapped the baby and placed it beside her before slipping quietly from the room. It was a hot day and Dr Hedley

Parker, who had been up late the night before, felt the first stirrings of a headache.

The family were waiting in the front room: big Wallace Hamilton, who looked as though he had been roughly hewn from a chunk of ironwood; his daughter and first-born, Julia, a quiet child of five with her mother's light green eyes; and Old Jack, Wallace's wandering brother. The curtains were drawn to keep out the noon glare and the room was dim and almost cool. The curtains did not quite meet and through the gap Dr Parker could see his old Cape cart and even older horse. The horse had pulled the cart into a small pool of shadow beneath the pepper trees.

"Just a simple old Cape cart, sir," Dr Parker would say of his vehicle. "Just your old two-wheeled Cape horse-cart, as used by the Dutchmen in the Cape. Not fancy, no. You must look elsewhere for that, sir. No chaise or gig or phaeton, certainly not. Made for a tough country, sir, like ours." And away he would creak, looking as dignified as it is possible to look in the blazing glare of an Australian day when one is covered in red dust and throbbing from head to toe with a blazing, rip-snorting hangover.

"Mr Hamilton," he said now, "my congratulations. A beautiful boy. Legs like little hams, sir. Kicked out, he did, like a little sprinter."

They shook hands, and then Old Jack and the doctor shook hands, and the new father said:

"A cuppa tea, doctor?"

The tea, Dr Parker knew, would have been brewing on the kitchen stove all morning. Dr Hedley Parker came from Sydney and had, many years ago, drunk freshly made, pale tea from delicate china cups. He sighed inwardly.

"Lovely," he said brightly.

Old Jack came to his rescue even as Wallace lifted the teapot.

"Perhaps," he said, "the occasion—something stronger? Eh, Wallace?"

Wallace replaced the teapot.

"Of course. Doctor—a whisky? Just a small one?"

Dr Hedley Parker pulled out his watch and squinted at it.

"Well, since it's an occasion—and the sun's over the yardarm, eh? Just a small one—don't make a habit of it, but—"

Wallace poured the whisky and they drank solemnly. Dr Parker, feeling considerably better, patted Julia on the head.

"A fine brother you've got," he said benevolently. "He's going to be a big boy."

"I want to see him," said Julia.

"Take her in, take her in," said the doctor. "Mrs Hamilton is tired, of course, but a few minutes—yes, take her in."

So Julia and her father tiptoed into the bedroom, and Old Jack poured Dr Hedley Parker another whisky, and one for himself; and a few minutes later Wallace came back and slipped something which chinked into Dr Hedley Parker's hand, and soon after that the doctor was gone, creaking along the road in his Cape cart with flies around his head and the red dust settling on his dark suit.

"An athlete, eh?" mused Old Jack as he and Wallace watched the doctor disappear into the heat haze.

"Funny how they can put their finger right on it, isn't it? Training, I suppose."

"Hmmm," said Wallace. To tell the truth, his new son had looked like nothing in particular to him: just a pink and purple scrap of a body, a crumpled face, a funny head with a few strands of thin golden hair, and a very loud voice. But if Dr Hedley Parker had given it as his professional opinion that the newly-arrived Archibald Orlando Hamilton was destined to be a butcher, a baker or a candlestick maker, Wallace would have taken his word for it. After all, Dr Hedley Parker *was* a doctor, and even if some people did say that his breath constantly smelled of acid pear drops so that it wouldn't smell of strong liquor, or that he carried slightly more of the local earth under his fingernails than was compatible with the standards of cleanliness expected of the medical profession, why, granting both these things, the fact remained that he was a doctor, qualified in Sydney, and, what's more, the only doctor for hundreds of square miles, and Figtree Crossing was damn lucky to have him.

So Wallace mused as he watched the doctor's cart, distorted by heat, now flattened, now elongated, now floating like a mirage, fade into silence and space.

"You've got to get them young," mused Old Jack, dreamily. "Like pianists, you know. Get 'em young and train 'em hard."

"He's crying again, Dad," said Julia, looking up from her doll: it was her best doll (she had only two), a store-bought creature called Emma all the way from Perth, with pink china limbs and a hard round red-cheeked face and startlingly blue eyes which slammed open and shut with sharp clicks when she was tilted.

Wallace got up.

"Let's go and get your mother some tea, Julia," he said.

2

Wandering Jack, they called him in Figtree Crossing. "That Old Jack, that Wal Hamilton's older brother, he's a real rover," they would say, with the deep envy of people who have spent all their lives in the same small town, always talking about moving ("I tell you, one day I'm going to get right out of here, right out, and never come back") but never plucking up the courage.

They were all glad to know him, too, and went out of their way to greet him when he walked down the dusty little main street in the grey moleskin trousers, heavy ankle-boots and old merchant navy officer's jacket he wore on all public occasions. The jacket, now sadly faded from its original navy blue, had four wavy gold rings on each sleeve which, said Bert the barman at the Royal, indicated a Master. In fact, the jacket was, or had been, a very good one, made by Gieves of London, tailors to the military and navy gentry for a century or two. It had, many years ago, been an extravagance on Jack's part: the African and Orient Line, in whose square-riggers Jack had trained and earned his Master's Certificate, did not care how its captains dressed as long as they ran taut ships. Jack had paid for the uniform out of his own pocket. The A and O Line did not run to captains' clothing allowances.

But even without the jacket and cap, nobody would have doubted that Jack had been in the navy. His lean face, still handsome despite his fifty-odd years, was tanned dark as a clipper's rubbing-strake; his prominent nose jutted like a prow from between two steely blue eyes. And his tattoos! A fouled anchor on one wiry brown arm, a scaly red and green dragon on the other—and, Lord, the places he could talk about! Cape Town, Rio de Janeiro, Hong Kong, Manila, Bombay, Calcutta, Macao, Tokyo, London, Sydney, Papeete—and some places nobody in Figtree Crossing had ever heard of, places that weren't even in the big atlas down at the town clerk's office, strange little ports in the Pacific and on the African coast. Other places whose names simply sang of adventure—Zanzibar and Mombasa and Tananarive and

Quantico. Jack had sailed in square riggers and steam-boats, wooden hulls and composites. Left the station in 1868, just as soon's he turned twenty-one—ran off the day after his birthday, he did; near broke old Cec Hamilton's heart. "Course," they'd say, watching Jack brush dust from his jacket, "course, he didn't leave the old man high 'n dry, like I mean Wal was growin' up, lemme see, in '68 Wal would've been, ah, eight, and a good promising lad. Can't say it was a surprise when old Cec left the place to Wal. I mean, he'd hardly heard from Jack for years. Years. For all he knew, Jack'd never come home. So Cec died and then poor old Ruby, just a few weeks later—worn out and heartbroken, they say, and I believe it—and Wal left alone to run the place. Luckily he'd taken up with that nice Broome girl, Rose, and they got married soon as was decent after Ruby died and look at the go they've made of that place! Worked their guts out! And then Jack comes back! Bang, just like that. Out of the blue. Train comes in one day, and there's Jack. Large as life, bold as brass. Walks into the Royal—ask old Tom there, he was here at the time—walks right in, has a beer, and asks me, 'How's things at Bindana, eh? How's the old man?' 'Your old man's dead,' I says, 'and your old mum, too. Years ago. And Wal's got the station. Lock, stock and barrel.' Well, that shook him, I can tell you. Really shook him. He finished his beer and walked out. The train was still standing steaming in the station and, fair dinkum, I reckoned Jack'd get straight back aboard. But no. He gets his suitcase and comes back. 'Give me a room,' he says, 'and can you get a message to me brother?' Then he has another beer and says, 'Well, I guess I haven't been a very good son. I been away eighteen years, you know. That's a long time. But the time just flew. Just flew. I always meant to come back sooner, but somehow—well, I didn't, and there's how it is. Back without a cracker and me brother's got the property.'

6

"So we got a message to Wal that night, by some bloke what was passing the station, and the next morning early Wal's here. Jack's in the bar having an early one, and Wal walks straight up to him and shakes him by the hand and says, 'Jack, welcome home.' Then he takes him out to the cart and loads his case aboard and comes back to old Mr Hemmings—you remember him, he run the Royal then, and said, 'What's the bill?' and he paid Jack's score and drove away. He took Jack home and he's been there ever since. And that's ah, lemme see, eight, coming on nine years ago. And Jack's happy as larry. Course, he does a bit of work around the place—mending fences, painting, gardening. But he ain't a cattleman. Never was. Knows nothing about farming. Always been a bit of a dreamer, Jack has. Wal and him built a room outside for Jack, and they tell me it's like a bloody museum. Full of maps and stuff from his travels. Souvenirs. They say he came home absolutely broke—down to his last sixpence. Reckon Wal slips him a couple of bob every now and then. Tried to tell me once he gets a pension from the shipping company he worked for, but I tell you what, if he does, they must be sneaking it out to Bindana, because it don't come through the post office here or the bank, and that's a fact, and it's a damn shame that a man like Jack should be short of a quid." So they nod sagely and change the subject as Old Jack approaches, and after a few beers they're listening to his sea tales with bated breath, and when he's finished they can smell the cloves, a mile off Zanzibar; they can see the skeletons back of Bagamoyo on the Tanganyika coast, where an Arab slaver murdered a whole coffle—more than two hundred black men, women, and children. And in that oven of a bar, with the wind hot as the devil's breath blowing the red dust through the door and the flies drowning in their tepid beer, they shiver when he tells them of a square-rigger fighting to windward off an ironbound Scottish coast, the sheets and halyards frozen hard, the

7

flying spray turning to ice and tinkling on the deck like broken glass.

He takes them on a small gunboat past the weird cliffs and savage rapids of the Lower Yangtze-Kiang, its screw churning the Chinese water to yellow foam. They stand beside Jack as he scans the river-banks for signs of a pirate ambush, feel a thrill run through them as he barks out: "Slow ahead. Close up the quick-firer's crew!"

And when Jack's finished they return to Figtree Crossing slowly, reluctantly, gazing about them as though waking from a dream. Then Jack finishes his beer, hauls out his gold watch, consults it, and says he must be off, gentlemen. The bar is a drab place when he has gone.

Of course, there is the occasional sceptic, usually an out-of-town commercial traveller, who resents the fact that he can't hold the bar-room floor with his town-sharp wit while Jack's there. But let him be foolish enough to say a word against Jack, or express any doubts about his stories, and he's soon left in no doubt that he's no gentleman and would probably be happier drinking elsewhere—which in Figtree Crossing means by yourself in your room, if you're a traveller, or down by the tracks with the town drunk, the Royal being the only licensed premises in town.

3

Archibald was never called Archibald, of course, even though he was baptised in that name. He was always Archy, even as a baby, even though his mother fought—not very fiercely—for the full name.

"You *can't* call a baby Archy," she said.

"Why not?" asked Jack. "I knew a bloke once, engineer in the old *Ottawa Queen*, well, he went ashore, married late in life, had a son. Called him Fred."

At which Mrs Hamilton threw up her hands and appealed to her husband.

"Archibald," mused Wallace. "Well, er, Rose, it is a bit of a mouthful . . ."

"It was good enough for my father—"

"It's a good name, Rose, I'll grant you that—"

"And I wanted a name that people wouldn't shorten. Like your father's. Nobody ever called him by his real, full name, Cecil. A lovely name. Dignified. He was always Cec!"

But Archy was always Archy, from the time he could toddle and before. And soon, Archy was whittled down to Arch; but by then Rose Hamilton had given Archy another sister, Mavis, then another, Helen, and two brothers, Edward and Albert, and had many other things to think about. Things like getting the children through measles and scarlet fever and whooping cough and colic and colds. Making one shilling do the work of ten during the lean years while Wal built up his herd. Washing. Cooking. Making clothes. Keeping Wal fed and fit and happy. Teaching Julia to read and write, trying to find time to play with Archy and the other children when she was so tired, so deathly tired that all she wanted to do was sleep. Rose never complained, not even to God in her prayers every night, because she was Rose Hamilton, a squatter's wife, and all squatters' wives lived the way she did: lives of hard, unremitting work, rearing and losing children, ageing, drying out, becoming stringy, faded, leathery, eyes bleached by fatigue, old at thirty-five. That was a woman's life.

She had almost cracked when Julia died. In a world in which things moved so slowly, even the seasons dragging

9

themselves reluctantly from one barely perceptible change to another, Rose's first-born died with shocking suddenness. One day she was alive, happy and laughing, playing in the wagon parked beneath the pepper trees: three days later she was dead.

Julia and Archy, now a stocky, brown-legged six-year-old with a cheeky face beneath a cap of blonde curly hair, had been playing coachman and horses, or something like that. Julia had been on the wagon-seat, pretending to drive, when she gave a sudden cry of pain. She had jumped down, and run into the house, clutching one hand with the other and crying. A splinter of wood from the wagon's old sun-warped boards had driven deeply into her right thumb. Closing her ears to the child's cries, Rose had dug the bloodstained sliver out with a needle, washed the wound, and bound it in a clean strip of cloth from the ragbag. A few minutes later Julia was out in the yard again, playing and laughing as though nothing had happened.

But the next day the thumb was swollen and painful. Rose washed it and replaced the cloth with a new piece. That night, sitting on the verandah with Wal after the children had been put to bed, she had looked at the dark horizon all around them, a dark line ending where the stars began, and had felt their isolation for the first time. Even Figtree Crossing seemed a world away.

"If that thumb of Julia's isn't better tomorrow we should take her in to Dr Parker," she had said, breaking a long silence.

"Are you worried about the lass?" asked Wal.

"Yes. A little."

Her husband patted her shoulder.

"Don't worry. Children are tough. But if you think the doctor should have a look, well—" She knew what the "well—" meant. It meant well, if the child's ill, we've got to take her to the doctor, even though we can't afford it. And we can't, thought Rose. It's been a very bad year.

Drought. Disease in the cattle. Repairs to the wagon. Ten calves, the nucleus of the herd Wal was trying to build, dead of some mysterious ailment. All the children need clothes, and we have about ten pounds in the bank. Ten pounds between us and the poorhouse.

"If you want her taken into town," said Wal, "you'll have to let me know early. I'm off to the Mile End at sun-up."

Early in the morning, when Rose crept into the children's room in the pearl-grey dawn, Julia was asleep. Her face was flushed. But that could have been the room, which was hot and stuffy. Rose pulled back the curtains to let in more air but even the dawn breeze was warm. Wal and Jack went to check on the cattle at the Mile End.

Julia awoke still flushed. She stayed in bed while the others got up. She would not have any breakfast. But Rose made her drink some milk. Then she undid the bandage and the panic suddenly rose in her and she had to bite her tongue to stop crying out. The thumb was grossly swollen, the flesh stretched like a pink balloon around the nail. Rose touched it, gently: it felt soft and pulpy.

"It hurts," said Julia, pulling her hand away. Tears spilled from her eyes and dried on her hot cheeks. "It hurts, Mummy."

Rose bathed the thumb in hot water. It was all she could think of. It seemed to ease the pain a little. She made Julia dress and sit on the cool side of the house, where the pepper trees overhung the verandah and made a green cave. Archy sat with his sister all day. Rose bathed the swollen thumb every hour. By early afternoon Julia was restless and burning with fever. Her thumb was now a grotesque pink sausage with a sinister dark stain spreading from it up towards the wrist.

"I wish Daddy would come home," said Archy for the hundredth time, and his mother clenched her teeth to stop herself screaming at him.

The day crawled slowly away through the heat and dust and silence, the bush suddenly seeming closer. In the late day the wind came, lifting the red dust in willy willies around the house; the corrugated iron roof creaked in the sun and the pepper trees stirred, dropping their small brown corn. When the day died, Julia lay in her mother's bed, her eyes staring at the ceiling, breathing short and fast. Shallow breaths that scarcely seemed to fill her lungs.

Then at last there were horses in the yard, boots gritty on the verandah: the men were home, exhausted, flayed by the sun, starving. Rose fed them and they sat dully, scarcely comprehending, when she told them about Julia. They examined the thumb again by the light of the big flaring pressure lamp and the child stirred and whimpered.

They went back to the front room, stunned, not daring to say what was in their minds.

"I'll go and get Doc Parker," said Jack.

Wal shook his head.

"You won't raise Parker in the wee hours, Jack. You know what he's like—"

"He'll have to be raised—"

"Wal's right," said Rose. "He'll be useless at that hour, anyway. So will you. Get some sleep, Jack, and leave at three. You'll be back here by nine."

"Nine! Twelve hours, thirteen hours! That child—"

He stopped.

"All right. Wake me at three."

Wal nodded.

"Thanks, Jack."

The husband and wife sat without speaking for four hours. The old house creaked as timber shifted and iron cooled. Rose woke Jack and came back to Wal at Julia's bedside and they heard the horse being led past outside, heard the hoofbeats as, away from the house, Jack mounted and cantered away.

Then there was only the beating of their hearts, Julia's shallow breathing, and the clock's measured chopping of the hours.

Tick.

Fred Barnslow's son had blood poisoning and died.

Tock.

Irene Richards squeezed a pimple and died.

Tick.

Norm Parsons cut a toe while timber-getting down south, and lost a leg.

Tock.

There's no cure for blood poisoning.

Tick.

None.

Tock.

Towards morning, with the first lemon light in the east, the wind rose. The old house creaked and the pepper trees stirred uneasily in the gritty wind. The wind lifted the red dust and brushed the house with a soft sighing in the dark. The skirts of passing ghosts are lapping us, thought Rose, cold and stiff in her hard chair. She looked at Julia. The child was sleeping restlessly, giving little moans. Her face was puffy and livid in the little pool of yellow light cast by the lamp.

Wal groaned and eased his stiff limbs out of his chair.

"How is she?"

"Shhsh. Sleeping."

"I'll make some tea," whispered Wal. Rose nodded, her eyes on Julia.

Wal tiptoed from the room. She heard his quiet passage down the hall. Suddenly she felt a wave of pity for him and the tears stung her eyes, sharp and salt.

Then he was back, his face alarmed. Rose started to her feet.

"Archy," he whispered urgently. "He's gone—not in his room. Not in his bed! I looked—" Rose flew past him, half-crying with anger and fear.

The open front door was a pale rectangle against the yard beyond. Rose and Wal crossed the hall in a silent rush and stood on the cool verandah. The fowls were waking in their run behind the house: curiously gentle chirrings and cluckings. The rooster crowed suddenly, a flamboyant welcome to the day.

"There," said Wal, pointing. "There, by the gate. The little bugger!"

They walked silently across the dry earth of the yard to the small figure, shivering in its thin cotton nightshirt as it clutched the cold fence wire with both hands, watching the road from Figtree Crossing. Rose knelt beside him and put her arm around him.

"Come back to bed, Archy," she said, her voice breaking. "It's so cold out here, darling."

"Waiting for Uncle Jack," said Archy, staring down the road. "Uncle Jack's getting the doctor to make Julia better."

"Do make him come inside, Wal," said Rose. "It's cold out here—he'll catch his death—" she broke off, shocked at the word.

Wal shook his head. He took his wife's arm gently.

"Let him stay, dear."

"Uncle Jack's coming soon," said Archy, tightening his grip on the wire as though expecting to be prised off like a limpet. "Waiting for Uncle Jack."

The light was growing fast. The sun lapped the yard and they could see the dried tears on Archy's face.

"Leave him," said Wal.

Reluctantly, Rose stood up. She felt old and exhausted.

"I'll get his dressing gown," she said. It was a maroon candlewick affair she had stitched together from an old bedspread.

When she came back, there were sounds down the road and movements in the shadows where the night still lurked below the ridge. The cart had made good time.

"Uncle Jack's here," said Archy.

"I must have light," said Dr Hedley Parker, so they pulled the curtains wide and lifted the bed right under the window so the morning sun fell full on it, making Julia wink, and sending slivers of pain shooting through Dr Parker's throbbing head.

Gently Dr Parker unwrapped the cloth around Julia's hand. The child moved restlessly.

"Oh," gasped Rose. Wal and Jack were silent, stricken, gazing at the thing Dr Parker had exposed.

Julia's hand lay on the sheets like some obscene sea-growth. A bloated polyp, ready to burst, leaking an evil yellow-green fluid.

Dr Hedley Parker touched it gently. He saw the spread of the infection up the arm. He moved Julia slightly and felt her armpit, felt the lymph glands there gorged hard as smallshot with their load of poison.

"Hot water," he said. "Please."

He opened his bag and took out a roll of clean linen, and his scalpel case. He snapped the case open and selected a scalpel with a small curved blade, like a sabre. The child watched him with unseeing eyes, breathing rapidly like a frightened kitten. Dr Parker felt her forehead. It flamed beneath his touch.

Rose returned with an enamel bowl of boiling water and set it on the bedside table. Dr Parker washed the scalpel, dried it on the clean linen.

"I'm going to lance the hand," he said. "Please wait outside. I'll call if I need anything."

Rose opened her mouth to protest.

"Please," he said.

They waited in the hall. The other children were about now; Jack shooed them back to their bedrooms.

A short, high cry. Rose buried her face on her husband's shoulder and sobbed aloud.

Dr Parker came out with the bowl.

"Get rid of that, please," he said to Wal.

"Will she—" began Rose.

"She's very ill," said Dr Parker. "I've drained the hand. But the glands—the infection has spread—" He shrugged helplessly.

Julia lay quiet. The ghastly hand was hidden beneath new bandages. The room smelled—the sharp tang of carbolic and something else under it, something rank and noisome.

Jack and the doctor left Wal and Rose with Julia. They went out on to the verandah. Archy was sitting on the edge, barefoot, still in his nightshirt and dressing gown.

Archy turned and faced the doctor. "She's going to die, isn't she? I had a puppy once that died."

"Well," said Dr Parker, "well—" He looked at the small earnest face turned up to him and the lies dried on his lips.

"I'm afraid so," he said. "I'm sorry." Archy slipped off the verandah and ran across the yard, scattering the fowls. He squeezed through the fence and streaked away from the house, his feet slapping up the dust, down the slope towards the creek below the house.

"Let him go," said Jack, watching the small figure disappear in the scrub and rocks. "He's got to cry." He turned to the doctor.

"You want me to take you back to town?"

"Not yet. I'll stay—until—well, I'll stay. I'm the doctor, after all."

Full morning and the wind whirling the dust. The sun a cruel flare. Dr Parker ached for a drink.

Two crows passed high overhead, flying in their strange shoulder-hunched way, chasing their shadows across the hot earth, calling kar! kar! kar!

Archy trudged back in the late afternoon, his dressing gown dragging in the dust.

Julia died.

They buried her the next day. There was no time to send to the undertaker in Figtree Crossing for a small coffin. And no money to pay for it. And in that climate no time to wait.

Jack made the coffin from a packing case that had once held a water-pump: he painted it with black wagon-paint that wouldn't dry and marked their hands and clothes when he and Wal lowered Julia into the hard red earth beside her grandparents.

Archy didn't cry at the burial; but he went down to the creek by himself and didn't come back until dark, when the bats were flying and the plovers whistling on the flats.

4

Archy loved Jack. Of course he loved his father too, and his mother, and, presumably, his brothers and sisters. But his love for Jack was special. Of course it was unfair: Jack had lived an exciting life while his brother Wal had stayed home and developed the station, or tried to, which was all one could do in that hard land. Try. And work and hope and keep trying despite droughts and floods and illness and slumps and constant worry about every penny.

And what stories could you mine from such a life to thrill your sons? The time a brown snake in the outhouse nearly bit your mum? The time that bludging, young, new hand Les McCann, eighteen and old enough to know better, got near drowned when he tried to cross the creek when it was raging full in the flood of '05? The day the new plough arrived? Milestones in the life of an outback cattle-man, maybe, but pallid fare compared to tales of battles and shipwrecks and fights with dacoits off Burma, Chinese pirates off Macao and Arab slavers off Zanzibar. And storms and earthquakes and typhoons. And Jack could read, too, beautifully ("Good enough to go on the stage," said Rose admiringly). His room was full of books, the walls lined with them, floor to ceiling, and piles of them beside his bed and on the windowsill. He had picked them up all over the world, crated and stored them, and for years after he returned to Bindana the books kept arriving in old tea-chests: a note would arrive from the station master at Figtree Crossing and Jack would hitch up the horse and go into the Crossing to collect them, returning late at night, a little slurry in his speech and smelling of beer. And the next night there would be a reading of some of the new books, Jack sitting with a pile of them beside him, dipping into them all night, reading in his beautiful voice while the children sat around entranced by Kipling or Jack London or Dickens, and Wal, sun-dried and exhausted, slept in his favourite chair and Rose mended clothes or made new ones, and listened as hard as the children, if the truth be known.

And Jack's room! It was an Aladdin's cave to Archy. It was, in reality, a creaking, bark-tiled, earth-floored, sun-seared hut, made of cracking paintless timber, tucked into a corner of the yard. "I don't want to intrude," Jack had said soon after his return. "Don't want to be underfoot in your house all day, giving you no privacy. Give me a place in the yard somewhere." So Wal had taken him at his word, and built Jack's room (with a little help from Jack) in two days; Wal was very good with his hands, being one of those lucky men who could do almost anything with tools and timber.

Over the years, though, Jack had transformed the dreary room. Most of one wall was covered with a map of the world: a great, garish Mercator projection. Most of it seemed to be coloured a bright red, and Archy, when he was eight, asked Jack why. Jack—it was winter, and he was wearing his navy captain's jacket, and, for good measure, an ancient naval officer's cap, crusted with verdigreed braid—puffed out his cheeks and looked important.

"That, Archy my boy," he said, running his hands across the map, spreading his arms to encompass the world, "that, them pink bits, is the Empire on which the sun never sets. The British Empire!"

Archy studied the map.

"The sun must set some time," he said. "It can't be day all the time."

So Jack explained.

"Oh," said Archy. "It must be big."

"It is," said Jack. "And we're part of it."

"We're Australian," said Archy.

So Jack explained again; and Archy got his first lecture about the Empire; and Rule Britannia; and Britons never, never being slaves; and about the Crimea's Thin Red Line; and Waterloo and Trafalgar and the Boer War; and the charge of the Third Light Dragoons at Mudki when the Sikhs were giving a bit of trouble; and how the British square worked, with Jack playing three different ranks of English infantry in his enthusiasm; and how to present, aim, and fire the Snider rifle (an imaginary one) —"*thumb* the round *home*, close the action *smoothly*—fire, squeeze, don't jerk—bang—swing the rifle sideways, snap down, *briskly*, the Martini-Henry loading action, making *sure* the cartridge case is clear, eyes on the enemy *all* the time . . . reload . . . present—bang!" It was all stirring stuff and, when he was nine, Jack said: "You're a big boy, Arch, and now I'll show you something really special," and he pulled his old sea-chest from under the rickety bed, opened it, and withdrew something metallic, oiled, and gleaming dully: a revolver, a big revolver, so big that Archy needed two hands to lift it. Jack eyed it with quiet pride as he carefully folded the soft chamois leather and clean cotton cloth in which it had been wrapped.

Jack took the big pistol and thumbed the hammer back, squinting along the barrel, making clucking sounds with his tongue.

"That, Archy, is a genuine—" he closed his eyes as though trying to remember a lesson, and recited "—Webley's Number Five Model Army Express 1880 pattern centre-fire six-shot double-action revolver with rebounding hammer, .450 calibre, with lanyard ring and ejector-rod—" he opened his eyes, "and there, young Archy, is a gun as will drop any man, even a Sudanese fuzzy-wuzzy, down stone dead in his tracks, dead as mutton!"

"Have you shot anyone with it?" asked Archy, awed.

Jack hesitated.

"Well—" he said. Then he winked. "Best not say anything, eh? Your mother—"

It was a most satisfactory answer for both of them.

Jack's room was filled with other fascinating things like, for instance, the cobra in a bottle of spirits. Once a beautiful thing, a live jewel of shimmering gold and black, now it stirred, flaccid and pale, in the murky fluid, its eyes, once bright as coals, glazed, blind shuttered windows. And there was a stuffed macaw, very ragged; the claw—two feet long—of a Japanese spider crab; a stuffed piranha fish from the Amazon, only a foot long, but with a mouth lined with teeth like razors—"Strip you to the bone, he would, in seconds," said Jack. "Why, in some of those rivers back of the Amazon I've seen—" and away he would go with more stirring tales of adventures on the high seas, on mighty rivers, on coral coasts; of encounters with piranhas and with crocodiles large enough to swallow bullocks whole, eagles in the high Andes which carried away peasants' children, snakes whose venom would "kill you quick as a wink, pfft!—just like that—set your whole body rotting in seconds," and fierce swordfish which attacked fishing boats for no reason, driving their swords through "five inches of *oak* planking—skewering sailors in the bunks, pinning 'em to the bulkheads like — like butterflies!"

And he had, hanging on his wall, the saw of a young sawfish, the dreaded sawfish which floated close to the shore in warm tropic seas and "Whack! Swish! One swing of its saw—look at those long sharp teeth on the blade—would cut a man in half—right in half!—easily as your mum cuts butter!"

No wonder, then, that Archy adored Jack and vowed, from a very early age, to be like him when he grew up, and See the World.

Not all Jack's mementoes were bloodthirsty or exotic. Carefully pinned to one wall, and protected with an overlay of tissue paper, was a large oleograph of the famous Harry Lasalles, the runner.

"Run!" he would say of Lasalles. "Like the wind! An express train—a—a leopard—yes, a leopard! That's the way you want to run, Archy—like a leopard going for its prey. It can run down an antelope, a leopard can, just run it down!"

By this time — Archy was eleven when this

conversation took place—Jack had decided that Archy was going to be an athlete. But not just an athlete. Another Harry Lasalles. Like many men who have never had children of their own, Jack had fixed ideas on how the children of others should be brought up, and he started Archy's athletic education at an early age.

An evening walk to the creek became a race; Jack's occasional trips to town in the cart always began with Archy trotting beside the cart for a mile or more along the road to Figtree Crossing, "limbering up", Jack would say; and even a game of throw-the-stick for the station's ageing cattledog, Blackie, became a race between boy and animal.

"*Flex* those muscles, Archy—*feel* them pumping *blood*, tense them like springs, let them *shoot* you away like a leopard springing—you're a leopard chasing its prey, and Blackie's a hyena trying to get it from you! Go!"

In fact, Jack had only seen a leopard once, and that was a very bored and rather moth-eaten animal in London Zoo. Years later Archy was to read that the leopard in fact isn't particularly renowned for speed, preferring to creep up as close as possible to its prey, or to drop on it from a convenient overhanging branch, being an intelligent cat and lazy to boot. It is the cheetah which runs like Harry Lasalles. Jack had got his cats mixed but Archy didn't hold it against him. After all, one big spotted cat is pretty much like another. And anyway, thought Archy, what if Jack did get a fact or two wrong? He had had so many adventures that it would be hard not to. And look at the things he *did* know! Why, he knew as much medicine as most doctors—certainly as much as Dr Hedley Parker over at Figtree Crossing. He could name every muscle and bone in the body, almost.

Thumping Archy's thigh with his gnarled seaman's fist he would bellow: "Build these femoral muscles! Feel them! Make them work! Flex those hamstrings! I want to see those gastrocnemiuses work like a bag of snakes under the skin!'' And if Archy didn't know how long Jack pored over his highly-coloured ''Home Physician's Chart of the Human Body'' (one shilling and ninepence in the Charing Cross Road) before each training session, well, what he didn't know wouldn't hurt him, would it?

5

So Archy grew from a child weeping alone at the dry creek over his dying sister to a youth: long-legged, wiry, tanned oiled-wood brown by the sun, his vivid green eyes staring fearlessly at the world, his thick dark blonde hair wild as a spinifex bush. He could swim like an eel, shoot like a Bisley champion with Wal's old Lee-Metford, and ride as though he'd been born on a horse.

And, thanks to Jack's coaching and en-couragement, run like the wind. Jack was convinced that Archy would one day, soon, run like a champion: and he drove Archy hard, beyond the barriers of pain, forcing the lad to keep training when every muscle in his body screamed its protest. ''You're not just going to be a runner, Archy,'' he would say, over and over again, ''you're going to be the best! You're going to be another Harry Lasalles, my boy!'' After a while, Archy believed him.

He grew and thrived as the station grew and thrived. Bindana had had a hard start but Wal worked it through, dragged it through, by sheer hard gut-wrenching physical labour and determination. Jack helped where he could, and so did Archy, from the time he could ride. The herd grew, slowly, but it grew. Wal put in a windmill.

There was money in the bank, not a lot, but it was there, a cushion against fate.

Wal could afford to hire help. First there was Les McCann, eighteen when Wal first took him on, a bitter young man from a dirt-poor family failing dismally at scratching a living from the hotlands west of Figtree Crossing. Les had bad teeth and a foul mouth to match, although he never swore in front of Wal, who would have fetched him out of the saddle with one sweep of his thick arm if he had, because Wal never swore—well, hardly ever, and then not very badly, an occasional bloody, or perhaps a damn.

There were other young hired hands later; they came and went, generally tall, whipcord thin young men who worked hard all day and went to bed early in the bunkhouse Wal had built behind the homestead; some were white, some were black, some were in between. Only Les McCann stayed, probably because he had nowhere to go, and because Bindana was a far pleasanter place than the hideous hovel in which his parents were slowly going insane, his mother from childbirth, poverty and loneliness, his father from drink and despair and endless, unprofitable backbreaking labour in the blinding sun.

If Les McCann did no more work than he had to it was probably because, Jack remarked, he had seen his own father slowly killing himself through work and being just as bitter poor at the end of forty years as he'd been at the beginning.

At which piece of philosophy Wal sniffed and remarked that people who worked on Bindana would earn their quid or quickly get their marching orders; but he never fired Les, all the same.

6

"There's Abos on the place, Mr Hamilton," said Les McCann one day shortly after Archy's eleventh birthday.

"Steal you blind, they will. Bunch of cattle-duffers if I ever saw 'em. You want to get 'em off the place, Mr Hamilton."

Wal sighed. He was sitting on the verandah enjoying a beer in the evening cool: it was a measure of his relative prosperity that he could now have a beer whenever he felt like one, and not only on special occasions.

"Here's trouble," he had remarked only minutes earlier, watching Les stride up the yard from the bunkhouse.

Les was invariably the bearer of ill news. Misfortune followed him with the persistence of an evil smell. He was always the first to report a lame horse, a sick cow, a dying calf, lost equipment, disease in the chickens, caterpillars in the vegetables.

So now Wal sighed and finished his beer and pulled out his watch—a heavy silver-plated striker which had belonged to his father—and said: "Too late to do anything about them now, Les. Where are they, anyway?"

"Up at the east corner. There by that big old dead gum, you know? An old man, couple of gins and kids—three, four. You want to go and chase 'em off, Mr Hamilton—"

"I'll ride over and look at them first thing in the morning, Les. Can't do much harm overnight."

Les shrugged.

"Well, if it were my place—"

"Don't worry, Les. I'll look at 'em."

Wal, watching Les McCann's slope-shouldered figure slouch reluctantly back to the bunkhouse, finished the last of his beer, upended the glass and let the froth dribble on to the hot red earth of the yard, and sighed again. Aloud he said: "Les McCann, you really are a miserable bugger—" and was startled when his wife hissed in his ear:

"Wallace! Must you use such beastly language? Thank goodness none of the children are around!"

"I'm sorry," said Wal, "but he is, you know. Some poor Abo family's moved on to the place and he wants me to chase 'em off—"

"They're a thieving lot," said Rose.

"Some of them," said Wal. "I'll ride over and give them the once-over in the morning. But I don't think they're going to murder us in our beds tonight, dear."

"Dinner'll be on the table in a minute," said Rose, disappearing inside. "Wash your hands."

"Yes, dear," said Wal. In the cool dark room off the pantry he washed his face and hands in the heavy enamelled washbasin, turning the water brick-red in the process with the accumulated dust of the day, dried himself briskly on the hard jack-towel behind the door, and went in to dinner. It had grown dark in the last few minutes and the big hanging lamp had been lit to shed a warm yellow glow over the table. Wal felt a stirring of pride: his family were all there, faces shining with friction from their before-dinner clean-up, Archy and Mavis and Helen and the two youngest, Edward and Albert, although of course only their mother ever called them anything but Ed and Bert.

The tablecloth, of good, heavy linen, was spotless; the dishes and plates were of the best china that Perth shops could provide; the cutlery was gleaming Sheffield plate. Rose Hamilton was especially proud of the cutlery: it was tangible evidence of the wealth and standing of Bindana Station. Her husband had his acres and his cattle; Rose had her tableware. It was a sign, every mealtime, that the hard days were over. Wal's parents had never had cutlery like that: Rose remembered the motley collection Wal had inherited—some of the knives and forks had plain bone handles, dyed gaudy pink or green or yellow; in several of them blade and handle were so loosely married that they swivelled in the user's fingers, making genteel eating difficult.

Rose set the large water carafe (of cut glass, and made in England) on the table, and covered it with a lace doiley, edged with tiny seashells, to keep the flies out, and then brought in a steaming platter of beef, flanked by a mound of roast potatoes, golden brown and sizzling in gravy; long green beans, grown by Mavis and Helen; and, from the same garden (a rather sandy patch of soil) some, it must be admitted, woody, pale orange carrots. A meal, as Wal remarked, and as he remarked at most meals, fit for a king. So now, healthily tired, he sat and ate and looked at his family—including Jack, doing more than justice to the roast beef—and glanced around the room, at the wallpaper which was almost new (it had only gone up two years ago), at the framed prints of Perth, Melbourne and Sydney, the green plush dining room curtains, faded now, but that was to be expected, but good stuff originally that had cost a few bob a yard, railed up from Perth. Why, Wal thought, we've done a bit of all right, I reckon, eh? And he ate with gusto and was just swallowing a large mouthful of beef and baked potato and carrot and beans when, he did not know why, he suddenly thought of the Aborigine family out at the old gum, squatting on the earth floor of their grim humpy, eating—what? Goanna? Witchetty grubs? What? And curling up naked, curling up close like animals to keep warm when the night wind blew. Les McCann, he thought, you really are a miserable bugger. And then he thought of Les McCann lying on his bunk brooding about the Abo family, exultant at the sight of people worse off than himself, lower down the scale of life, longing to see them driven away, their humpy wrecked, burned, dust in their faces. Les lying there brooding lonely in the dark while the other stockmen joshed and laughed and told tall stories about where they'd been and where they were going; and Les hating them as much as he hated the Abos because he was never going anywhere or coming from anywhere because some time back along the line something had addled in his mind, something had turned permanently sour and lay at the back of his eyes, like a stagnant pool in a dry creek, dirty water rimmed with bitterness and regret. And Wal swallowed his mouthful with a painful gulp and thought: poor Les. Poor poor Les.

"Are you feeling all right?" asked his wife, looking at him with concern.

"Of course."

"You looked—strange for a minute."

"Just thinking. Just thinking, that's all, dear."

"Never think and eat," said Jack. "May I have some more potatoes? Thank you. No, never think and eat. The one interrupts the other. First things first. And after a long day, it's eating first on my list."

"So I've noticed," said Wal drily.

7

They rode out just as the sun was turning the eastern rim of the plain into a line of fire. It was still cool and the birds were calling; over in the east, where the sky was still dark blue, Venus ascending flamed like a jewel.

They rode quietly through the yard, Wal and Archy, the horses' hooves falling soft on the dew-damp earth. Les McCann came out of the shadows of the bunkhouse and fell in with them.

"Morning, Mr Hamilton." He seldom greeted Archy.

"Morning, Les."

They rode in silence away from the homestead. As it grew lighter Les glanced at Wal, ran his eyes over rider, horse and saddle, and said flatly:

"You didn't bring your rifle."

"No," said Wal. "What for? I'm not going hunting."

Les snickered.

"Thought we was hunting Abos, Mr Hamilton."

Wal reined, turning his horse across the path of McCann's grey. Archy stopped, too. The sun was just over the hills now, yellow as lamplight.

"How many Abos did you say there were, Les?" asked Wal quietly.

"Oh, an old bloke, couple of gins, few snotty-nose kids," said Les uneasily.

"Well, if you think they'll be too much for us to handle without firearms, Les, perhaps you'd better go back and give my wife a hand around the house, while Archy and I sort things out," said Wal.

McCann's face flamed red, then white. With a violent wrench he spun his horse and galloped back the way they had come. Wal and Archy sat silently until the beat of hooves died away.

Wal exhaled. "I shouldn't have said that, should I? He just got under my skin. C'mon, son, let's go."

"Perhaps he'll give notice," said Archy. "You know, leave Bindana."

"Not him," said Wal, with conviction. "Not Les."

Wal clucked to his horse.

"Because Bindana's all he's got, Archy. The best home he's ever had."

"He's got people at the Crossing. Uncle Jack says so."

They were trotting side by side now. Wal turned and looked at his son.

"You ever seen his people, Archy? Uncle Jack ever show you where they live?"

"No, Dad."

"Perhaps if you saw them and the place they call home you'd understand Les better."

"I know they're poor. But we were poor once, Uncle Jack says."

Wal laughed.

"Jack's never been poor. Not the way it counts. Yes, your grandfather and grandmother were poor, I guess. But they had a dream and they worked for it—"

"You work too, you and Mum—"

"Not the way Grandpa and Grandma did. They worked, really worked! This place was nothing when they came here in the eighteen-fifties with no money and Jack a child. Nothing. They lived in a leaky tent for months while Grandpa got some crops in the ground, something to live on. Then they lived in a shack made of timber, gum-bark and clay. My father made 'em with his own hands—couldn't afford to hire anyone. Soon as he got money he got a real bricklayer out from the Crossing to build the new house, where we live now. Just one room at first. Then he added to it whenever he could afford it. Look at it now! One of the biggest places around. More rooms than my father ever dreamed of. I wish he was alive to see the whole place now."

They jogged along in silence for a few minutes, Archy deep in thought, automatically flicking away the flies which had risen with the sun.

Wal glanced at him surreptitiously. Archy's brow was furrowed. Wal put out his big hand and slapped him on the shoulder.

"Aye. I know what you're thinking. Les's folks must've come out here about the same time as Grandpa. So why did Grandpa make a go of it and not them, eh?"

Archy nodded, grinning. "I was! That's just what I was thinking, Dad! You could go on the stage like that man at the Crossing last year! Percepto the Mind-reader!"

Wal smiled.

"Wasn't that hard, son. Didn't take a Sherlock Holmes—that the name of Mr Conan Doyle's detective?—to get your train of thought. Thing is, I can't answer the question. The McCanns and the Hamiltons both had about the same chances. Guess Grandpa was a harder worker than old Mr McCann. Or luckier. Could have been a lot of things. I reckon luck must've been part of it. Some people work hard and never come right, like old Mr McCann. Anyway, I know Les's father tried hard enough before he gave up. Just couldn't get anything to work right for him. And Les—well, it knocked the spirit out of Les. So I—we—must make allowances for him."

"I don't like him much," said Archy.

"You don't have to."

And Archy sensed the conversation was closed.

The dead gum speared the red earth like a frozen bolt of lightning. It had stood there for years—Wal could barely remember when it had died, thirty or more years ago. It was a stranger to that place: a huge red gum. One day, perhaps sixty years before, a seed, carried miles from its native habitat by a bird or a freak wind-current, had fallen to earth. Unusually heavy rains had seeped into the soil near the seed and established a tiny underground lake, which later rains had kept full. The seed sprouted; grew; sent a long tap-root deep into the soil, searching for water. It found the water and thrived, sent its roots deeper, picked up and tapped other sources of moisture.

And the tree grew, soared almost seventy feet high

before a succession of dry seasons sucked the water out of the little lake, dried up the underground streams, seared the earth. Desperately the tree sent its roots deeper and deeper, but the water had retreated beyond its reach. The tree died. Slowly, slowly, first the top new leaves, then branch by branch, the sap gradually sinking, the bark curling, flaking off in great sheets, the dead leaves whirling away on the hot wind. Over the years the wind and sun blasted and bleached the tree so that now it gleamed white as a skeleton. On windy days it creaked and split, and every year a little more of it crumbled away.

A faded, much-patched tent flapped dismally beside the old gum.

The Aboriginal family stood before it, stiffly, as though posing for a photograph, as the white man and his son cantered up.

From the saddle, looking down at the awkward little group, Archy had a sudden almost overwhelming impression of *blackness*, strangeness: it seemed briefly, impossibly, that the group was one solid alien being, not six different people. Wary, dark faces, frozen in the hard light, watched him, eyes sharp as lizards'. Then the old man moved, lifted his hand, and the spell snapped. The two younger children hid their faces in their mother's tattered cotton skirt while the eldest, a boy of about Archy's age, regarded Wal gravely.

All wore ill-fitting cast-off white man's clothing. The remains of a suit flapped against the old man's body, a stained, collarless shirt and a worn waistcoat under the coat. The boy wore only fraying drill trousers, tied at the waist with string.

Behind the old man an incredibly ancient woman half-crouched, mumbling to herself.

Silence. The old gum creaked.

Wal swallowed. He almost wished Les was with

them. He didn't need another Aboriginal family on Bindana; he had two living out at Mile End. Besides, Bindana had never employed many Aborigines. There were not too many of them in the area, and there hadn't been for years. It was a hard, unforgiving country which had taken backbreaking toil to make productive, and the early settlers, back in the 1850s and on into the sixties and seventies, and even later, had made it brutally plain that they were not going to share the rewards of their toil with anyone.

"Where you feller from?" he asked, lapsing automatically into pidgin.

The boy stepped forward. He was thin but wiry, with large white teeth.

"The mission at Currawong," he said. He waved vaguely westward. "Over there. They kicked us out."

He spoke clearly in a high, rather piping voice, in perfect English.

"Currawong? That's twenty, thirty miles," said Wal. "How'd you get here?"

"Walked," said the boy. "It took a long time."

"Why'd they kick you out of the mission?"

"My father fought with another man."

"Where's your father?"

"Dead. The other man killed him. Then the priest said it would be better if we went. So we went."

Didn't want a feud brewing, thought Wal. He looked at Archy.

"What do you think, son? Let 'em stay?"

"Yes," said Archy. "Let them stay."

"All right," said Wal, talking to the boy, because the old man, staring straight ahead, seemed to be taking no interest in the proceedings, "you can stay, but not here. Too hot, and no water for miles. You get your stuff down to the creek, eh? There—see?" and he pointed back down the long shallow slope of the valley to where the bush grew in a solid green wall along the hidden water. "There. All right?"

"All right, boss," said the boy. He looked up at Wal. "I work for you, right? Tomorrow."

"We'll see," said Wal. "Come on, Archy. Can't stay here all day." They swung round their horses and cantered away, raising a little cloud of dust which blew and settled on the bushes. The boy watched them until they were out of sight.

"Should have told 'em to keep moving," shouted Wal to Archy. "But what can you do? Them just arriving like that. And the old man looked dead beat. Still, if they cause any trouble—never can tell, not with Abos. Never know what they're thinking. And if they get into the drink, well . . ."

They galloped home.

Les McCann, after getting orders for the day, stamped irritably into the kitchen the next morning as Wal was finishing his tea.

"One thing I can't stand," he said, "it's a cheeky black."

Wal raised his eyebrows.

"Didn't know we had any, Les."

"You have now, Mr Hamilton. That young black from the new lot that you—" Les hesitated "—sorted out yesterday morning. Trying to talk like a white man. Bloody mission schools—I tell you!"

"What are you talking about, Les?" asked Wal. "You've lost me. What young black? Where?"

"There—under the tree," said Les, pointing through the kitchen door. "Sitting there large as life and twice as ugly! Asked him what he was doing and he said cheeky as anything, 'I've come to work.' Just like that."

Wal stared at the small black figure sitting cross-legged in the shade of the pepper tree.

"Well I'll be—" he said. "The little—" He turned and opened the inner kitchen door, shouting down the passage.

"Archy!"

His son appeared. Wal indicated the small figure under the tree.

"That's your job for today, son. Find out what he can do. Keep him useful around the yard. Give him some tucker—"

"And watch he don't steal enough for the whole family," said Les.

Archy walked across the yard, blinking in the hot morning sunlight. The young Aborigine stood up. He smiled: his whole face shone when he smiled.

"My name's Zac," he said. "It's short for Zachariah." He put out a slim dark hand.

"Pleased t' meetcha."

Archy could feel Les McCann's eyes on him.

Slowly he put out his hand. The dry black fingers curled around his. He looked into the smiling brown eyes.

"Mine's Archy," he said.

In the kitchen, Les McCann shook his head in disbelief.

Chapter 2

FREMANTLE

1913

1

Platt Street, Fremantle, would have run into the harbour if
it hadn't stopped abruptly at the railway lines as though
some giant had trimmed it with an axe—whack—slicing
the end house on either side so abruptly that even
compared with the other houses of Platt Street they seemed
unnaturally pinched and poky, almost too narrow for
normal people to live in.

The wharf at the end of Platt Street was empty this
hot December afternoon; but a British tramp had just
coaled and left and the coal dust lay on the smooth water
like streaks of strange black foam.

Unfortunately, as any Platt Street housewife could
tell you, the coal dust not only decorated the harbour: it
crept up the street, and got in at front doors, and soiled
window curtains; and seemed to fall heavily from the

bluest and clearest of skies minutes after the weekly wash had been hung out. There was always coal dust in Platt Street; coal dust and old newspapers, either blowing about and wrapping themselves around people's legs, or stuck quivering to walls like great moths; and surreptitious cats, and barefooted children and old men and women sitting on verandahs (but there were not many verandahs in Platt Street, most of the houses opening straight out on to the pavement, so that the interested passer-by could make a third party at the most intimate discussions in the tiny front lounge rooms).

The houses in Platt Street—all long gone now—were erected in the 1860s by a benevolent council in the pious hope that the waterside workers and seamen for whom they were designed would lead modest, sober and industrious lives, and have small families. Reflecting these hopes, the houses were narrow, high-waisted, small-windowed affairs, consisting of a lounge room and kitchen below, with a short passage and steep stairs leading to two hot and tiny bedrooms tucked away under the tiles above. The backyards, constructed on the same economic principles, enclosed a few square yards of dusty earth (in which some hopeful householders tried to grow scarlet runner beans or geraniums) and housed the wash-copper, a long stick to hold the washing line up, and a bucket-lavatory in a shed which buzzed with bluebottles all summer, and smelled horribly all year round.

The inhabitants had long since confounded the council by steadfastly refusing to live up to any of its hopes but one: they lived modest lives, unencumbered by much property, either portable or otherwise, because they could not afford any other sort. The one real indulgence of the Platt Street people (apart from beer, when there was money to pay for it) was children. They seemed to spring from the gritty pavements overnight, like mushrooms, and although they were cropped regularly by diphtheria, scarlet fever, measles, mumps, whooping cough, pneumonia and sometimes by exotic fevers brought in on the ships, there seemed to be more of them every year—"Like one of them tropic creepers," remarked Patrick Dunne in the Royal Standard one night, "what comes back, year after year, and blooms better the more you prune it"—a philosophical remark occasioned by his having seen Mrs Dunne safely delivered of her ninth (a girl) only that morning, at about the self-same time that a small coffin was being carried from Number 15, just across the street.

The Dunnes lived at Number 16; a tall, thin, flat-fronted house with the usual number of Platt Street rooms. Patrick and Mrs Dunne shared the back upper bedroom with the youngest girl, aged two and, from that morning, the new baby; five boys (a set of twins among them) occupied the front bedroom; an older daughter made up her bed on the settee in the lounge every night (which meant that the whole family had to go to bed early), and Maureen and Patrick's oldest child, a strapping youth of twenty, had the luxury of his own apartment—a lean-to shed in the backyard, uncomfortably close to the lavatory, but a blessed oasis of quiet and privacy.

Maureen Dunne worked hard: the house was as clean as the best on Platt Street, despite the coal dust; the few feet of timber floor in the tiny hall shone; the children always had clean, if sadly worn, clothing. An eternal fire blazed under the copper in the yard and drying shirts and undervests and socks flapped day and night before the oldest son's lean-to.

The Dunnes had neither the time nor the money to develop or indulge any taste for decoration: a bucket of whitewash every couple of years was all Patrick's pay as a wharf labourer could run to. But over the years Maureen, a devout Catholic, had snipped pictures of gory crucifixions and haloed Virgin Marys from coloured magazines, and dipped into the sparse housekeeping funds to have them framed; and over the washbasin, to inspire Patrick when he shaved on Sundays and Wednesdays, were fading prints of Irish heroes—Wolfe Tone, Robert Emmett, Shane O'Neill, Dan O'Connell. And a photograph, in a black iron frame, of Patrick's father, Sean Dunne, hanged by British soldiers—with his own belt, so the family story went—at a crossroads outside Dublin in 1889, for being a member of the Sinn Fein. Patrick's mother had died, of grief and shock and shame, the same year; Patrick's two older brothers, unable to get work, had gone to America and Patrick himself, at nineteen, with seven pounds in his pocket, walked to Dublin, full thirty miles from their little village; paid a few shillings for a deck-passage to Liverpool, where he signed up on the first ship which would take him away from the accursed English oppressors. The first ship was a crowded steamer, the *Mollymook Castle*, taking Irish migrants to Australia. Patrick scrubbed decks, peeled vegetables and emptied the first-class cabins' slop buckets for sixpence a day and his food: he slept in a crowded, hot and filthy forecastle alive with the biggest cockroaches he had ever seen, and he deserted when the *Mollymook Castle* reached Fremantle. Maureeen Flynn, who had arrived a year before, was working as a chambermaid at the Royal Standard; Patrick married her within a month; they moved a few yards up Platt Street to Number 16, and their first child, Frank, was born in the upper front bedroom less than a year later.

Patrick did not like Australia much—although, to be fair, he had only seen Fremantle and once taken a day trip to Perth—but his early plans of "moving on" to some vague destination where things would be better were always foiled by the arrival of another child. So after a few years he became reconciled to his life—after all, everything he required, job, pub, and home, were within a few yards of each other; it made things rather convenient.

There were only two clouds on his horizon: he was amazed and affronted by the number of English in Australia ("I tell you, I'd never've come if I'd known," he often said), and the sad fact that his first-born, Frank—his son!—showed not the slightest interest in the Sinn Fein, in the Irish martyrs, in Ireland itself!

"I'm Australian, Dad," he said one day. "I'm sick of all that Sinn Fein stuff."

"Oh, ye are, are ye," roared Patrick, outraged, unbuckling his belt. "Ah, so yer not Irish, ye young bastard! C'mere—!"

But Frank, then only eleven, was out of the door like a gazelle.

That was the first of many battles.

Frank Dunne at twenty-two was good-looking, lithe, with a wry sense of humour and a set of sparkling white teeth, all his own—a rarity among the inhabitants of Platt Street.

He was also something of a hero in the street—and for several streets around. The speed which had enabled him to dodge many a belting simply by out-running his father had been turned to good account at school, where a sports-minded priest had turned the Platt Street tearaway into a polished young athlete. He had even won a cup—a silver-plated affair the size of half a hen's egg, which his mother kept on her chest of drawers, beside her prayer-book and crucifix.

There was money in running, too, as he found after leaving school, when some worldly young men had introduced him to the illicit betting which went on at amateur athletic meetings in Fremantle and Perth. By the time he was twenty Frank had won just about every race in his age and class for scores of miles around, and was hard pressed to find a gala, fete or fair at which he would not be instantly recognised as The Platt Street Marvel.

Which is why, on this hot February afternoon in

41

1913, he was standing at the bar of the Royal Standard with several friends drinking beer, playing a desultory game of darts and generally feeling that he had had enough of Platt Street and his job as a tally-clerk at Messrs Howson and Grimm, clearing agents and forwarders.

"But it's good money, Frank," said his friend Snowy Lane, a serious young man of about Frank's age who kept a diary and, it was rumoured, had almost gone in for the priesthood.

Frank snorted.

"Good money! Nineteen and six a week!"

"It's more than I get," said Billy Morrow, who was apprenticed to a carpenter. "A lot more!" His habitual frown creased his nut-brown, puckish face, and his eyes, usually alive with laughter, clouded as he mused on the unfairness of the apprenticeship laws.

"Gawd! Nineteen and six! I'd go wild with all that money."

"But you're learning a trade," said Snowy seriously. "Frank and I, we're just clerks, but you're learning a trade! You'll always be able to earn a living, whereas Frank and I, we'll be stuck with a few bob a week for years. Don't be a fool, Billy, you stick with it!"

"Well, you two can stick it all you like," said Frank, finishing his beer. "But I'm not. I'm off—"

"Off?" said Snow. "Off where?"

"Outback," said Frank, signalling the barmaid for more beer by holding up three fingers and nodding. "Here we are, sitting in one corner of a huge brand-new country that's just crying out to be opened up, just begging for people to go out and grab what's there for the taking, and we sit here in one tiny little isolated corner of it and whine about our piffling wages without having the guts to do anything about it. If we stick around here, we'll all end up like our fathers—a swag of kids, no money, wasting our lives in Platt Street!"

Silence. A rather embarrassed silence, because it was true. Outside the bar the dust and newspapers stirred on Platt Street.

"You need money to move," said Snowy at last.

"Ever think of the railways?" said Frank. "They pay you to move, and they're looking for men now. Fettlers. Saw it in the paper the other day."

"What's a fettler?" asked Billy, frowning.

"Yeah, tell us, Frank," said Snow, winking at Billy. "What exactly is a fettler?"

"It's useless talking to you blokes," said Frank angrily. "Well, you can all just stay here in Platt Street and rot."

He slapped his hat on his head and strode out of the bar. Snowy and Billy watched him stride up the hill.

"Think he means it?" said Billy, frowning again.

Snowy, still watching Frank, nodded.

"I reckon," he said.

They drank another beer in silence, thinking their own thoughts. Thinking of another forty years in Platt Street.

There was a terrible row at Number 16 that night. Old Patrick, awash with beer and whisky, and so Irish in his rage and grief at his son's treachery that the neighbours hanging out of the windows across the street and up and down the hill could only understand one word in six. Maureen weeping. The children howling. The mixed-breed dog at Number 11 catching the prevailing hysteria and alternately barking and wailing.

Only Frank was calm. He sat out the storm, pale-faced but determined.

"It's my life, Mum," he said. "And I'm going to do something with it. I'll send you something from my wages, don't you worry."

"Ye ungrateful little bastard," said Patrick. "After

43

what we done fer ye. And that good job! Ye'll niver git another like that, ye bastard!''

"I'll get a better one, Dad.''

"Ye'll bloody starve, ye will! Oh, I tell ye, Maureen, it's the bloody English—this bloody country's crawlin' with 'em—they've put this rot in the boy!''

After an hour or two of this, though, Patrick began to falter and show signs of lapsing into a fit of the maudlins. Frank promptly sent one of his brothers down to the back door of the Royal Standard for a bottle of whisky (the hotel being long shut), and with half of this under his belt Patrick turned from the abusive to the jolly by way of the tearfuls, and ended the evening roaring Irish rebel songs—to the great political edification of Platt Street—before falling under the kitchen table and to sleep, simultaneously.

The next morning Frank gave Messrs Howson and Grimm one week's notice of his intention to leave.

"Mad, you are,'' said Billy Morrow's father, a thin, pale man with great purple circles around his eyes. He worked as a night watchman six nights a week and slept badly during the day. Platt Street was not the quietest thoroughfare in Australia, what with carts and wagons rumbling down to the wharf from dawn until dusk and children and dogs.

"Mad,'' said Mr Morrow, blinking his purple eyes. "To throw up an apprenticeship—more of a chance than I ever had. But—'' He shrugged his thin shoulders, looking around the shabby front room. Six nights out of seven for thirty years Mr Morrow had sat alone in his council tent, watching over some pile of rubble, some mysterious hole in the public road, some exposed water or gas main. Crouching over a tiny coal brazier in winter. Tending his red warning lamps, and thinking. He had done a lot of thinking in those thirty years. Looking at his son now he remembered some of those thoughts, some of the impossible dreams he had dreamed while watching the lamps flicker in the midnight wind.

"Well," he said, "well—I think you're mad, son, but—good luck!"

"And you'll not forget the way you were brought up, Dennis," said Mrs Lane tearfully.

"Of course not, Ma," said Snowy.

"Oh, I do wish you'd thought harder about the Church, Dennis."

"I did, Ma. That was a long time ago. I made up my mind, and I haven't changed it."

"You'll say your prayers every night?"

"Of course, Ma."

Mrs Lane wept a little more and then dried her eyes.

"You were always a good boy, Dennis. You will write?"

"Every week, Ma. I promise."

"And go to church?"

"Might be hard to find one, out in the bush, Ma. But I'll look."

"Then you *must* say your prayers, Dennis, and twice on Sundays."

And Mrs Lane fell to weeping again.

Ten days later, with the wind blowing in salty gusts from the tumbled blue Indian Ocean, a puffing, oily, wheezing engine rattled and clanked north-eastward. Fremantle was soon left behind, and then Perth and the beautiful Swan River, and the bush began soon enough.

"It's bloody—*big*," said Billy Morrow, frowning at the passing landscape.

"It's—" Snowy fumbled for words. "It's—it goes on for a long way, doesn't it?"

Frank leaned out of the window, clutching his hat

45

with both hands, squinting against the slipstream. He gave a wild rebel yell: "Yeeeaaaahooo! Australia, we're coming! Yeeaaahooo! Look out, world! We've got ya by the throat!"

Chapter 3

BINDANA STATION
1911

1

Archy went to school for the first time in the cool dry winter of 1911, a small school that had been opened on the neighbouring station with assistance from the State Government and seven or eight surrounding station families, because there were now enough children of school-going age to justify it. And it was an easy hour's ride from Bindana Station homestead, a fact which delighted Wal and Rose Hamilton and outraged Archy.

"An hour!" he said when the news was broken to him. "That's two hours a day! I don't need to go to school. I can read and write, and do arithmetic. And Uncle Jack's also teaching me geography, and history—"

"That's enough, Archy," said his father. "Uncle Jack's been very good to you, I agree. But there's a lot of things he can't teach you. Mathematics, for example.

47

Algebra. Geometry. Things I never had a chance to learn—"

"What good are they, anyway—on a station?" asked Archy.

His mother sighed.

"I always knew we should have sent you away to school in Perth."

"Don't start that again, Rose," said Wal. "Please." He looked at his son's aggrieved face and tried again.

"Look, Archy. Some day you might want to go to university, eh? Or to one of these new agricultural colleges, to learn scientific animal rearing. And I'll tell you what, my boy, what you've learned from Uncle Jack won't get you in the front door!"

"I don't want to go to university. I want to stay here. On Bindana."

Wal was exasperated.

"How the hell do you know what you'll want in six, seven years' time, Archy?"

"Please don't swear, Wal," said Rose. "It does no good, you know."

"I just know," said Archy stubbornly.

Wal stood up, his face set in the rigid lines which meant, Archy knew, that talking was over.

"When I was fourteen," said Wal, "I did what my father bloody well told me—"

"Please don't swear, Wal," said Rose. "I ask you and ask you."

"I did what my father told me," repeated Wal, "and so will you, my boy."

So Archy walked slowly outside to where Zac waited patiently beneath the pepper tree and said resignedly:

"I'm going to school, Zac."

Zac opened his eyes wide.

"Fair dinkum, Arch?"

Archy glanced hastily at the house.

"Fair bloody dinkum, mate," he said.

Mr Digby Scone, brought (at great cost, it was said in Figtree Crossing) to educate the children who came by horse, cart and on foot to the new school on Naturi Station, was tall, pale and, although he habitually wrinkled up his nose and lips as if he had just bitten into a lemon or detected a bad smell, a dedicated and kindly man.

Apart from education, which was meat and drink to Mr Scone, he held sacred three other things: God, King, and Country.

In fact, he had greatly impressed the interviewing board in Perth by assuring them (and striking quite a pose, too, standing with his right hand inside the breast of his best coat, rather like a pallid Napoleon) that, "As well as my primary duties, that is, my educational duties, I consider that I, and indeed any teacher, gentlemen, has another duty, a sacred duty, to *systematically* develop devotion to the sovereign, love of country—in short, gentlemen, true patriotic *sentiment*—in the bosoms of the youth in his care—"

Mr Scone would probably have been good for another hour or two if the board had not stopped him and, after a whispered consultation, given him the job.

Before leaving for Naturi Station, Mr Scone bought a Union Jack from the Education Department stores. It cost him six shillings and sixpence, but it was six feet by three feet, and he thought the expenditure worthwhile.

He had planned a regular morning ceremony at his new school; and as he perspired and wiped the cinders from his eyes during the long hot train journey from Perth, he envisaged the patriotic little ritual before classes each morning. He would group the children in a circle around

49

the flagpole; the boys would salute as the flag was raised, and the girls would stand to attention. Then there would be three cheers for the King. But on arrival he was disappointed to find that the tiny school did not boast a flagpole, and he had to console himself with pinning the flag to one wall, and having a somewhat reduced ceremony.

For the rest, Archy's lessons were frequently interspersed with talks on the life of King George V, patriotic songs and verses (he rather liked "Rule Brittania"), and vignettes about Heroes of the Empire.

Mr Scone, for all his learning, was a simple man. He lived in a world of black and white (or rather red, white and blue) standards. He would cheerfully have given his life for King and Country had it been required of him; but as it seemed unlikely that any such request would be made before he was ready to draw his pension, he devoted his efforts to ensuring that the younger generation would know what was expected of them when the time came. And the time *was* coming, he mused. Why were the Germans frantically building up their navy? Didn't they know Britannia ruled the waves and always would?

But it was from Zac that Archy received what he considered his real education. Zac, after all, taught him practical things—how to dig for water in a long-dry creek-bed. Which roots and bulbs were edible. How to make a fire without matches, to weave carrying-baskets from shaved sticks, to watch the dawn and evening flights of birds which usually led to water or ripening fruit or berries. He taught Archy the secret meanings of the hieroglyphics around the waterholes and on smooth patches of rock and sand, and the faint shirrings and almost invisible scratches suddenly opened like a book to the white boy:

". . . see them scratches on the rock, that's a big old goanna's claws done that, Archy . . . and them marks on the sand here, like someone's brushed the sand with a feather, that's a big snake done that, perhaps a python. Here's a roo's back feet marks—she had a joey, see, an' it jump out the pouch here—and here—and here it jump back in again . . . here's a dove's feets, where he's been drinking . . . and, boy, a dingo's bin here—three, four dingo—you better tell your dad, you better tell Mister Hamilton he better watch those new calves . . .'

It was a vivid education, and poor Mr Scone's offerings paled in comparison. Archy's mother would have paled, too, had she seen her eldest son, heir to Bindana Station, squatting beside Zac at a smouldering fire and eating half-raw goanna with gusto, or swallowing sweet grubs, or digging down through the baking sand to find the hibernating water-frogs, so blown up with stored water that they could be squeezed like a sponge. She and Wal knew of, and, up to a point, approved of, Archy's friendship with Zac. But any suggestion that the future owner of Bindana was "going native" would have horrified them.

It was Archy's feet—and Les McCann's inquisitive eyes—which almost put a premature end to the association.

Archy and Zac ran together: to the creek, across the yard, down the dusty road. Often Uncle Jack timed them with his big silver watch, which had a sweep secondhand that could be stopped to give times in fractions of seconds. Zac was fast, Archy faster.

They both ran barefooted; Zac because he had no shoes, Archy at first because he felt uncomfortable wearing store-bought boots while his mate Zac was barefoot; later, after his feet had toughened, because he liked the feel of the earth beneath him, the texture of rocks and grass against his skin. He got to taking his shoes off as soon as he came home from school, and only putting them on when called to tea.

The Great Big Foot Row, as Jack always called it, took place one Sunday evening. It was autumn and the bite had gone from the sun when Jack measured out a hundred-yard course at the bottom of the yard, along the fence near the bunkhouse. Les McCann sat on the fence, arm looped around a hardwood post, smoking. It was a quiet, still evening: the slender branches of the pepper trees, with their green herringbone leaves, hung straight down; the blue smoke of Les McCann's pipe drifted slowly away.

The boys ran back panting and laughing to where Jack stood studying his watch.

Jack nodded. "Not bad, Archy, not bad. Ten and a bit—couldn't read the fractions—Les's smoke got in my eyes."

"I was yards away," muttered Les, who had no sense of humour.

"Like to give us a race, Les?" asked Archy mischievously.

"Got better things to do with me time," said Les.

"These lads can run," said Jack. "Arch has got the makings of a champion. He's faster than Zac now, and Zac is damn fast."

"Guess if you've got feet like a black, you'll run as good as a black," said Les, expelling a cloud of smoke.

"What do you mean?" said Archy angrily.

Les withdrew his pipe and pointed with the stem. "Look at your feet. Those ain't a white's feet. They're bloody Abo's feet—look at them toes!"

"Leave the kid alone," said Jack. "Come off it, Les."

"It's true," said Les. "Look at 'em, just look at 'em—"

In the still evening air their voices carried to the verandah, where Wal was having a beer. He heaved himself to his feet and strolled across the yard just as voices began to be raised.

"What's the row?" he said quietly.

"Les says I've got—" he looked at Zac "—bad feet."

"I didn't say bad," said Les doggedly. He took out his pipe and pointed again. "Look at 'em, Mist Hamilton. Them toes—all splayed. Like a black's. Comes from not wearing shoes like a Christian. Couple of years' time, Archy won't get shoes on them feet. Can't get blacks to wear shoes, you know. Cause of their feet—"

"Nonsense," said Jack angrily.

Wal studied his son's feet.

"They look all right to me."

Then Rose, who had come out on to the verandah to summon the family to tea, came down to see what the argument was about.

Zac retreated quietly into the purpling night.

Jack, muttering imprecations, went to wash for tea.

Les sat and smoked, smugly.

Wal, Rose and Archy went up to the house; and Archy was told that in future he would wear shoes unless engaged in some occupation such as bathing for which they were unnecessary.

All Archy's protests were useless. And, when the argument threatened to continue over tea, Rose put a swift end to it:

"I'm not going to argue, Archibald. Perhaps I should tell your father to forbid you to play with that Zac any more . . ."

Thereafter, Archy wore shoes after school, and never dared to take them off until he and Zac were out of sight of the house.

Snowy Lane, a dutiful son, wrote to his mother in his large, unformed hand:

> *Well, we are in Geraldton. It is very hot and nothing much has happened except that we've become the Four Musketeers. D'Artagnan is really Barney Betts. Of course he doesn't know that. Nor does Frank know that I call him Athos, Billy Porthos, and myself Aramis. Perhaps they would get a good laugh out of it, but I can't bring myself to tell them. I call Frank Athos because he likes to skite about girls, and talks as though he left a lady-love in Perth!—which I know is not true! And I call myself Aramis, because he was interested in religion (became a priest or went into a monastery, I'm not sure, and my copy of M. Dumas's book is at home in Fremantle and Billy is Porthos not because he is loud and fat but because that's the only name left.*
>
> *Too tired to write more tonight, so I will continue tomorrow.*
>
> *Well, it is tomorrow. In your last letter (which took a long time to find me!) you asked if we had made our fortunes yet. No, we haven't made much money yet, but Athos says it's early days! Hope he's right!*
>
> *Nothing much happened again today. It is still pretty hot. I had better tell you how we met D'Artagnan (B. Betts Esq).*
>
> *Well, here goes: just across the tracks from our tents there's this pub, the Railmen's Arms, and a poor place, fair dinkum. Dirty windows and very common women drinking in the saloon bar, which*

is a small dirty room. The publican is a big man with thick arms covered with black hair and he treats his staff (1 dried-up old woman, must be at least 40, and a bloke) like dirt. The bloke, who's about our age, is a real long streak of misery, as Athos says, not too bright, I'd say, talks real slow, and at first we gave him a bit of a going-over—well, just smart-talking, talking about the big city, and how slow bush people was and that, and he used to get mad, poor bloke, wearing a dirty apron all week, and all the time getting a real hard time from the publican, Harry Hairy-arm Finch Esq: "Clean them dishes, mop the kitchen floor, wipe those glasses, fetch that keg," etcetera etcetera, so that after a few days we stopped chiacking him and got to feeling a bit sorry for him. One night when he'd finished work (v. late) we had a few beers with him and took him to the local Chow's for a feed; poor bloke didn't want to come at first, seemed he had no money, but after a couple more beers he let us shout him on condition he paid us back on pay day. So we had a good feed at the Chow's and when Athos heard what Barney was being paid, and all the work he did (NB: Barney an orphan, and no one to stand up for him) he said: "You wanta come along with us, Barn, join the railway and see the world." Porthos and Aramis laughed at that, we having seen v. little of the world except part of the Western Australian desert, and less money. But we agreed that anything was better than Hairy-arm Harry and the Railmen's Arms (NB: I miss the Royal Standard!).

Well, we're in the Railmen's Arms the very next evening. Barney is getting as hard a time as ever from H. Finch Esq. I guess us sitting there gave him some guts. Because suddenly he whips off his dirty apron and throws it in H. Finch's face and says: *"I've taken enough of your abuse. Gimme my money, I'm leaving."* Well! H. Finch Esq goes purple and rolls up his sleeves and I reckon he's going to really stoush young Barney Betts, when Athos pushes his chair back with a loud noise and stands up, and so do Porthos and Aramis, and Athos says: *"Hey, Mr Finch, you lay off our mate, hey? You treat him like dirt and if he wants to leave that's his business."* Old Finch glared—I thought he was going to take us all on! Then he opens the till, takes out some money and chucks it on the counter. *"I won't charge for all the glasses you've bust,"* he says. *"Just get out—and take your friends with you—when they've paid for their drinks."*

Barney B. scoops up the money, shoves a couple of bob along the counter to H. Finch, says, *"Take it out of that"*, and swings over the counter himself.

"Get out get out get out," shouts H. Finch, and we go into the street.

"What now?" asks D'Artagnan.

"A feed at the Chow's," says Frank, *"and then you can come and spend the night in the tent, if you don't mind Billy's snores, and tomorrow we'll fix you up on the railway."*

NB: The next day got Barney (D'Artagnan) Betts a job in our gang on the railway. A good bloke but like I noted earlier not the brightest. However it takes all kinds to make a world and as you always say, Mum, judge not lest ye too be judged. Must close now.

Your loving son,
Dennis

*PS What's the news from Europe, Mum? Don't get
many newspapers out here. Has England declared
war on the Hun? Last time we heard they were
trying to make up their minds. Most of us out here
reckon they should jump in and give those Germans
a lesson they'll never forget.*

Sister Alice Cooley, just off duty, sits in her private room
in Sydney Hospital and writes in her diary, in the clear firm
hand which is the envy of the junior nurses:

Sydney, September 1914
    *Forty today. Forty! And no husband, no
children. And alone in my little room. I feel that
Life is passing me by. But today I took a step!—if
life will not come to me, I shall come to life! I
accepted an appointment in the Australian Army
Nursing Service. I believe everyone should do their
bit in this dreadful war which they (Memo: who are
"they"?) promise will be over by Christmas. Heard
some patients in the ward today asking why
Australia should be "in it". Felt like giving them a
real dressing down! Of course we should be "in
it"! if Britain and the rest of the Empire are "in
it"!*
    *Who knows? Perhaps I shall be sent abroad!
That would be fun. I feel more cheerful already at
the prospect. La Belle France, perhaps! (Memo:
Tell Matron tomorrow without fail that I shall be
leaving. She is bound to be* furious!*)*
    *NB: The AANS is to pay me 9s 6d a day
and a uniform allowance of £10 10s 0d and give me
£16 a year for what they call "maintenance or
renewal of uniform". Well, I doubt that the war
will continue long enough for me to draw this
generous allowance, but it is a nice thought.*

The next day Sister Cooley gave her potted geraniums to a friend (Sister Steele, on men's surgical) and made another entry in her diary:

>*I was right. Matron* livid. *I'm sure she thinks I'm an*—adventuress! *Seemed quite scandalised. Sniffed pointedly before*—most *reluctantly*— *agreeing to release me in two weeks, and said (sniff again),* "Of course, at your age it is highly unlikely that you will be posted abroad"—*and then went on to say that the hospital* "simply cannot *be expected" to keep posts open for people who throw away good positions to go on* wild goose chases. *We parted not very warmly.*

3

The dry season ended with a great bang of thunder. The clouds that had been banked over Bindana Station all day, turning darker and darker until at sunset they hung gorged over the homestead like a monstrous bruise, burst as the sun set. Lightning shivered the sky, paling the dying sun, and the first big drops pocked the red earth in the yard, raising little puffs of dust. Then the drops fell faster and thicker, until the yard was a muddy sea, the bunkhouse and the pepper trees hidden by solid sheets of water falling from the black sky.

The break had been threatening so long that Bindana was not taken by surprise, except by the violence of the rain: it roared on the homestead's corrugated iron roof, rushed down the overloaded downpipes in great torrents which burst into the yard.

Earlier in the day Wal had moved the station's Aboriginal families closer to the homestead: Zac's and the people from Mile End were now housed in the grain and tool store beyond the bunkhouse.

The family had an early tea of cold beef, ham and salads. The clouds made it so dark that the lamps were lit an hour earlier than usual.

The deafening roar of rain on the iron roof made conversation difficult, but Jack tried gamely, with tales of other storms, other places:

"In Hong Kong in, oh, ninety-six, it rained six and a half inches in an hour—"

"Come on, Jack," said Wal, dragging his mind away from worries about his stock—he had ordered them driven to high ground earlier in the day, but were they high enough? And his lucerne—well, that was gone, and the homestead vegetable garden, too. "Come on, Jack," he said. "Six and a half inches in an hour—why, that'd be solid water, very near."

Jack nodded.

"It was, Wal, it was. Damn—sorry, Rose—damn near solid, Wal. Hurt you to stand up in it! Just after a typhoon, it came down, middle of summer, and the rain so warm that you could have bathed in it! Junks sank at their moorings, just went down like stones—sunk by the rain! I tell you, that rain was so thick it beat you down!"

"How terrible," said Rose, thinking of her garden.

"It was," said Jack. "They were dragging Chinese—dead, of course—from the harbour for days afterwards. Hundreds of 'em. Washed down from the hills. Men and women and kids. With their pigtails coiled around 'em like dead black worms—"

"Please, Jack," said Rose, shuddering.

"Sorry," said Jack. "Well! That was a storm, I can tell you. This is just a shower."

"She'll do me," said Wal drily.

But Jack was still in Hong Kong.

"You know," he said, "funny thing. Funny what sticks in your mind. You know what I really remember about that rain? A strange noise. For hours there was this odd pok-pok-pok-pok-pok noise. Couldn't work out what it was—"

"And what was it?" asked Wal. "Chinese rolling down the hills?"

"Rocks. You know Hong Kong island is very steep—very steep. Goes almost straight up. The pok-pok-pok noise was the big stones and boulders which had been loosened by the rain bounding down the roads and lanes from the upper levels. Went out the next morning and the streets were full of boulders!"

"For pity's sake, Jack!" said Rose. "The children'll have nightmares!"

"Off to bed," said Wal. "All of you! Archy—there'll be no school tomorrow, so we'll be out early to look at the stock. You can come along—if you're in bed in five minutes."

The children disappeared. The rain roared and rushed. Jack slipped and slid across the yard to his room and left his Wellingtons outside for the rain to rinse: then he sat drinking brandy-and-water until a late hour, listening to the rain and remembering the dead Chinese and the boulders in the streets of Hong Kong.

The rain stopped just before dawn. The clouds were still low and heavy and the lower yard sloppy as a swamp, but because of the slope of the land the water was not lying near the house.

But slowly, as the sun rose and struggled through the grey haze, they began to see the land below the house: the creek had filled rapidly and run over its banks to fill lower-lying depressions with sheets of water which gleamed dully in the early light. As far as the horizon there was the sheen and glint of water, marked here and there with dark islands of gum-tree tops.

The stockmen were waiting for Wal, their horses moving uneasily in the mud. Wal gave orders quickly, sharply:

"Jack, you and Les and Archy—ah, you're here, Zac, you'll do for this—Jack, get up to the East End, see if that mob up there've had the sense to get on to high ground. Me and the rest of the boys'll check Mile End. There's only about twenty head up at East End—you should be able to handle them. Right. Let's go!"

The horsemen wheeled and trotted out, the horses' hooves throwing up great gobbets of red mud.

Jack and his small party went east, skirting the swollen creek. Sometimes they had to put the horses stirrup-deep through fingers of floodwater leaking out on to the plain. As it got lighter and the sun burnt away the haze, the water around them shone like molten gold. Sodden birds sat, fluffed and plaintive, in the bushes and trees thrusting out of the water. The party learned quickly to gauge the depth of the water ahead by the thickness and height of the trees it lapped: on a few occasions a miscalculation lead to one of them getting a soaking as his horse suddenly started swimming.

There were casualties, too: drowned kangaroos and wombats, stiff-legged and glassy-eyed, caught in the branches of flooded trees. On a dead gum dozens of coppery skinks stirred uneasily as the horses splashed past. And once they saw a large goanna, fully six feet long, perched awkwardly on the very pinnacle of a crumbling anthill, his long tail lashing the water irritably. Zac, with an eye on the family supper, was all for catching it, but Jack made him ride on.

"Hell, Mister Jack," protested Zac, "that's a hell of a big goanna! A good meal there, Mister Jack!"

"Poor bugger's trapped, Zac," said Jack. "Can't

take advantage of him. Not cricket."

"Who's playing cricket?" asked Zac.

Les McCann snorted.

The goanna watched them until they were out of sight, its long black forked tongue flickering inquiringly.

The cattle had moved to higher ground as the water spilled from the flooded creek. Now they stood, looking muddy and miserable, on a long, low island rising above the red sea.

The riders splashed towards them and rode out on to the dry ground. The cattle moved nervously, backing away until they could go no further.

Archy counted them. He frowned and counted again, moving slowly around the milling beasts.

"Seventeen," he said. "Three missing."

Les McCann, disbelieving, counted them himself. "Seventeen," he conceded grudgingly. "Your Dad's going to be ropable, I can tell you."

Archy looked helplessly around the waterlogged plain. Like the others, he was plastered with red mud kicked up by the horses.

"There's some thicker bush and higher ground over there," he said, pointing to the north. "They could have split away from this lot, got on to a dry spot—"

"There's a branch of the creek runs up there," said Zac. "If they got caught in that, they're dead, sure."

Archy hauled himself into the saddle. "Let's go and take a look. Uncle Jack?"

Jack, who had been gazing at the sky, turned.

"I reckon we'll have to. I was just looking at the weather. Looks like rain over there—" He pointed to the northern horizon, where the dark rolling clouds seemed to be spilling down into the low hills. Lightning flickered through the murk. "Reckon it's already raining up there, Archy."

He swung himself into the saddle. "We want to get out of here before the run-off from that lot comes down."

They forced the reluctant horses into the water again and sloshed north. The land got rougher, with large boulders sticking out of the red floodwater like raisins in a pudding.

They picked their way carefully up the creek branch, the horses stumbling on the uneven, invisible ground. The creek had been deep-cut by centuries of rain and the walls were higher here than further down: they towered above the riders as they lurched and cursed through the muddy water, thick with debris from the surrounding bush—small trees, branches, great dead trunks, whole thorn bushes.

They found the missing beasts. Bodies bloated, stiff legs in the air, they were wedged against a large fallen gum, forced in hard by the pressure of the water. The water backed up and poured over the bodies with a steady roaring. The dead eyes, curiously blue and cloudy, seemed to stare accusingly.

The riders sat with the water swirling around their feet and looked at the swollen carcases.

"Damn," said Archy.

"Should've let me catch that old goanna," said Zac.

"Knew it was a waste of time," said Les.

Jack lifted his hand.

"Sshh," he said. He turned his head, mouth half-open, listening. "Hear anything?"

Zac's eyes opened wide.

"Water!" he shouted. He pointed to the indigo clouds, shot with lightning flashes, hanging over the lower northern hills. "Water—it's been raining up in the hills and now it's coming!"

Then Archy and Les could hear it too: a rolling deep rumble, ominous, like the distant sound of the sea.

Zac pulled his horse around, sending showers of muddy water over the others.

"Let's go. Let's go." He looked at the high creek walls. "We don't get out fast, we'll soon be like them—" he pointed at the swollen carcases stirring as the water thrust against them.

With desperate but careful haste, they floundered back down the creek, away from the looming sides which ringed them like prison walls. Soon the horses, already tired, were panting and distressed, lathered in mud, streaked with foam.

Every time they stopped to give the horses a breather they could hear the ominous rumble from the north.

Soon they could hear it over the horses' snorts and laboured breathing. And then Archy realised that they were not going to make it. They were almost at the junction with the main creek, and the roar of the approaching water drowned out all other sound.

His stomach a tight ball under his ribs, Archy cast around desperately for a way out. Then he saw the little island, steep and rocky, against the south wall of the main creek. About twenty feet across, it was fifteen feet higher than the water. Just a tumbled heap of boulders and scrub, but it would give them a chance.

He shouted at Jack and pointed:

"Ahead! Our only show, Uncle Jack!"

Halfway across the creek, the horses whinnying with rising panic, Archy looked up the main waterway, northwards: ghastly in the livid light leaking from the black low clouds, a solid wall of water, foaming white and red, was roaring towards them. A four-foot-high bore of water thick with the debris it had scoured from the plain—trees, shrubs, thorns, dead animals.

The horses plunged and reared and then they were on the island, forcing the horses up, up to the very summit, crouching among the rocks while the flood raced past, retreating even higher as it rose, until they were standing pressed together, a tight smelly heap of men and horses, on a few square yards of precious earth, dripping mud and sweat and horse dung.

In the afternoon the water dropped, inch by inch, as the flood spread out across the plain. The sun came out and the water around them sparkled and shone. By mid-afternoon their little island was forty feet across, and getting bigger every minute.

"Now I know how Noah felt," said Jack, looking at the falling waters. "And he had forty days of it!"

The water continued to fall rapidly all afternoon as the thirsty, long-dry land drank it in. It ran into fissures and cracks, renewed underground streams and filled artesian basins which had been dry for years.

Trees and bushes began to appear above the water, and the water turned to fine red mud, which dried in crazy mosaic patterns, diamonds and rectangles and squares. Frogs which had slept for many dry years awoke, and dug themselves out of their cells, and croaked.

It was Zac who noticed the snakes first. He saw a fine new-sloughed brown snake regarding him with a shining eye, and walked around the island before telling the others.

"We got company," he said.

As they watched, with mounting apprehension, Zac pointed out the snakes lying among the flotsam and jetsam of the flood, coiled among the rocks, lying, like mud-covered sticks, on the shore left by the falling flood.

"Tigers, browns, death adders," said Archy after making a cautious tour with Zac. "Washed out of the hills by the rain."

Les, who had retreated to the very highest point of the island, asked uneasily:

"What are we going to do?"

Zac pointed to the sun.

"That sun's coming through, and it's warming those snakes. They're cold now, from the rain and the storm, and snakes don't like moving when they're cold. But once that sun heats them, they'll move. They're just as scared of us as we is of them, you know."

"Hate the bastards," said Les McCann, shuddering. "Filthy, slimy, stinking—"

Zac looked at him with contempt.

"You ever held a snake, Mist McCann? Well, I c'n tell you they're not slimy, nor filthy neither." He grinned maliciously. "Poison? Yes, sure. Why, I saw a boy got bit by a tiger snake over by Currawong Mission, man, he swelled up—"

"Cut it out, Zac," said Archy. "I'm not too keen on them myself."

"I'm not bloody budging till they're all gone," said Les. "Should've brought a gun. Slimy buggers."

"Tricky blighters, snakes," said Jack. "I remember once, in Tanganyika—"

"Not now, Uncle Jack," said Archy.

"They're moving," said Zac. "Look."

The snakes, their cold blood warmed by the sun, and alarmed by the sounds of men and horses, were sliding away, slipping into the dropping water, swimming, heads raised, to the land which was rapidly reappearing all around.

"Reckon we can go now," said Zac. "I can't see any."

"Not me," said Les.

"You want to stay here in the dark, Mist McCann?" asked Zac innocently. "Most snakes come out in the night, you know. Hunting mouses and stuff like that. You want to take that horse down there in the dark?"

Les looked at the mud-smeared rocks and the matted debris packed between them and shook his head.

"Better mount then," said Zac. "Be dark in an hour. I'll go first, scare away any snakes that's left. Keep your eyes open."

They edged their way down slowly, the horses stepping daintily into the drying, slippery silt which covered everything.

The others were clear, their horses already knee-deep in the creek, when Les shrieked. His horse, startled, bolted into the water, stumbling on the hidden stones, and Les, his mouth open in a great wide O of pure terror, reeled back in the saddle as he shrieked and sobbed and tried to shake off something lithe and brown dangling from his left forearm. Digging his heels into his pony, Zac grabbed the reins that had fallen from the screaming man's hands; he soothed the plunging horse and led it back to the island.

Les threw himself off. He huddled on the damp mud, clutching his forearm and moaning. The snake, finally detached, flopped hissing to the ground: Jack broke its back with two savage blows of his thick stockwhip. Then he dismounted and squatted beside Les.

"Let's have a look, Les," he said quietly. "Where'd he get you?"

"I'm gonna die," moaned Les. "Pumped me full of poison, he did. I could feel it! Feel it!" His voice rose to a scream: his face was twisted and there was spittle running down his chin.

"Let's look at your arm," said Jack.

The two small puncture wounds on the dark forearm leaked drops of deep red blood.

Les turned his face away, sobbing.

"Got your knife?" Jack asked Zac softly. Zac slipped out his sheath-knife. Repeated honing had worn the blade down to a thin sliver: it winked wickedly in the sun.

"You c'n shave with that," said Zac.

67

"Good," said Jack. He handed the knife to Archy. "Pee on it," he said briefly.

"What?"

"Pee on it. Urine's got uric acid. Sort of weak disinfectant. Kills the microbes. Well, some of 'em. We should make a fire, heat the knife red hot, clean it that way. But we haven't got the time. And—" he glanced around the sodden landscape, "—nothing dry enough to make a fire with, anyway."

"I—I *can't*," said Archy. "I'm sorry, Uncle Jack. I can't—just, you know, just like that—"

"I can," said Zac. "Give it to me."

Jack glanced at the young Aborigine and then at Les, hugging his knees in utter misery and terror.

Jack grinned slightly and handed the knife to Zac.

"Sure, why not? I'd do it myself, but I reckon at my age—well, you young blokes must have cleaner pee, eh?"

Zac turned his back and after a minute or two turned around and handed Jack the knife.

"Clean as a whistle," he said.

"You're not gonna cut me," screamed Les, scrambling to his feet. "Jesus Christ, you're not gonna cut me!" He lurched towards his horse. "Not gonna cut meee!"

"Grab him, Arch," said Jack, and Archy brought Les down with a low tackle around the legs. He thrashed about, cursing and weeping, while Zac got behind him and held his arms to his sides.

"Won't take a minute," said Jack. He was sweating.

Swiftly he made a tourniquet of strips torn from the tail of his shirt and bound it above the punctures, tightening it with a stick. Then he sliced the flesh of Les McCann's forearm, across and across, despite the man's struggle and screams, and put his lips to the bloody wound. He sucked and spat for several minutes while Les lay back panting and groaning and Archy and Zac watched him, horrified and fascinated.

"That'll do," said Jack finally. "Should've got most of it out. How are you feeling?"

"You cut me," said Les accusingly. "You bloody cut me! I'll have the law on you."

"I've saved your life," said Jack mildly. He waded into the creek and washed his mouth out several times. He washed Zac's knife off and gave it back to him. "Thanks, Zac. Like a razor."

"If you're feeling all right, Les, we'd better ride," he said to the injured man, who was staring with wide eyes at the bloodstained cloth around his forearm.

"You—you reckon you got it all out?"

"I hope so," said Jack. He swung himself into the saddle. "Learned the trick from a bloke in Kenya. Archy, Zac, give Les a leg up. It's getting dark." His glance fell on the dead snake. He pointed at it with his whip handle.

"Zac, stick that in my saddlebag, please. I'll see if I can identify it from one of my books when we get home."

"I don't know this bugger," said Zac, examining the thin bronze corpse.

Then they heaved the groaning Les into the saddle and trotted home through the twilight.

At Bindana homestead a horrified Rose put Les to bed in the spare bedroom (no bunkhouse for him that night) and applied fomentations to the arm and made him a special invalid broth. In the morning, rather to Archy's surprise, he was still alive and ate a large breakfast of bread and butter, steak, sausages, eggs, chips and at least a pint of tea, and Wal, after looking at his arm, expressed the opinion that it was hardly worth bothering Dr Parker—"I mean, dear, he's alive, isn't he? And no sign of swelling or what you'd expect from poison—" but Rose insisted that medical advice be sought, so after breakfast

Zac drove Les into Figtree Crossing in the cart, and Archy strolled down to see if Uncle Jack had identified the snake.

Jack's small room was even more crowded these days—he had recently added model ship building to his hobbies, and spars, masts, winches, guns, blocks, tiny belaying pins and cordage from His Majesty's ship *Resolution* were scattered everywhere. HMS *Bounty* in full sail cruised across one wall, and scale plans of the tea-clipper *Taeping* were pinned to another. And on a plank of wood on the windowsill, with Jack's big magnifying glass and a thick book full of pictures of fearsome-looking serpents beside it, was the snake, looking considerably less formidable in these surroundings than it had out in the bush.

"How's Les?" said Jack. "Shut the door, Archy."

"Gone to town to see Doc Parker," said Archy. He nodded at the snake. "Have you found out what it is? Les reckons he can still feel the poison burning him. That was really brave, Uncle Jack, sucking poison like that, but you must've missed some."

Jack's face twitched.

"Latch the door, Archy," he said. "I want to show you something. Right. Now look here—"

He prised the dead snake's delicate mouth open with two thin slivers of wood. The small sharp teeth, slightly recurved, lay in rows. Jack held the upper jaw up with one sliver and ran the other down the tiny needle-like teeth which lined it.

"What do you notice, Archy? Look at the teeth."

"A pretty good set of fangs," said Archy.

Jack shook his head.

"That's just it. They're not fangs. They're just teeth."

"I don't understand."

"Look—all those teeth are even, right? If a snake's a venomous snake, then two teeth in the upper jaw, the poison fangs, are going to be longer than the others. They can be right at the back of the jaw, in which case the snake's a back-fanged snake and usually not very poisonous, or right at the front, like a cobra's, in which case it's usually deadly. But all this feller's teeth are the same—and do you know what that means, Archy?"

Archy stared at him, dumbfounded.

"It means, Archy, that this feller here isn't a venomous snake! In fact, far as I can identify him, he's a poor little grass snake."

"But he bit Les!"

"Yes. He did. He was probably washed up in those bushes brought down by the flood; Les brushed it out of the way, the snake got a fright and lashed out— whack—into Les! But it was only a nip. Wouldn't have done any harm, no more than a cat scratch or a dog bite."

"Les is going to be wild," said Archy. Then another thought struck him. "The knife!"

"Abo's pee," said Jack. He seemed to be choking. His face swelled and turned red. Archy looked at him in alarm as Jack continued to show all the signs of apoplexy. Then it burst out: roar after roar of laughter. Soon Archy was roaring, too. They laughed until they cried.

They laughed until their stomachs hurt. Then they wiped their eyes and looked at each other, still grinning.

"My old Mum used to say," said Jack, "Least said, soonest mended."

"I'm sure," said Archy, with a very straight face, as Jack picked up the snake to take it out and burn it before the cart got back, just in case Dr Hedley Parker had decided he wanted to examine the vicious reptile, "I'm sure, Uncle Jack, that Les will always be grateful to you for saving his life—"

And then they burst out laughing again.

Chapter 4

BLACKBOY CAMP
Western Australia, October 1914

1

It was so hot in the brigadier's office that even the flies were still, clinging exhaustedly to the cream walls. But the brigadier, nearing sixty, still had his tunic buttoned up to the neck, and held his barrel-shaped body erect in the hard chair behind his cluttered desk.

From outside came the multitudinous sounds of a big military camp preparing for war: shouted commands, clump-clump of marching feet, rattle and clash of small-arms drill, jingle and creak of harnesses, rattling, grinding motor-lorries, the occasional protesting whinny of one of the Light Horse mounts.

The brigadier jerked his head towards the sounds and said to the man sitting opposite him:

"Still coming in, eh?"

Major Rex Barton, a solid, rather taciturn man, deeply tanned, nodded and smiled.

"Can't keep 'em out, sir. Reckon we'd have a riot if we shut the gates."

The brigadier grunted.

"Can't beat a volunteer army, you know. Bet the Hun's not getting the same response. Not the same over there, you know. Decadent old empires—not that I'm against empires, as such, but those Europeans—too much inbreeding—you a farmer?"

Barton shook his head. "No. I was a teacher. History, mainly."

"Ah. But you'll know what I mean. Any farmer'll tell you you can't use the same bloodstock over and over again. Weakens the breed. That's what's happened in Europe. All those old decaying empires—blow on them, whoof! Down like a pack of cards—"

"We've got one of them on our side—"

The brigadier puffed out his cheeks, in which the veins had exploded into little purple, spiral nebulae, and bristled his bushy white moustache. For a frightful moment he had thought that Major Barton was going to poke fun at the Empire. Then he let the air out of his cheeks with a quiet hiss and sat back.

"Hmmn—yes, of course. Russia. Well, I don't know much about the Russians. Probably no better than the rest. So it's up to us, eh? And the French, of course."

They were silent while a motor-lorry laden with stores rattled past, its gearbox grinding horribly.

"Which way do you think Turkey will jump, sir?" asked Barton. "Think she'll join the Triple Alliance, or us? The Turks are furious because Britain has refused to deliver those two battleships she built for them and now I hear Germany has given them two to replace them. *Goeben* and *Breslau*."

74

The brigadier snorted disdainfully.

"The Turks! My dear boy, Abdul will never get involved in a white man's war—"

"They might want to have another go at Russia, sir. Finish what they started in 1853."

The brigadier snorted again.

"The Crimea! Yes, to be sure—and they had to get us *and* the French to help—and still made a mess of it! No, no, Barton, Abdul may brood over his lost battleships, and pray more than usual, but that's all he'll do—why, look here—" the brigadier pushed back his chair and stumped across to the big map which occupied a whole wall of the tiny office.

"See here, Barton—" the brigadier stabbed the map with a thick thumb "—here, and here. Say Abdul is foolish enough to join the Triple Alliance and move against Russia, eh? Right. Ivan swings his forces south, keeps Abdul occupied in Thrace and along the Black Sea coast, and the Royal Navy forces its way through the Dardanelles and reduces Constantinople to rubble! The classic pincer movement—"

Barton looked doubtful. He stared at the map. "That still leaves a lot of Turkey, sir."

The brigadier tapped the map again. "There's the key point, Barton! Constantinople! It's like killing a snake—blow the head off, chop the head off, well, the body may twitch for hours, but the blighter's finished, eh? Same thing with Turkey. One quick push up the Straits and it'll be over in a week. No, you can forget Asia. If Abdul does do anything silly, which I doubt, because he's quite cunning, it'll cause a brief little sideshow, that's all. No. It's Europe you'll be going to, major."

The brigadier sat down again and sighed sentimentally.

"My God, my boy, I envy you. That'll be a real

war—a real by-the-book war. Not like South Africa, by God, where you couldn't bring those damned farmers to stand up and have a proper battle!''

Barton settled back in his chair, and the brigadier, moustache bristling, cheeks flushing a deeper purple with the heady wine of reminiscence, launched into a long and rambling description of the Boer War, which would have been finished much sooner, the brigadier suggested, but for the strange reluctance of the enemy to stand up and be killed like gentlemen.

He concluded at last, his rather large, pale eyes quite damp with emotion, and Major Barton retired to his quarters to write to his wife and son before dinner.

After dinner, although he was tired, he spent several illuminating hours with the *Light Horse Pocketbook*, in which the handling of mounted riflemen was lucidly explained by Lieutenant Howell Price; made some notes from *Hints on Health For Soldiers*, and fell asleep while barely halfway through *Map Reading and Field Sketching Simplified*.

2

A few days later Major Barton took a quietly malicious delight in showing the brigadier a small item in a Perth newspaper. It said:

"Reuter reports from London that in consequence of the German battleships *Goeben* and *Breslau*, sailing under Turkish colours, shelling the Russian ports of Odessa and Sevastopol, the British, French and Russian ambassadors have requested their passports from the

Turkish Foreign Office, preparatory to quitting the country; and that, from October 31, the Ottoman Empire may be deemed to be in a state of war with the Allied Powers of England, France and Russia."

The brigadier snorted.

"Bloody fools," he said, and stumped out to inflame a platoon of young Light Horsemen with tales of how British lances had sent the Boers packing at Verneukpan or somewhere.

3

It was round-up and branding day at Bindana: a long, brutal day of burning flesh and hair, bellowing calves, heat and sweat. An exhausting day all round, but especially so for the cattle, which is why, probably, they resisted so strenuously the efforts of Wal Hamilton and his men to drive them into the stockyard.

Wal was everywhere that searing afternoon, weaving his stocky cattle horse around the bucking, rearing animals, his long silver-handled stockwhip cracking like rifleshots. Archy rode almost stirrup to stirrup with his father, seeming to know what was required of him without being told: a nod, a gesture with the whip, and Archy was there, chivvying, chasing, heading off, turning back.

Wal reined his horse and took a breather, fanning his face with his hat, watching Les McCann and the two new hands, Norm and Jim, bring up a dozen stragglers.

"Wish Coop was down here and not up at Mile End with Zac," he muttered to Archy, watching Les's attempts to steer the milling cattle. Coop was Wal's foreman, a quiet, efficient man of close to sixty who had drifted on to Bindana a year or two before and stayed.

"If he and Zac get things started up there we'll be finished sooner," said Archy. "They make a good pair. Oh oh. Les's in strife again."

The stragglers had split into two. Les, shouting incoherently, gazed about him indecisively.

"Bloody hell—" said Wal. "Talk about hopeless! Bloody war's taken all the good men! Wish it would take Les!—Les! Les! Don't just sit there, man, or they'll be back in the mulga! Get 'em!"

"I'll do it," said Archy. He wheeled his horse and cut off the stragglers, shepherding them back into the main mob, before Les had decided what to do.

"Good boy," said Wal. Les and the new men sat on their lathered horses beside the suddenly passive cattle.

"I'll go and give Coop and Zac a hand up at Mile End," Wal said. "You finish off here, Archy." He glanced across the heaving backs at the other stockmen.

"Think you can handle 'em?" he asked, pointing with his chin.

"I can handle 'em, Dad," said Archy.

Wal handed Archy his stockwhip and Archy felt himself flushing with pride. Wal's stockwhip, with its handle inlaid with real silver, not gilt, was something special—a symbol of authority, like a crown, or a mace, or a field marshal's baton.

"Thanks, Dad," he said. Wal slapped him on the shoulder. "Right. Keep 'em moving. See you later."

He cantered off. Wal watched him for a few seconds. Then he wiped the sweat and dust from his face and trotted around the herd. He gave quiet, concise orders to the two new men and, exchanging amused glances, they rode off.

Watching Archy ride up, Les began rolling a cigarette with insolent deliberation.

"There's a few strays out there still, Les," said Archy. "Go after them, will you?"

Les continued rolling his cigarette. He wet it carefully, removed a piece of tobacco from his tongue, and spat wetly.

"Zac can do that when he gets back," he said.

"He won't be back for a while," said Archy, fighting rising anger. "So you do it."

Les lit the cigarette and inhaled. He let the smoke out in long lazy puffs.

"Right. When I'm ready."

"No, Les," said Archy quietly. He raised the whip and pointed. "Now."

Les looked at him thoughtfully. Then he shrugged his shoulders and jerked the reins.

Sister Cooley wrote in her diary:

Aboard the troopship Benalla: *we are off! We sail for Western Australia, where we are to rendezvous (it sounds almost illicit!) with "other units" of the Australian fleet and several ships bringing across the New Zealanders who are with us in this great adventure. We are to sail to Western Australia—to King George Sound, on which the little port of Albany stands—without any escort of warships at all, which does seem a little unwise, as that dreadful German ship the* Emden *has, according to the newspapers, been sinking all sorts of ships not far from our shores. However, we must trust in the people "up top", I suppose.*

4

Round-up days on Bindana ended at the dam: a great saucer of coffee-coloured water in a red clay hollow. The stockmen threw themselves into it gratefully, laughing and splashing each other like children. There were layers of water in the dam: the top inch or two, heated by the sun, was almost blood-warm: after that it got colder and colder and on the hottest day the lowest layer, on the mud ten feet down, seemed almost freezing. Archy dived to the bottom and came up spluttering. He swam to the bank and got out, bare feet squelching in red ooze. Zac, dripping wet, joined him. They sat in companionable silence for a while on a fallen tree trunk, watching the stockmen's horseplay in the water.

Les McCann, sitting nearby and rolling one of his interminable cigarettes, glanced sourly at them. He finished making the cigarette and put it between his lips while fumbling in his shirt for matches.

"Prefer the company of blacks, eh, Archy?" he said unpleasantly. The unlit cigarette jiggled on his lower lip, dribbling tobacco.

The stockmen abruptly stopped their rough-housing. The dam's small ripples licked the mud with soft chuckles.

Archy looked at Les. Careful now, he told himself. You're the boss's son and he's an employee. Think of what Uncle Jack'd say. Or your Dad.

"Zac's my mate, Les," he said. "All right?"

Les shrugged and grinned.

One of the new stockmen chuckled quietly.

Old Coop stood up, frowning.

"Arch and I—we run together—" began Zac.

The stockmen laughed. The tension was broken.

But Les McCann never knew when to stop. He

grinned again, showing his stained teeth as he blew a disdainful cloud of smoke.

"Fancy yourself as a runner, do you, Archy?"

Zac stood up, balancing himself on the log, and began to pull on his boots.

"He's more than a runner, mate," he said to Les. "He's a top bloody athlete!"

Les frowned. "Who're you mateying, boy?"

"Take it easy, Les," said Old Coop. "He's a good kid."

"Which one?" asked Les. "The boss's son, Coop, or are you a black lover too?" He spat out the damp remains of his cigarette as Old Coop opened his mouth to protest. "Anyway, girls run. Men box."

"Ah, lay off, Les," said one of the new men.

"Archy can run faster than you can *ride*," said Zac hotly, and all the stockmen, even Old Coop, laughed.

Les pretended to be engrossed in rolling another cigarette.

"That so?" he inquired idly. "That really so? You'll be going to the Olympics next, I guess, eh?"

Archy said, flatly:

"Two to one I'll beat you to the home gate."

One of the stockmen gave a whoop. "Take him on, Les. Take him on!"

Les stopped making the cigarette.

"You mean me on horse, you afoot?"

Archy nodded.

"Yeah. I run cross-country, you take the track."

Les hesitated.

"Well, now, I don't want—" but one of the new men interrupted him, grinning.

"It's a fair bet, Les. It's a couple miles further by the track, but you've got a horse under you. Four legs agin two."

Les thought for a few seconds.

"Okay," he said. The stockman whooped again. Archy began pulling on his boots. Les pointed at them, shaking his head.

"Not like that. Barefoot."

Archy looked around. The ground was rough and stony. Les smirked and lit his cigarette.

Archy handed his boots to Zac.

"You're on," he said to Les. The stockman stared at him, then shrugged.

"You want anything on it?"

"I said two to one," said Archy. "I've got two pounds I've been saving, and a bit. You beat me to the home gate and I give you two. I beat you and you give me one. All right?"

"Can't say fairer than that," said Old Coop.

Les walked across to his horse and prepared to mount.

"Just one thing," said Archy, as Les put his foot in the stirrup. Les looked over his shoulder. "Yeah?" he said, impatiently.

"Bareback," said Archy. Zac and the stockmen hooted with laughter.

"Barefoot, bareback," said Archy, smiling sweetly.

"Fair enough," said one of the new men.

Slowly Les unbuckled the saddle. He glared at the other stockmen.

"Thanks, mates," he said.

"I'll be starter," said Old Coop, pulling out a soiled handkerchief.

They told about that race for years afterwards. The story was passed from stockman to stockman. How Archy took off like a kangaroo, bounding away in great long land-eating strides until Zac caught up with him and told him to slow down, to save himself; how they ran, black boy and white, away from the dam, through the scrub, jumping stumps, raising great pink and white flocks of galahs and white clouds of screeching cockatoos; how Zac dropped out, almost fainting with the heat and the pace. How Archy ran with one eye cocked on the track, looking for the cloud of dust that would tell him that Les was over-taking him. They tell, with some exaggeration, how the rocks tore Archy's feet and how you could follow his trail by the blood splashes; which was not quite true, although the rocks and small hidden stones (they were the worst) damaged him cruelly.

They tell, too, how while Archy was hanging on the home gate, panting and bloodied, a riderless horse cantered up, reins trailing, followed by Zac, mounted now, carrying Archy's boots, and laughing until the tears ran down his face, pointing back down the dusty track where, ten minutes later (some even said half an hour) a dusty, dishevelled Les McCann appeared around the bend.

"Slid off that bare back soon's he started," explained Zac when he had controlled his laughter sufficiently to talk. "Got on again, and fell off again—I tell you, Arch, he's been on and off that horse twenty times 'tween here and the dam!"

("And all old Les got out of that caper," the tellers of the tale would add, years later, "was the sorest backside from here to Sydney—fair raw, it was.")

But that was later, when the dust had settled. On the day itself, while Archy was getting his breath back and Zac, no longer laughing, was clucking over his ruined feet, a furious Uncle Jack, attracted by their laughter, suddenly appeared at the gate.

"You bloody young fool," he shouted, pointing at the torn feet, "perhaps you'll tell me how you think you'll be running in the big race—the Kimberley Gift!—next week? Or will you pray for a miracle?"

"Oh hell, Uncle Jack," said Archy, his face falling. "I'd forgotten about that!"

"Forgotten about it! Forgotten about it! Come up to my room—Zac, give us a hand—we'll clean 'em up before your mother sees 'em."

Jack did not spare the hot water, carbolic soap and some generous splashes of iodine, and Archy had to grit his teeth to stop himself crying out.

"That's the best I can do," said Jack finally, to Archy's great relief. "What a bloody mess."

"Will they—be all right in time?" asked Archy. Jack shrugged.

"Maybe. You're young and fit. And they're pretty hard feet—like old leather, thanks to your running barefoot—" he looked up from his bandaging and grinned "even after your father forbade it. But you're going to have to rest them for a while."

"What'll Dad say? It's a busy time."

"That is your problem, Archy." Jack looked at the poster-portrait of Harry Lasalles. "You know, Archy, I don't understand you. You've got the God-given ability to be one of the country's greatest runners—and I'm not just saying that—you could be up there with Harry Lasalles—and I don't just mean on the wall of my room, Archy, I mean up there, among the sporting *greats*—"

"Uncle Jack," began Archy, embarrassed, but Jack cut him off, impatiently:

"Yes! You could be greater than Lasalles. And three days before your first big race you go and do this!"

Jack seized the bandages and glared at Archy. He saw the years of training and preparation—the dawn runs, the lectures on the finer points of style—"Elbows and knees, lad—concentrate on your elbows and knees"—the careful build-up to this first vital race, all put in jeopardy by one foolish and impulsive act.

"I'll still win," said Archy. "If you did a good job on those feet."

"I did the best I could," said Jack curtly. "I'm not a miracle worker."

"Anyway," said Archy, hesitantly, watching his uncle's face, "anyway, running's not all there is to life, is it?"

Jack looked up from the bandages and stared at Archy in disbelief.

"I mean," said Archy , "well, there's a war on—"

Jack eyed him acutely. "Yes?"

"Peter Trevellian joined up last week. The Light Horse."

Jack hauled himself to his feet.

"Let's hear no more of that nonsense, Archy," he said firmly. "You're under age."

"You ran away to sea when you were young—"

"I was twenty-one. Of age. And I didn't run away to a war where I might get me head blown off! Or anything else!"

"You'd been right around the world a couple of times while you were still a young man! The Spice Islands, the Barbary Coast, China, Zanzibar—"

"Oh, perhaps I made some of those stories up, lad."

"No you didn't. Dad says you nearly got yourself killed half a dozen times."

Jack looked at the big map, the sawfish saw, the Japanese crab, the piranha fish, all the other lovingly preserved memories of other times, and sighed; looking at his nephew's eager young face, he sighed again.

"I know how you feel, Archy," he said. "But look, my adventures were different. I judged the risks and took my chances according to how they weighed out. But war—war's different, Archy."

"How is it different? You've been shot at by Arab slave traders and dacoit pirates. How's it different, being shot at by enemy soldiers?"

Jack sat down and scratched his head.

"It's a good question, Mist Jack," said Zac.

"Well, for a start," said Jack, "for a start,

generally speaking, you're usually, being a European, better armed than an Arab slaver or a dacoit. The ancient old muzzle-loaders the Arabs used in East Africa couldn't hit a barn door at fifty yards. And the same with the dacoits. Old brass rifles made in Sumatra or somewhere. Bloody useless. Now in a war, a proper war, duly declared, between civilised nations, well, you've got trained soldiers—trained, mind you, not like poor savages who'd be happier with bows and arrows, most likely—trained soldiers using modern weapons. Why, the Huns've got the best rifle in the world—the Mauser, boy!"

"We've got good guns too," said Archy stubbornly.

"And another thing," said Jack. "If you're just an adventurer, like I was, well, you can call it quits when you've had enough. Go home! Well, you can't just go up to your commanding officer and say, 'I'm tired of this game now, sir, can I go home.' No sir." He broke off and fixed Archy with a sharp eye. "And anyway, even if you were old enough, you know there's no chance in the world of your father and mother letting you go. So what's the point of talking about it?"

"I thought you'd help me," said Archy. "Sort of—talk to them."

Jack opened his mouth to protest but at that moment, after a perfunctory knock, the door was unlatched and Archy's sister Mavis, sent to summon Jack for supper, thrust her tousled head through the gap.

"Mother says—" she began, and then saw Archy's bandaged feet. Her eyes widened. "Mothersaysare-youcomingtosupper," she shot out, and then the door was slammed and they heard her racing up the yard, shrieking, "Mum! Mum! Archy's hurt his feet!"

Jack sighed and stood up. "I think we've been blown upon, as the criminal class say. Let's go and eat."

After supper the family sat on the balcony enjoying the cool evening air. Wal and Jack drank cold beer.

"Now when's this big race?" asked Archy's father, mellowed by the beer and the peace and cool.

"Saturday," said Jack, shortly.

"How long will you be gone, Archy?" asked Wal.

"Just over the weekend," said Archy quickly.

His father wiped beer froth from his mouth.

"Hmmm. Fine time you pick to go gallivanting—right in the middle of the bloody muster—"

"Please don't swear in front of the girls, Wallace," said his wife.

"I'm going to have another beer," said Wal, getting up. "Thirsty work out there today. Another, Jack?" His brother nodded. Wal paused at the door.

"Anyway, Archy, just see that you put in your share of the work before you go. The men shouldn't have to work harder just because you're off in town."

"I'm afraid the lad's going to have to rest for the next three days, Wal," said Jack mildly.

Wal spun around. "Rest? Why? He's not a racehorse! Perhaps you'd like me to spell him after the race as well?"

With all a child's pride in privileged knowledge, and a little girl's special malice, Mavis looked up and cried:

"Because he's cut his feet up and they're all bloody! I saw the water where Uncle Jack washed them! All red!"

"I thought it was just a blister or two?" demanded Wal.

"Well, a little more than that," admitted Jack. "A bit of a white lie, Wal. Didn't want to worry Rose."

Wal thumped the doorpost with his large hand.

"Bloody hell," he said, and went inside to get another beer.

"I wish he wouldn't swear," said Rose. "And Archy, I'm most annoyed with you for deceiving me."

"Sorry, Mum," said Archy. "But they're not that bad, really. Mavis is exaggerating—"

"The basin was all *red*," said Mavis firmly.

"You youngsters come inside and I'll read to you before bed," said Jack diplomatically, and Mavis's little treachery was lost in a delighted chorus of approval and the subsequent scramble for the best seats. Archy stayed outside.

His father had finished his beer and was sitting reading a newspaper by the light of a patent lamp, screwing up his eyes in the inadequate light. Archy stepped off the porch and walked slowly down the yard. The night was very still and the sky cloudless. He sat down and looked at the stars: they seemed brighter than usual. The Southern Cross was hanging over the pepper trees. He ran over the star names he knew. Sirius. Proxima Centauri. Alpha Centauri. Canopus. Aldebaran. And far Arcturus.

Footsteps behind him in the yard, and the weak yellow glow of a hurricane lantern. Uncle Jack going to bed.

The old man stopped beside him, looking up at the sparkling arch sweeping from horizon to horizon.

"Makes you feel pretty small, doesn't it? The universe. Earth's just a speck of dust in a huge sea—an insignificant speck of dust. And our sun's smaller than a lot of those up there—swallow up our whole solar system, some of them would. Betelguese could do it and not hiccup."

"Hmmm," said Archy, overwhelmed.

"I'm going to bed," said Jack, and took himself and his light away, leaving Archy alone with the stars and the night.

Snowy Lane, who was of a philosophic turn, described the rails as stretching "from here to infinity".

The rails! Snow had come to hate the rails over the last two years. They lay straight as though drawn with a ruler across that featureless red plain, winking at the sun by day when they seemed to writhe and waver in the heat; a cold twin ribbon under the stars at night. And when a train was coming, long before the men tending the rails could see or hear it, the rails hummed a high secret song about it to themselves.

The rails pointed to infinity from here, and here, to Snowy Lane, Frank Dunne, Barney Betts and Billy Morrow this dusty 1915 autumn afternoon was—well, they weren't too sure. It was "somewhere along the track", a drab collection of corrugated iron huts, rusting in patches as though afflicted with some metallic acne, and faded and patched fettlers' tents. And dented fuel drums, piles of sleepers, rusting rails, worn picks, sledgehammers with splintered handles.

They sat and drank stewed tea, it being their mid-afternoon break, while old Angus, the foreman, dozed in his stifling hut.

Barney was laboriously reading aloud a two-week-old Perth newspaper. Two-syllable words unsettled Barney, and words such as "Gallipoli" and "peninsula" which he was reading now brought him down heavily. In fact, he crashed so badly over Gallipoli, and became so hopelessly entangled in "expeditionary" and "reconnaissance" that Billy snatched the newspaper with a shout of exasperation, causing a little nankeen kestrel hunting lizards along the track to wheel away in alarm.

"I'll read it," said Billy, "for gawd's sake."

Barney surrendered the newspaper reluctantly.

"Before you tear it to pieces," said Frank, "pass me the sports pages."

"Don't you want to hear about the war?" said Billy.

"No," said Frank, picking up a small local newspaper, the *Figtree Crossing Examiner*. "Doesn't interest me at all."

"Oh, bugger him," said Barney. "Come on, Billy, read it to us."

"Let's hear it," said Snowy.

Billy rustled the paper importantly.

"Listen to the headlines. 'Australians in action. Troops establish themselves on Gallipoli Peninsula . . .' "

"Get on with it," said Snowy. "Angus'll be chasing us in a couple of minutes."

Billy cleared his throat again.

"Hrrmm. 'Reports reaching us—' "

"Who's us, Billy?" asked Barney.

Snowy groaned.

"The newspaper, you dill. *The Editor*."

" 'Reports reaching us,' " continued Billy, " 'via correspondents in Cairo and Alexandria, indicate that, despite encountering heavy opposition from the entrenched Turkish forces, Australian and New Zealand troops have made good their landing of April 25, and are now settled in some strength on the western extremity of Gallipoli Peninsula—' "

"Jeez, I wish I was over there, with 'em," breathed Barney.

Frank looked up from the *Examiner*.

"You would," he said. "Get your head blown off, eh, that what you want?

"Wouldn't do much damage," chuckled Snowy. "Sorry, Barn. Just a joke."

"You want to finish or not?" asked Billy, rustling the newspaper impatiently.

"Yes, yes," said Barney. "Get on with it. Only two minutes to go."

" 'Military observers are confident that it is only a matter of days before the Australian and New Zealand Army Corps and the British and French, occupied elsewhere on the Peninsula, are able to form a solid front and sweep the enemy back towards Constantinople.

" 'As yet unconfirmed reports from the Peninsula state that the Turks, in defiance of the conventions of war, are using barbed-wire entanglements and deep pits, the bottoms of which are studded with sharp spikes, to impede the advance of our troops.' "

"The bastards!" said Barney.

"That's it! I'm going to join!"

Frank sighed. "Come off it, Snowy. Do you want to be a hero, then?"

Snowy bridled.

"Crikey, Frank, I want to be part of it. I'm proud of what our blokes have done!"

"I reckon they're mad," said Frank. "Why volunteer to fight thousands of miles away! I'll do my fighting when they get over here."

Foreman Angus, sweaty, dirty, pig-eyed, foul-mouthed, sleep-crumpled, appeared across the tracks, buttoning his collarless shirt.

"Two minutes, you blokes! Two minutes from—" he glanced at his watch, "now!"

"Right, boss," said Frank cheerfully and, under his breath, "you old bastard."

Billy folded the newspaper and tucked it inside his shirt.

"I dunno, Frank," he said. "I reckon Snow's right. I think we should be in it."

Frank glared. "We? Who's we, Billy?"

"Blokes like us. Every man who can fight."

"Right," said Snowy. "Absolutely right. I mean it.

I'm joining up. What about you, Barn?''

"Dunno," said Barney, his forehead creasing in a troubled frown.

"Be in it," said Billy impishly. "The girls go mad about blokes in uniform." He laughed. "Course in your case I don't reckon anything much would help, but you might as well give it a go."

"You going to join, Billy?" said Snowy.

"Too right," said Billy. "I've just made up my mind."

Frank suddenly felt a bit out of things.

"Tell you what," said Snowy excitedly,. "let's all join up together, eh? We're mates and mates should always stick together and look after each other."

"And write to each other's parents as we get killed," said Frank. "No thanks."

"Come on, Frank," said Billy. "You've got to be in it."

"I haven't got to be in anything, Billy. If you all want to get yourselves shot, go right ahead."

"I'm not scared to die for my country," said Snowy.

"Good on you, Snowy," snarled Frank. "You be a dead hero, and I'll be a live coward, right?"

"You've got to admit, Frank," said Billy, "the army couldn't be worse than this," waving his arm to take in the desert, the shacks, the piles of sleepers and Foreman Angus.

"Can't argue with that," said Frank. "No sir."

"You'll join up with us then?" asked Barney.

Frank shook his head firmly. "No. But I'm not going to stay here, either."

"You lot not back working in ten seconds I'll dock your pay," bellowed Angus from across the tracks.

Reluctantly they got to their feet and strolled back

to their tools, beneath a barrage of abuse from Angus.

Working on the rails near the platform the next morning, Snowy felt rather than heard the rails begin their secret song.

"Train coming," he said softly. They all stopped work and looked up the long shimmering tracks. The air quivered. Far away a faint, lonely whistle drifted on the hot wind.

"Keep working or Angus'll smell a rat," said Frank.

They plied their picks until the sweat dripped from them. The foreman watched them sourly for a few minutes and then retreated to the shade of his hut.

A speck appeared down the line, trembling and twisting in the liquid air.

"Perth, here we come," whispered Snowy.

They watched the train grow.

Then it was at the platform, panting and steaming and smelling of hot oil, exhaling great gasping clouds of steam.

"Now," said Frank quietly. "We've got about two minutes!"

Hidden from the foreman by the train, they dashed for their tent, where four cheap small suitcases stood in a row, packed and ready.

"We can wash and change on the train," said Frank. "Let's go—Barney, get moving, you can comb your hair later! There—she's going! Run for it!"

With great metallic groanings and squealings, its smokestack belching great gushes of greasy fumes, the train was dragging itself past the tent.

They rushed out, watched with idle interest by a few pale-faced, cindery passengers, and hauled themselves aboard the nearest coach just as the train picked up speed.

Panting and laughing, they sprawled across their suitcases in the narrow corridor. Frank disentangled himself and crossed to the window on the other side of the train. They were just passing Angus. Frank opened the window and shouted, "Bye, Angus. Thanks for everything." The others crowded around him, shouting and waving.

It took several seconds for the foreman to realise what was happening. The smile that had started to form on his face melted into an enraged bellow of rage.

"You young bastards!" he screamed. "You come back here. You young bastards! I'll—"

He ran after the departing train, alternately screaming abuse and stopping to scrabble for rocks to hurl at the grinning faces now rapidly disappearing down the track. There were heads peering out of all the coaches now, and ripples of laughter which became a roar as Angus tripped and fell hard across the rails.

Frank stuck his head as far out of the window as it would go and, cupping his hands about his mouth, shouted: "Keep it up, Angus—it's the hardest work you've done for years!"

Frank, still grinning, pulled his head back inside.

"Now," he said, "let's find a seat."

Twenty minutes later, washed, wearing clean shirts and trousers, they were leaning back watching the desert roll by, as quiet and respectable a foursome of young men as would be found for miles around.

A sign flashed by. Frank took his feet off the seat opposite and got his suitcase off the luggage rack.

"This is where I leave you lot," he said. "For a while."

"*Here*?" asked Snowy incredulously.

Frank took the *Figtree Crossing Examiner* from his pocket.

"While you were getting steamed up over the war news, I found something in this little rag that I reckon will make me a bit of money—"

"Go on," said Billy. "You're not going to work out here any more, are you?"

Frank smiled. "Hardly work. There's a big commemorative athletic meeting here tomorrow. Thought I'd do a bit of running again. Maybe pick up a few quid—"

"You haven't run in months, Frank," said Snowy.

"I can beat anything they've got up here," said Frank.

The train stopped. Frank looked out of the window at Figtree Crossing, wrinkling his nose.

"Won't be here long. Be back in Perth in time to wave goodbye to you lot."

Snowy shook his hand.

"Good luck, Frank."

"You'll need the luck, not me," said Frank. "But thanks." He shook hands with Billy and Barney. "Keep your heads down, fellers, eh?"

Then he was gone. They watched him stride away down the platform. The train whistled impatiently.

6

The cart was at the gate, and the whole family except Wal was lined up on the verandah to say goodbye. Jack shook the reins and clucked to the horse, which was eager to go.

"Come on, Archy," he said. Jack was driving Archy in to the Figtree Crossing meeting, and staying overnight. He felt a little awkward about it: there was Wal out in the bush with the stockmen, and there was a lot of work to be done, but Jack wouldn't have missed Archy's first race for the world.

So now Jack sat in the sun and waited while Archy said goodbye to his mother and brothers and sisters. He hugged his mother close.

"Goodbye, Mum," he said, and something in his tone touched his mother's heart.

She kissed him again.

"Good luck, son," she said.

"Thanks." Abruptly he turned and bounded down the stairs and hauled himself up into the cart.

"Let's go," he said to Jack.

"Thought you'd never get away," said Jack. "We've got a race to run, you know."

The whip snapped, the horse pricked up its ears, and they jounced away at a swift trot. Archy turned and waved until a bend in the road hid them from the house.

A dark figure burst from the stand of scribbly-barks near the creek: Zac, loping smoothly over the rough ground, easily overtook the cart and ran beside it for a while, grinning hugely.

Archy held out his hand and Zac seized it.

"Good luck, Arch," he said. "Good luck! You show 'em how to run, hey?"

"You bet," said Arch. "See you, Zac."

Zac ran beside them for another half mile and then slowly dropped back. The last glimpse Archy had of his friend was a small dark figure dwindling in the distance, still waving. He swallowed suddenly and hastily turned his face from Jack.

Oh yes, Figtree Crossing could put on a show when it felt like it, make no mistake. The day of the annual athletic championships was always a good one, but people would talk about the 1915 event for years to come. The food! The beer—why, the Royal Hotel must be making a mint, knowledgeable men said, eyeing the kegs set up in the shade of the grandstand, and there's more back at the hotel, soon as that lot's finished!

Dr Hedley Parker, glowing a little from the combined effect of the sun and a few early snorts with wellwishers, eyed the grandstand's alarming tilt to the left and declared it reminded him of the famous leaning Tower of Pisa, which he had seen on his visit to Italy in '03.

The grandstand was, in truth, a rickety affair of cheap timber which creaked alarmingly and drove splinters into unwary backsides. Dr Hedley Parker, eyeing its crowded benches, speculated on the medical profits if it collapsed. Not that he was a mercenary man; on the contrary, he attended the athletic meeting every year and offered his services gratis to the contestants. It was understood, though, that spectators who required his services would have to pay for them . . .

"My dear lady," he said now to a woman who had expressed doubts about the grandstand's ability to survive the day, "my dear lady, if the leaning Tower of Pisa, built by Italians, has lasted several hundred years, I rather think that that edifice, constructed by Australian craftsmen, will . . . last, eh? I should think so." And, touching his hat, the doctor strolled away.

There is really nothing like a war to create a sudden paroxysm of mateship. The very highest levels of Figtree Crossing society—even the solicitor and his family!—had come to this year's meeting. The carts and carriages of the well-to-do circled the main oval like the wagons of frontier settlers preparing for an attack by Indians, and on the grass beside them were travelling rugs and folding stools and tables and smart wickerwork picnic baskets spilling white linen, silver cutlery, cold roast chicken, cool salads, and bottled beer and lemonade chilling in the Royal Hotel's plated ice-buckets. The army was there, too, in the shape of several officers of the Australian Light Horse, smart-looking men striding about in trim khaki uniforms, hatted and gaitered and belted and putteed enough to make many a young woman's heart flutter and many a young man's swell with envy. The Light Horse were not bent on idle pleasure, though; oh no. Between events they were beating the drum for recruits, and, rumour had it, were going to put on a "real show" before the day was over.

Frank Dunne wandered among the crowd and glanced from the kegs beside the grandstand to the elegant preparations for lunch going forward around the perimeter, and had no doubt as to which he preferred. His father would have been shocked at the depth of Frank's yearning. Frank strolled past one of Figtree Crossing's few motor-cars: a large maroon Rover, and his heart ached. Its owners ate cold chicken and drank beer on a tartan rug in the car's shadow; their clothes were good, the daughters were pretty, the voices educated. Frank's heart ached again, and he thought of Number 16 Platt Street and turned away.

In the shadow of the grandstand he saw an old man coaching a strapping youth of about eighteen through a set of warm-up exercises. Frank turned away, hiding a smile. These country bumpkins. He would show them. Would he show them! He fingered the money in his waistcoat pocket: twenty pounds, sixteen shillings and nine pence. Well. By tomorrow, that would be—he grinned. Well, a lot more. Then back to Perth. With a decent stake, I can start that bike shop, that's where the money is, personal transport.

Get a franchise for one of those imported makes. Perhaps, in a few years, get a motor-bike dealership! Dreaming, he walked away, smiling condescendingly on the country people who looked his way.

The Officials' Tent was hot and close.

"The main event," said the younger official to Frank, "is the one hundred yards Kimberley Gift. The prize is ten guineas and a gold medal, and the event is closed. Entries had to be in a week ago."

"I just got in from outback," said Frank.

"What's your name, son?" asked the official.

Frank told him.

"It's not too big a field, Lionel," said the older official mildly.

Lionel looked at Frank.

"You registered?"

Frank nodded.

"Where do you usually run?"

"In Perth."

The official's eyes narrowed. "I know you. Dunne, the stand-up start."

Frank nodded again.

"Give him a go," said the official's offsider.

"Anyone take bets?" asked Frank, smiling innocently.

Lionel whistled and looked knowing.

"It's against the law," he said, filling out an entry form. "How much were you wanting to lay?"

"Twenty quid," said Frank.

"You're pretty confident. Let's see it."

Frank put his money on the table. Lionel looked at the little pile of old notes.

"Even money?" he asked.

Frank nodded. "Fair enough."

Still Lionel hesitated.

"I want to be fair," he said. "This is a lot of money. Young Archy Hamilton's running."

"Who's he?"

"Probably the fastest kid in Western Australia. If not the entire country." He put out his hand for the notes.

"What's he do the hundred in?"

"Under ten," said Lionel. "Don't want to take your money without warning you."

Frank considered for a moment. "What's my mark?"

"Same as the local lad," said Lionel.

"All right. You're on," said Frank.

Lionel scooped up Frank's money and put it in his breast pocket.

"Changing room's behind the grandstand."

"Thanks," said Frank.

Jack inspected Archy's feet and sighed.

"They're still a mess," he said. "I could wring your neck."

"They'll do," said Archy.

"They're still bloody raw!"

"Don't worry. They feel fine."

"You're a liar, Archy Hamilton."

"Never, Uncle Jack."

Jack replaced the bandages, sighing again.

"Saw Les McCann in the crowd. Surprised your Dad gave him time off."

Archy shrugged. "Les's joining up. A surprise, eh?"

Jack grunted. "I'll be surprised if the army's desperate enough to take Les." He finished the bandaging and stood up.

"You can still pull out, Archy. Lasalles himself pulled out of the Barlow Cup and nobody thought the worse of him."

"I'm running, Uncle Jack," said Archy quietly. He cocked an ear toward the noise outside the first aid tent. "Listen. They're calling the race. Let's go."

Outside a slight breeze had risen. The gay bunting on the grandstand fluttered and the stand itself uttered wooden groans as the crowd stamped and cheered the runners.

"Frank Dunne?" said Archy as he walked up to the starting line with Jack. "Never heard of him. Not from around here."

"Don't worry about him, whoever he may be," said Jack. "Start your breathing, boy. Deeply, now. Get those lungs *full. Fuller!* Here—" he gave Archy's thighs two stinging slaps. "Brace them, flex them, boy—"

Some of the other runners, passing them to take their places, grinned, and Archy smiled back, rather embarrassed. Jack ignored them.

"They'll laugh on the other side of their faces soon," he snorted. "Come on. What are these, eh? These things in your legs?"

It was a ritual they had fallen into over the years, a question and response litany which set Archy's heart pounding.

"Springs," he said. "Steel springs."

The grandstand was a pink and brown wall of inquisitive faces.

"Again," said Jack. "Don't take any notice of those people. Again!"

"Steel springs!"

A murmur rippled through the crowd. The starter was strolling towards the line of runners, holding the small starting pistol.

"What are they going to do?" asked Jack remorselessly.

"Hurl me down the track!" Archy was trembling.

"How fast can you run?"

"Fast as a leopard!"

"How fast are you going to run?"

The starter was almost at the line. People were staring at Archy and the old man.

"As fast as a leopard!"

Jack slapped him on the shoulder.

"Go, then. And let's see you do it!"

Archy crouched as the starter consulted his watch and raised the pistol. The crowd fell silent. Archy glanced down the line. The stranger was looking at him curiously. Archy looked to his front, down the track. The pistol cracked.

The pain was there instantly, the very second his feet thrust into the gravel. Each footfall was a blaze of agony: he felt as though he was running on glass. There was blood in his running shoes: he could feel it squirting between his toes.

He clenched his teeth and felt his face twist into an ugly mask. The crowd roared, rushing past him in a great blur of sound and gaping mouths.

Someone was coming up fast beside him! The stranger, Dunne, running with his handsome head high, coming up, passing him, the crowd going mad, now, screaming standing up pounding feet roaring Archy! Archy! Archy! Yards from the tape! You're a leopard! Dunne's a gazelle! Catch him! Catch him! His lungs aflame, he drew level, overtook Dunne, passed him, feeling the skin on his feet tearing, the blood soaking through his running shoes. Then the tape was against his chest, snapped, and he was rolling, writhing on the ground, tearing off his bloody shoes, biting his lips to stop himself crying out with pain and the crowd was around him, hauling him up, half-carrying him. Then whispers, hushed, awed, "Jesus, look at them feet, eh? Mincemeat!" And Dr Hedley Parker cluck-clucking and Jack bouncing around on the outskirts of the crowd like a buoy in a tide-rip, grinning and waving.

They gave him ten golden guineas, which he gave to Jack to keep for him, and a golden medal, which they hung around his neck on a watered silk ribbon. They gave him a glass of beer which he gulped so fast that it went down the wrong way and sent him spluttering, and the crowd cheered and gave him another and slapped him on the back and lifted him on their shoulders and carried him to the first aid tent, where Dr Hedley Parker was waiting with bandages and bottles of carbolic and iodine and creams and ointments.

He saw Dunne in the crowd, and leaned across several people with his hand out, but the stranger pretended not to see him and, turning away abruptly, shouldered his way through the pressing throng. Archy watched him go, feeling suddenly deflated. Hell, the bloke had run a good race. A *good* race. Why suddenly go crook? It was only a race, after all.

Dr Hedley Parker burned his ragged feet with one potion, and cooled them with another, wrapped them in clean bandages, and made cutting remarks about the mental competence of both Archy and his Uncle Jack.

Then, grudgingly, he said: "All right. You'll do. I wouldn't do any running on those feet for a while, if I were you."

"I won't, Dr Parker," said Archy with a grin.

"Or marching," said Dr Parker pointedly, looking at an infantry recruiting poster, exhorting young men to "Fall In!" pinned to the tent-pole.

"The infantry, Dr Parker? No fear!"

"He's too young, anyway," said Jack.

"And with luck this war'll be over before he's old enough," said Dr Parker, washing his hands in a tin basin. "Well! I hope so."

Jack helped Archy hobble to a bench in the front row of the grandstand. Something was happening, or about to: the field was deserted, and all eyes were on the entrance to the oval, across which a gaudy banner proclaiming "The Kimberley Gift, 1915" strained in the wind.

A brass band struck up outside the gate and the crowd stamped and cheered. Whips cracked, harness strained and timbers creaked. Something moved in the shadows beyond the gate: something monstrous, twenty feet high. It lumbered forward, breasted the banner, sent the two pieces fluttering away—a giant, staring-eyed wooden horse. For a moment the mere sight of it silenced the crowd: then the whips cracked, the carrying-wagon lumbered forward, and cheers broke out: across the huge beast's wooden chest hung a sign, lettered in crackling red: "THE LIGHT HORSE—JOIN NOW!"

After a moment of stunned silence the crowd erupted: dozens of young men, full of athletic fervour, patriotism and the Royal Hotel's keg beer, spilled across the oval, clambered aboard the wagon, fell off and clambered aboard again, snatching recruiting forms; while some quieter spirits soberly joined the squad of mounted Light Horsemen and recruits (enrolled during the horse's passage through the town to the oval) trotting sedately behind the wagon.

Dr Hedley Parker, watching the scene from the door of the first aid tent, frowned.

"The last wooden horse was a bad omen for a lot of people," he said sourly to his assistant, a stoutish man called McClicker who bank-clerked by day and ran the Figtree Crossing Boy Scouts on Friday nights. "Let's hope this one isn't."

"Why, Troy was a glorious victory," said Mr McClicker, bridling. "This horse is a *symbol*, Dr Parker—a symbol of Empire!"

Any minute now, thought Dr Parker, and he's going to give me a lecture about Mafeking and Lord Baden-Powell and I really would prefer a drink.

"Mind the shop for a while, would you please, Mr

McClicker?'' he asked, and strode with determined tread towards the refreshments tent. Mr McClicker, rolling bandages, watched him disapprovingly.

Jack tapped his stopwatch.

"Nine and five-sixteenths seconds, lad. You've equalled Harry Lasalles—cut feet and all!''

"Uncle Jack—'' began Archy, but Jack was in full flight and would not be stopped.

"No, lad, nothing can stop you now. Nothing!''

"Uncle Jack!'' Archy was almost shouting. "Listen to me.''

He put his hand on Jack's sleeve.

The old man looked at him, suddenly silent.

"I'm not coming home.''

Jack looked at Archy and across the oval at the grotesque wooden horse. Some soldiers were pitching tents around it: their mallets rose and fell with a steady whok-whok.

"I knew it,'' the old man said. "I knew it all along. This bloody war! Your bag weighed a ton. What the hell you got in there, lad, bricks?''

Archy laughed.

"Books, mostly.''

He smiled. "And my lucky arrowhead—the one you gave me.''

Jack shook his head. "You're only eighteen—a long way from twenty-one. How're you going to get them to take you? You'll never get your parents' approval.''

"They won't ask me too many questions when they see how I can ride—and shoot—'' Then a thought struck him. "Uncle Jack—you wouldn't—''

Jack shook his head. "No. I won't blow the gaff, Archy. I promise you that. I was young, once—'' he stopped, and his eyes became remote: looking at them, Archy imagined Jack gazing at long lonely seas under the moon, at Zanzibar at dawn, Hong Kong climbing around the Peak, swift dacoit canoes trailing a lugger in the Celebes.

He held out his hand.

"Goodbye, Uncle Jack—and thanks. Thanks for everything. I'll write. I promise I'll write. Here—" he fumbled in his shirt pocket and produced a crumpled letter. "For Mum and Dad. Try to explain to them, will you."

Jack smiled grimly. "Your mum's always thought me a bad influence, Archy, but I'll try."

Archy turned away. It was suddenly hard to speak.

"And—say goodbye to Zac for me, will you? He was always a good mate. Say goodbye properly to him for me, Uncle Jack."

"I will," said the old man. "Don't worry."

He watched Archy shouldering his way through the crowd, surrounded by wellwishers.

"God bless you, boy," he murmured, "and look after you."

"Got religion at last, eh, Jack?" said a voice in his ear, and he turned to see Dr Hedley Parker, glowing like the sunset and nodding sagely.

"Celibacy and Scotch, I find, Jack, induces the state," said Dr Hedley Parker, oscillating slightly about his axis.

"Haven't had a drink all day," said Jack indignantly, "and as for celibacy—"

"Too old, too old," murmured the doctor. "Don't worry. It's nothing to be ashamed of."

Jack was indignant. He nodded at the young men clamouring around the wooden horse.

"I was just thinking . . . all those young men, so keen . . ." Dr Hedley Parker nodded.

"That horse, my dear Jack, my dear Jack, that horse—well, the horse of Troy took its soldiers to glory.

That horse, dear Jack, may take our young men, our best young men, the cream of our young men—to *hell*!"

"You're drunk," said Jack in a rage, and left.

Snowy Lane sent his mother a postcard:

> *Dear Mum,*
>   *Nothing much to report except that we've packed in our jobs on the railway and are coming home to join up. Except Frank, who has other plans. We are disappointed because we would have liked to stick together. Still, it can't be helped. We are working our way home with odd jobs and should see you in a week or so.*
>
> > *Your loving son,*
> > *Dennis*

Major Barton lay in his underwear on top of the bed in his quarters (it was very hot) and, after writing to his wife and son, read a few chapters of *The Signalling Handbook for Australian Military Forces* and *How to Instruct in Bayonet Fighting*, before falling asleep.

8

Frank Dunne sat at the window of his small hotel room and watched the country boys galloping up and down. He envied them their horses and the easy way they handled them. In Platt Street the only horses one saw were exhausted old nags hauling delivery wagons. But, he consoled himself, the horse was on the way out; the motorcycle was the coming form of personal transportation. He had a momentary vision of himself, goggled and gauntleted, roaring through the middle of Figtree Crossing on the Birmingham Small Arms Company's latest machine, scattering the country boys and their mounts. Then his eye fell on the pitiful pile of silver and copper coins on the bedside table, and he sighed.

Business was brisk at the Light Horse recruiting post in the oval. In fact, business was so brisk that the army could afford to be selective; only the best were taken. Some young men wept—actually wept—when they were turned down because they were considered too short or too tall, too fat or too thin, or had flat feet or bad teeth.

The recruiting officer conducting the riding test—the last hurdle for would-be Light Horsemen—was an acerbic bottle-nosed captain. His habitual frown deepened as he scrutinised Archy:

"You sure you're old enough?"

Archy blushed.

"Yes, sir," he said, cursing the guilty blood flooding his face.

"Hmmm," said the captain. Then he shrugged. "All right. But you don't look it. Well, go on, boy, mount up. Let's see you ride."

Archy swung lightly into the saddle and was just about to do the prescribed trot around the oval when a familiar voice seemed to freeze his blood.

"'Scuse me, sir," the voice said. "I know the lad. I'm afraid he's only eighteen."

Les McCann, smiling apologetically, shook his head admonishingly at Archy. "And his father'd skin him alive if he knew he was here, sir."

The bottle-nosed captain sighed wearily as he tore up Archy's form.

"Off the horse, lad. We can turn a blind eye if it's a matter of six months or so, but—hey!"

Archy, furious and humiliated, dug his heels into the horse and sent it flying around the oval. Tears of rage stung his cheeks. He took the animal around the prescribed course—walk, trot, canter, gallop—and then returned it to the bottle-nosed captain who opened his mouth to say something but wisely changed his mind. Archy glared at Les McCann and stalked away through the crowd, his face rigid. The captain vented his anger by snarling at a few recruits and then got back to the business of signing young men on for the Light Horse.

Frank Dunne sipped a small beer, fingered his dwindling pile of cash and searched the crowd for Archy's face. Frank, as well as his financial worries, was suffering a bad attack of guilt. He bitterly regretted having snubbed Archy after the race. After all, the country boy had won, fair and square, and Frank, in his grief over his lost money, and in his hurt self-esteem, had acted like a poor sportsman. Like a very poor sportsman indeed.

He could not know that Archy was upstairs in his room, nursing in solitude feelings very similar to those Frank was nursing in the crowded bar. Anger at Les McCann's treachery mingled with shame at his childish display of horsemanship. Archy's face flamed again at the memory of it. He lay and listened to the jollity downstairs and wished he was back at Bindana. Well, he would be soon enough. No sense in hanging around here. He wondered if Uncle Jack had given his father his farewell letter yet. Archy thought of the letter and squirmed inside. To have to go home with his tail between his legs, rejected. Not even the sight of the medal winking in the lamplight could cheer him. A medal! For *running*! Those blokes downstairs would come back with medals for more important deeds than winning a race! He almost wept with rage and humiliation. Later, the bar closed and the revellers dispersed noisily into the night, Archy still lay awake. And so, several doors away, did Frank Dunne.

Frank rose early the next morning. He bathed and shaved and packed his small bag and counted his money for the tenth time. He had enough to pay the hotel bill, and perhaps buy a cup of tea. Certainly not enough to buy a good breakfast or a ticket to Perth. No; he would have to jump a train that morning and get back to Perth before he starved to death. And if he was spotted jumping the train and sent to prison, well, at least he would eat.

He walked slowly downstairs, tantalised by the smells of frying bacon and sausage drifting up from the dining room. He paid his bill and was walking resolutely past the dining room when he saw, through the open door, the youngster—what was his name?—who had beaten him the day before. He hesitated and then walked into the room. Archy was the first to breakfast. The Royal prided itself on its breakfasts, and the cook had done Archy proud: eggs, crisp bacon, sausages and a mound of toast. But Archy, still brooding, had no appetite: he slowly munched a piece of buttered toast while the giant breakfast cooled on its plate. He looked up when Frank approached and frowned.

Frank put down his bag beside the table, and held out his hand.

"I'm sorry about yesterday, mate. You ran a great race. Name's Frank Dunne."

Archy hesitated, then shook the proffered hand.

"Archy Hamilton. Sit down."

Frank sat down slowly, trying to ignore the breakfast.

"Just gave me a hell of a shock being beaten right out here. I won everything there was to win, back in Perth."

"I was lucky," said Archy modestly. He pushed the untouched plate away.

Frank shook his head.

"No sir. Anyone who runs like you did with crook feet isn't lucky."

Frank glanced at Archy's bag alongside the table. "Joining up?"

Archy grimaced.

"No. I missed out. Under age."

Annie, the Royal's pretty young waitress, emerged from the kitchen with Archy's tea.

"You want somethin' to eat?" she asked Frank. He looked up at her with his nicest smile.

"You mean do I wish to order, I suppose?" he asked.

Annie bridled.

"You from the city?" she asked with open contempt. Annie disliked city people; only two years ago a city girl—from Adelaide, of all places—had stolen the affections of her young man. So now she glared at Frank and curled her lip at his diction and asked again: "You from the city, eh?"

"I am," said Frank.

Annie stepped back a pace and looked him up and down before saying:

"Yeah well, I can tell you we don't put on the dog up here, mate. What d'you want to eat? Quick now, I haven't got all day, you know."

"Nothing, if that's your attitude," said Frank loftily.

"Suit yourself," snapped Annie, and flounced away.

"Better have something if you're going back to Perth today," said Archy.

"I'm not hungry," said Frank. "Anyway, I can get something on the train."

A pathetic lie, with his mouth watering at the smell of the eggs, bacon and sausages under his nose.

"Well, I'm not hungry either," said Archy, pushing the plate away. He looked at Frank, reading the blazing hunger in his eyes.

"Look, why don't you peck at that? It'll be wasted otherwise."

"Don't you really want it?" asked Frank. His hand, almost of its own volition, stole toward the loaded plate.

"No. I'm too browned off to eat. Besides, I'll be home for lunch."

"Well," said Frank, drawing the plate towards him and reaching across the table for Archy's unused knife and fork, "well, no sense letting good food go to waste, is there?" And he fell to with such a will that bacon, eggs, sausages and the rest of the toast were gone in minutes. "Ahh," he said, mopping up the last of the egg with a crust of toast, "that was good!"

Archy grinned.

"I'd hate to see you eat when you are hungry."

Frank grinned back. "I lied," he said simply. "Fact is, mate, I was bloody starving." He sat back and patted his stomach. "Whew! Feel like a new man." He looked across the table at Archy.

"You going to try again? For the army, I mean?"

"I can't," said Archy. "They know I'm under age. Wouldn't get as far as the recruiting desk."

Frank shook his head.

"I don't mean here. In Perth."

Archy stared at him.

"Hey," he cried, his face lighting up. "You're right. I could. Nobody knows me there—" He stopped, shaking his head.

"No go, Frank. I've used up most of the money my Dad gave me to pay the bill here. Got a couple of bob left. Not enough for a ticket to Perth."

"How do you think I'm getting to Perth?" asked

Frank. "I've got no money for a ticket. Blew it all on that blasted race."

Archy looked at him blankly. Frank explained.

"I'm bloody sorry, Frank," said Archy. "I really am. If I'd known, I think I'd have let you win. Dinkum I would."

Frank laughed.

"No you wouldn't. You had your heart set on that medal, mate. And that old bloke with you would've kicked your backside from here to Sydney if you hadn't won it."

"You're right. Uncle Jack would've done his block. Anyway, how do we get to Perth without money?"

"Easy. There's a train coming through here at eight tonight. I checked the timetables yesterday. A lot of the trains running south have empty freight cars. I know. I used to work on the railways. So we use the few bob we've got between us to buy a packet of sandwiches to last us until we get to Perth, and when the train's pulling out of town, we jump aboard one of the empty trucks. It's dark by eight; nobody'll see us. And tomorrow night we're in Perth. My folks'll give us some tucker and you can share my room until the army takes you."

Archy finished his tea. He stood up.

"You're on," he said simply.

They walked out of the hotel together. Annie the waitress watched them go.

9

Crickets sang in the rank grass along the railway embankment. Beyond it, the lights of Figtree Crossing trembled in the warm evening air.

"She's coming," warned Frank.

Far down the line a spray of sparks shot skyward and a glaring light sliced the darkness. Metal screamed as the train began its steep haul out of the station.

"Get ready," said Frank. "The bags aboard first. Then us. But let the driver's cab and the passenger coaches get past us before you show yourself, all right?"

They ducked as the tracks were bathed in a harsh yellow light.

Then the engine was past them in a gush of flame and steam: they caught a fleeting glimpse of a sweating man shovelling as though his life depended upon it. Then lighted passenger coaches, a dining car with tables laid with white linen.

The train was picking up speed now, furnace roaring, smokestack spewing sparks, raining cinders.

A high-sided rattling stock truck drew abreast of them, open doors advertising its emptiness.

Frank tapped Archy's shoulder.

"That one. Now!"

They flew after it, cursing the slope and the uneven ground. The train picked up speed, faster and faster, drawing slowly away from them. Archy forced his aching legs to make one last monstrous effort, and got his hand on the edge of the truck's door. In went his bag—almost out the other side, too, but no matter! He hauled himself aboard, sprawling, lungs bursting, in wisps of straw and horse manure. Frank—where was Frank! He leaned out: Frank's face, an agonised white blob in the gloom, was falling behind. Archy hung on with one hand and stretched as far as he could. Frank's hand locked into Archy's as the train, reaching the crest of the hill, increased speed with a burst which almost pulled Archy out of the truck. Then Frank was aboard, sobbing, laughing, choking for air.

"Thanks, mate," Frank gasped when he had got his breath back. "You nearly lost me. Whew!"

They lay back in the straw while the train rocked and swayed through the night. Outside, the stars were vivid unwavering points in the clear air above the endless dark plain. They sat and watched the stars for a while and ate the sandwiches they had bought with the last of their money: stale bread and pale ham, sliced so thinly it was almost transparent. Then, as the night became cool, they pulled shut the truck's doors, made themselves comfortable as best they could on the straw, and fell asleep.

Some time before dawn there was a great deal of shunting and rattling of couplings and backing and puffing and clanging. Archy lay, half awake, listening to the activity outside. Once lanterns passed the truck and he heard men talking, but they were left undisturbed, and after a while he fell asleep again.

When they awoke it was broad daylight. Shafts of sunlight streamed into the truck through the ventilation slits.

Archy sat up, groaning.

"I'm a mass of bruises. Oh, boy!" Then realised something.

It was terribly quiet.

And they were no longer moving.

He shook Frank into full wakefulness.

"Hey. Notice anything?"

"Can't say I—hell, yes, we've stopped."

Frank leaped up and beat the straw from his clothes.

"Let's get out of here before someone comes along."

"It's very quiet," said Archy. They listened. Not a sound except the dry rustle of wind in grass.

Carefully Frank opened the door. It stuck, and he hauled it aside with an angry curse.

"Shhhh," said Archy, squinting in the sudden glare.

"Shhh be damned," said Frank. "Look at this! My God, look at this!"

The desert was outside: it rolled from the very door of the truck to the horizon. Stones and sand and sparse scrub shimmered in the heat.

"Perth?" asked Archy.

Frank turned away from the open door, grinning savagely.

"No, mate," he said. "Not quite."

Then Archy saw it, too. His jaw dropped.

"Oh gawd," he said, stunned.

They had been shunted on to a small spur line during the night, a sort of metal appendix on the main north-south line.

And around lay—nothing. The shining rails ran into the immense distance. A lonely kite wheeled high in the cloudless blue.

And, in a chair tilted against the shady wall of a small tin hut—the only building from horizon to horizon—a solitary Aborigine watched Archy and Frank jump from the truck. As they approached he reached under the chair and retrieved a faded Western Australian Railways peaked cap, which he dusted hastily and placed on his head at a jaunty angle. Then, having established his officialdom, he stood up, shedding little puffs of dust and sand from his creased and patched khaki trousers and collarless white shirt.

"G'day," he said.

Archy and Frank stared at him in amazement. The official cap had been decorated with a band of snakeskin; and now that they were out of the sun's vicious glare they saw that one entire wall of the hut was covered with dry snakeskins, hundreds of them, pinned to timber slats and making a fine dry rustling in the wind.

"Name's Billy Snakeskin," said the stranger. "Full-time snake skinner and part-time railwayman. What can I do for you young gentlemen, eh?"

"Where the hell are we?" asked Frank. Billy Snakeskin took off his official cap and scratched his head. His hair had a coppery tinge which hinted at a mixed ancestry.

"They call it Salt Flats Junction."

"Why in—in blazes," said Archy, "was this truck dropped off here?"

Billy Snakeskin replaced his cap and shrugged.

"Dunno, boss. Somebody wants it, I guess." He waved his arm. "Somebody out there must've ordered it."

Frank and Archy looked at the truck, squatting in solitary splendour on its spur line, and then at the surrounding countryside. To the south-west the desert wore a strange glitter and weird shapes seemed to dance in the heated air. Who on earth, Archy thought, would have ordered a truck to be left for collection in this godforsaken hole?

He turned back to Billy Snakeskin, who had resumed his seat and appeared to be dozing.

"Do you work for the railways, Mr, ah, Snakeskin?" he asked.

Billy Snakeskin opened one eye.

"Part-time," he said. "Part-time. When a train's coming, I run this station—fill in forms, load, unload and such like. Rest of the time I catch snakes. For their skins. Got a bloke sells 'em in Perth for me. You know—to shoe shops, ladies' handbag shops, belt shops and such like. Good business. Plenty of snakes around here, boss."

"You live near here?" asked Archy. Billy waved his arm in a gesture which embraced the surrounding desert. "Around here, boss."

"Look," said Frank. "We're in a hell of a fix, Billy."

Billy Snakeskin opened both eyes and grinned, displaying several quite good teeth.

"I'd say you was, boss."

"Can you tell us when the next train to Perth goes through?"

Billy Snakeskin straightened the official cap.

"Course I can," he said. "I know all the trains."

"Well, tell us," said Archy.

Billy Snakeskin grinned again.

"Two weeks," he said. He hunched forward in his chair, hugging himself. "Two weeks, boss."

"I don't believe you," said Archy, stunned.

"No, and nor do I," said Frank.

Billy Snakeskin was affronted. He got slowly out of the chair and adjusted his cap, which his recent mirth had sent awry.

"All right." He beckoned with one finger. "Come here and I'll show you."

They followed him into the gloom of the hut. The Western Australian Railways Department did not cater much for the creature comforts of its employees. The hut held an old deal table, much stained and scarred; a calendar advertising a Perth printing company (and, i that oven of a hut, displaying a robin redbreast on a snow-covered windowsill) and a forty-four-gallon drum of water.

"There, boss," said Billy Snakeskin, slapping a worn and thumbed timetable on the table.

"That's the official timetable, see." He ran a thick finger down the closely-set type. "Look fer yourselves."

Frank studied the timetable and groaned.

"He's right."

"Course I'm right," said Billy Snakeskin.

"What are we going to do?" said Archy, appalled. "We can't stay here for two weeks."

"Buggered if I know," said Frank dismally. "What a bloody mess."

"There's always the lake," said Billy Snakeskin, grinning again. "If you're game."

The lake? Archy and Frank looked around the seared landscape in bewilderment. There was surely no water anywhere on that aching plain.

Billy Snakeskin laughed.

"Course, it ain't had no water in it for years, but." He gestured to the south-west, where a strange light shimmered in the sky.

"Salt flats, now. But there's a big station over there, and another line to Perth. But it's hard out there on the old lake, boss. Don't even get snakes out there."

They stood in the doorway and looked at the strange light.

"How far is it?"

"Forty miles to the other side of the salt," said Billy Snakeskin. "I been there. Not many snakes there, but. I worked once on old Len Stanton's station. He'll give you a feed and see you right till you get the train to Perth. You tell him Billy Snakeskin sent you—he'll laugh. Knows me, he does. Knows old Billy. Wanted me to stay working for him but I said no boss thank you very much and come back."

"Why?" asked Archy.

Billy Snakeskin took off his cap and scratched his coppery head again. He looked around at the land trembling in the sun.

"I like it here," he said.

Archy made up his mind quickly.

"If we go, we've got to go now," he said.

Billy Snakeskin grinned and pointed.

"That way, boss, to Mister Len's place. Good luck."

"Let's go," said Archy. He walked out of the hut into the blazing morning. "Whew! Well, come on, Frank."

Reluctantly, Frank followed him. They crossed the

tracks and as the land fell away beyond the siding they got their first glimpse of the dead lake: an evil glittering empty pan of caked mud and salt stretching as far as they could see. No birds, no life. Silence and heat.

"Jesus, Mary and Joseph," whispered Frank.

Billy Snakeskin had run after then, still chuckling. "Boss," he said, "both bosses, you're mad. You better take this." He handed them a canvas waterbag. "Give you a chance, anyway." He lifted his right arm, pointing across the lake: "There's forty mile of that, boss. Forty mile! You'll cook." He swung around again, and sought the shade of his hut.

When Frank and Archy were tiny black specks on the vastness of the lake, Billy Snakeskin stood up, balanced on his rickety chair, cupped his hands to his mouth and bellowed:

"You'll never make it!"

The hot wind whipped his words away, tearing them into pieces, scattering them across the sky so that Archy and Frank heard only a faint wailing.

Frank, almost running to keep up with Archy, looked around the dead lake uneasily. The dried crust, baked by day, half frozen by night, crackled beneath their feet.

"Archy, this's mad," said Frank. "We should've waited. And what about your feet?"

"Two weeks? That *is* mad. And my feet'll be all right, don't worry."

"Perhaps that Snakeskin bloke was wrong."

"Not according to the timetable he wasn't. Don't worry, Frank, it's quicker this way, mate."

"That's what Burke and Wills thought, and look what happened to them."

"That was in—well, it was a long time ago. You can't get lost today, in 1915."

"Why?"

"Because—well, things are different. People'd look for us."

"They've got to know we're lost before they start looking for us, Archy."

Archy stopped. He looked around at the featureless lake bed.

"You've got a point, Frank. Still, nothing we can do about it now. Let's keep going."

"Forty miles, that Abo snake bloke said."

"The average man can walk four miles an hour. We're not average. Let's go."

"Hope you're right."

They plodded on. The sun was almost vertical now. They took off their shirts and wrapped them around their heads to shade their eyes and give them some relief from the frightful glare of the lake bed.

At two o'clock they had their first drink of water. It was lukewarm and seemed to make them thirstier.

"What if we run out of water?" asked Frank, shaking the bag.

"There's always water if you know how to find it," said Archy stoutly.

"All right, I'll bite. How?"

"Cockatoos. At sunset they lead you straight to it. It's their drinking time."

Frank threw up his arms.

"That's lovely—we put our lives in the hands of a flock of bloody galahs!"

Another thought struck him: "Anyway, where are the galahs? Or anything else? There's not a living thing for bloody miles! There's not even a flaming tree for your galahs to sit on!"

Archy trudged on in silence. They walked without speaking for an hour, the only sounds the faint hiss of the wind and the squinch-squinch-squinch of their feet.

They were having their second drink of water when Frank voiced another fear.

"How do we know we're not walking around in circles? Blokes do, you know. I've read about it. Walk around in circles till they drop and the vultures eat them."

"No vultures around here, Frank."

"No, nor anything else."

"Don't worry. I know where we're going. Or at least I can make sure we don't walk in circles."

"Follow some sort of bird?"

"No. Listen and you'll learn something."

Archy tapped his watch.

"See, I've got the twelve pointing straight at the sun, right? See that reflection of the sun on the glass right over the twelve? Got it? Now the hour hand is on three o'clock, right? Well, north is slap in the middle of three o'clock and twelve—right there between the one and the two."

"So how does that help us?"

Archy sighed.

"If we know where north is, Frank, we can work out where south, east and west are. At present we're walking—" he squinted at his watch, "I'd say a little east of south. We'll check again in an hour and make sure we're still going in the same direction. All right?"

"Make sure you keep the bloody thing wound."

They walked. When they could bear their thirst no longer they drank some more water: a mouthful each, tepid and tasting of old canvas. The wind came up and lifted the dried salty earth and flung it into their faces.

"Should've got some tucker off that snake bloke," said Frank. "I'm starving."

"I saved us a sandwich," said Archy. "I've been hanging on as long as I could."

"Let's have it."

"Let's take a break," said Archy. They sank down gratefully. Archy took a small parcel from his pocket and unwrapped it carefully.

"Don't lose a bloody crumb," said Frank apprehensively.

The bread had dried and curled in the heat, and the ham was decidedly past its best, but Archy and Frank ate as though it was the Royal Hotel's extra-special businessman's dinner in front of them. The meal was washed down with a mouthful of water, and then they were walking again.

The sun set at last: at times it had seemed as though it would ride in the sky above them for ever. Its last slanting rays sent their shadows striding across the cracked mud like grotesquely distorted giants. Then it was gone in a blaze of orange and purple. Night swept quickly over the lake and the wind turned cold.

By the last glow in the sky they hastily collected handfuls of the sparse, dead scrub which had tried to grow in the saline mud. Then Archy tripped, in the growing dark, over the remains of a tree, drowned many years ago, and with the scrub and the tinder-dry tree they soon had a blaze going. They crouched close to it, shivering, and soon had to rifle their bags for extra clothes.

They sat in silence for a while, overawed by the silence and the vastness of the universe.

"Can you ride, Frank?" asked Archy suddenly.

"Of course," said Frank, and Archy sensed a defensive note in his voice. "Of course. Why?"

"Just wondered why you didn't try for the Light Horse back in Figtree Crossing."

"Because I didn't want to," said Frank shortly.

"Going to join the infantry?"

"I'm not going to join anything," said Frank snappily. "All right?"

Archy was shocked, and his voice betrayed it.

"Frank—you've got to be in it," he protested.

Frank stirred the embers with his boot and said irritably: "I don't have to be in anything, mate, if I don't want to be. This is a free country—or haven't you heard?"

"I'd be ashamed of myself if I didn't fight," said Archy warmly. "Bloody well ashamed."

"Well, that proves only one thing, Archy," said Frank.

"And what's that?"

"That you and I are different, eh? And let's leave it at that."

He covered himself as best he could with his spare clothes and, with his face to the fire, was soon asleep. Archy sat awake thinking and looking at Frank for a long while before he curled up on the other side of the fire.

Sister Cooley had written in her diary:

October 19, 1914

Aboard the troopship Benalla: *We are just one of a mighty fleet! There is the* Medic, *the* Euripides, Ulysses, Afric, Ascanius, Honorata, Athenic—*it almost seems, as we are bound for the lands of classical antiquity, that the authorities have chosen ships with appropriate names! To escort us we have our own H.M.A.S.* Sydney *and* Melbourne—*great grey cruisers bristling with guns. And—there is a Japanese ship among our escort, the Japanese warship* Ibuki! *She shepherded the New Zealand fleet across the Tasman Sea. And now we are all assembled here and waiting for the "off"—a great armada riding on the lovely lonely sapphire waters of King George Sound.*

November 1: Sailed today. I have just counted the ships. There are forty-two—the greatest fleet ever to sail from Australia. Noted a few more ships' names today—I am trying to keep a full record of this historic event: the Wiltshire, the Southern (I heard one of our ship's officers saying she was "too slow" and would reduce the speed of the whole fleet) and the British warship H.M.S. Minotaur (another classical reference!) which has been sent all the way from the Royal Navy's China Station, wherever that may be, to help escort us.

November 8: At sea. Many of the men ill. Very hot and the ship's metal walls (bulkheads, the sailors call them) "sweat" moisture most of the time, which I think accounts for the absolute epidemic of colds and sore throats aboard. Have started typhoid inoculations, a company at a time. What a sight this great convoy makes as it ploughs across the brilliant blue sea: the lines of ships, the slower troopships shepherded by the warships, the wakes churning the water to foam, the strings of flying fish which dart away from the bows, the huge pillars of black smoke from the mighty engines! At night, for fear of the Emden, all ships are darkened except for a few hooded lights to prevent collision, and the ships "speak" to each other with blinking signal lamps. Many of the men flee the crowded stuffy quarters below deck and sleep on deck under the stars—and aren't there shouts of protest at dawn when the sailors begin hosing down the decks without bothering to wake the sleeping soldiers!

November 9: H.M.A.S. Sydney left us at high speed, her four tall funnels belching great clouds of smoke as she disappeared over the horizon. A rumour has flashed around the ship that she has gone to fight the Emden, which is lurking somewhere to the north.

November 10: The Sydney has sunk the

Emden *after a dreadful battle off Cocos Island!*
The whole convoy rang with cheers when the news
was announced. We all feel much safer.

Snowy Lane sent his mother a brief postcard:

> *Home very soon now. Will be great to see*
> *the old place again. We are still all very keen on*
> *joining up. I am sure we are doing the right thing.*
> *The news from Europe sounds very bad. Wish*
> *Frank was with us. We three still have a lot of fun*
> *together, but things aren't the same without Frank.*
> *Oh for the good old days of the Four Musketeers.*

Love,
Dennis

10

The day began with a sip of water. The waterbag felt
frighteningly light, and the lake bed still stretched around
them as far as the eye could see. They started walking while
it was still cool and barely light. The sun rose fast enough,
though, and lapped them with its scorching tongue. Their
skin blistered and peeled, their lips cracked and bled. And,
sip by sip, the water level in the bag sank.

They walked mainly in long brooding silences, each
occupied with his own thoughts, the only sound the fluting
wind and their feet breaking the salt crust.

"You of all people should be going," said Archy

suddenly, breaking a silence which had stretched for two hours. "You, of all people."

Frank stopped and swung around to face him, his eyes blazing in his seared face. Little sun-blisters on his cheekbones had burst and leaked serum which had dried on his cheeks like tears.

"Why?" he asked angrily. "Why the hell me of all people?"

"Because you're an athlete," said Archy. "They need fit people."

"Well, they're not getting me, mate."

"I've got mates who'd be lucky to run the hundred in twelve seconds, and if they're prepared to do their bit, why shouldn't you?"

"Do their bit! Do their bit!" Frank mimicked him. "I'll tell you what they'll do, Archy—they'll do their bloody lives, that's what they'll do!" He leaned towards Archy and tapped him on the chest. "And I'll tell you why Frank Dunne won't be doing his bit, mate—because it's not our bloody war, that's why!"

Archy gaped at him in amazement.

"What do you mean, not our war? Britain—"

"Exactly—Britain! It's an English war—nothing to do with us. We're Australians."

"You mean you wouldn't fight for the Empire?"

"Look, I don't believe in that King and Country stuff. What's His Royal Highness ever done for me? And if I got my legs blown off, or blinded, what would he do? Give me a pat on the head, a medal and sixpence a day pension. No thanks."

"You know what you are? You're a bloody coward!" The frightful word hung on the heated air between them.

"There's only one reason I don't knock you down for that, mate," said Frank, through clenched teeth.

"What's that?"

"Because I don't feel like carrying you the rest of the way! Now give me a drink, and don't open your mouth about the bloody war again!"

They laboured on in a deepening silence, avoiding each other's eyes.

A strange haze grew with the day, a filmy milk-and-water cloud which gradually covered the entire sky and blotted out the sun.

Squinch-squinch-squinch.

The last of the water.

Squinch-squinch-squinch.

Thirst grew. And a griping hunger.

Suddenly Frank stopped.

He pointed.

"Look at that. Jesus, Mary and Joseph, look at that." A double line of footprints intersected their track at right angles and marched off into the trembling distant glare. Their own footprints.

They stared, appalled.

"We've made a circle," whispered Archy. "A bloody great circle!"

They fell silent, stunned by the enormity of it.

"Well, what price your bloody trick with the sun and your watch now, eh?" snarled Frank. "Bloody marvellous!"

"Been no sun for hours," said Archy. "Look at the sky." He pointed at the haze where a diffused glow merely hinted at the general direction of the sun.

"Thought you were a bushman!" said Frank bitterly. "Oh, sure, he can find water by following birds—trouble is, there's no birds. Oh yes, he can navigate by the sun—only there's no sun!"

"At least I didn't pick the wrong blasted train!" shouted Archy, stung.

"It was the right train, just the wrong bloody coach! Could've happened to anyone!"

"All right," said Archy, "all right, Frank. Blaming each other's not going to help." He stuck out his hand. "C'mon, we're mates, eh? Shake on it."

So they shook on it. Then they sat down on the hot earth and had a council of war, the outcome of which was that they were agreed on one thing: that they were lost, without food or water, and didn't know which way to walk next to put them back on course.

They sat, drearily contemplating the landscape. Then Frank suddenly jumped to his feet, staring, shading his eyes with his hands.

"Archy—something's coming—look!"

Archy scrambled to his feet and stared in the direction of Frank's gaze.

Something had taken solid form out there where the tortured air trembled and shivered in the heat.

It came steadily closer, a tantalising shape, now tall and thin and wavering, now squat and distorted, like something seen through rippling water or flawed glass. They watched it draw nearer, fascinated, almost expecting some weird creature of the desert to materialise. Then it grew closer and took on the solid form of a camel with a man sitting high on it. They could hear the steady shou-shou-shou of its splay hooves on the salt. The driver saw them and clucked to the beast and it swerved toward them.

They surveyed each other in silence for a few minutes. The camel grumbled and harrumphed and showed its ugly long teeth and the rider, a man in his late fifties or early sixties, with several days' growth of grizzled beard on his brown weather-worn face, fanned himself with his sweat-stained felt hat and shook his head in amazement. It was several moments before he spoke. When he did it was to the point. He unslung his waterbag and handed it to Archy.

"Take a drink," he said. He waited until they had both drunk their fill. Slowly, still regarding them, he took the waterbag back and slung it from the saddle again. Then he said:

"D'yer mind tellin' me what in th' bloody hell yer doin' out here? Eh?"

They explained, both talking at once. The driver shook his head in disbelief.

"You know," he said, shaking his head again, "This must've bin yer lucky day. Name's Stumpy." He looked at the intersecting sets of footprints and shook his head yet again, even more vigorously. "Yep. The old story. Walkin' in circles, eh? Bin dead in a day or two. Yes. Yer bloody lucky day, mates."

"We were told there was a property over this way," said Archy.

Stumpy nodded. He gestured at their footprints.

"But yer certainly weren't gonna find it! Not any of the ways youse was going."

"How far are we from it?" asked Archy.

"Ol' Len's place? 'Bout ten mile or so."

"Can you head us there?"

"Sure. Passin' quite close to it meself." A thought struck the camel driver. "Youse 'ad any tucker? Thought not! My oath, what a pair. 'Ere—" he opened his saddle-bag. "Get yerselves around that. Bit o' cold mutton an' damper. Go on, eat it!"

They fell upon it like wolves. Stumpy watched them, chuckling.

"Ol' Len give yer a bed an' some grub an' probably give youse a ride to Wollamby. Where yer headed?"

"Perth," said Archy, through a mouthful of damper.

"I nearly went there once," mused Stumpy, rolling a cigarette. "Smoke? Don't use 'em? Yep, thought I should see one big city before I die. Youse lookin fer work?"

"No," said Archy, looking at Frank. "I'm off to the war."

Stumpy frowned.

"What war?"

Frank and Archy stared at him.

"Why—the big war, the war against Germany," said Archy.

"Never heard of it," said Stumpy. "Don't read the papers much. Don't see no one sometimes fer weeks. Knew a German once, though. Out Alice Springs way. Not a bad bloke. So now we're fightin' 'em. 'Ow'd the war start, then?"

"Gawd," said Frank wearily, "don't get him on to that."

"Well, I don't know, exactly, how it started," admitted Archy. "But it was the Germans' fault."

"And are the Australians fightin' already?" queried Stumpy.

"Yes," said Frank, "in Turkey!"

Stumpy smoked for a while, considering this. Finally he removed the cigarette and looked at Frank sternly.

"Don't make sense ta me. Yer mate says we're fightin' the Germans, 'n you say we're fightin' in Turkey. What the hell're we doin' in Turkey?"

Frank shrugged.

"Don't ask me."

"Because Turkey's an ally of Germany," said Archy shortly.

Stumpy nodded wisely.

"Well, y' learn somethin' new every day, eh? But I still can't say I can see what it's got ter do with us."

Frank grinned.

"If we don't stop them over there," said Archy firmly, "they could end up over here—"

Stumpy sat up and tilted his hat over his eyes and looked around at the blasted desert landscape.

"Far as I'm concerned," he said, "they'd be bloody welcome to it."

Frank shouted with laughter.

Stumpy and his camel took the boys to the edge of the salt: it stopped quite suddenly, and there were living things around again—green things, and birds, and a different colour in the sky.

They thanked Stumpy, and shook his hand, and even patted his camel, at which the beast did its best to bite their hands off. Then Stumpy was away, without looking back and they were rolling in grass—grass! green grass! slapping each other on the back and shaking hands again and again.

As the sun was setting they toiled up a slope. And at its crest, sitting on a good horse, a girl sat watching them, her eyes wide with wonder at the sand- and salt-encrusted figures. She wore cool linen and a wide-brimmed straw hat secured under the chin by a band of muslin. She was as fresh and delectable as a new salad.

Archy spoke first, when he had got his breath back.

"G'day," he said.

She looked at them, still wondering.

"I'm Mary Stanton," she said in a cool, quiet voice with a hint of laughter in it, and pointed back the way they had come with a delicate whip made, surely, for display only: "You've come across the lake?"

"Yes ma'am," said Frank.

She smiled.

"You must have met Stumpy, or you'd be dead."

Shamefacedly, they admitted it. She looked at them dispassionately.

"Can you walk another mile?"

They nodded. For her they would have walked another ten, and ten.

"Right. The homestead's straight over the hill. I'll tell my parents you're coming."

And she whirled the horse and was gone in a swirl of linen and a hint of perfume—lavender water, Frank thought. Coming from the city, he knew about these things. He looked at Archy. "Well, what are we waiting for? Walk!"

They walked.

It's hard to look smart and sophisticated when one's wardrobe consists of clothes which have been dragged across—well, not forty miles of desert; Billy Snakeskin was wrong there—but certainly thirty; but Frank Dunne tried. For Mary Stanton, he tried. He brushed his teeth and combed his hair as best he could in the tiny fragment of mirror the Stanton homestead bunkhouse provided, and thought he didn't look too bloody bad, all things considered, and his sun-scarred cheekbones made him look, well, interesting, you know. And he could talk well—being from the city and all that. He grinned. Ah ha. Oh yes. Not a bad catch, Frank Dunne. And all the annoyances, frustrations, discomforts and dangers of the past few weeks were swept away, forgotten.

Then Archy walked into the room. Frank stared at him. Archy had put on his best shirt. Brushed his hair. Cleaned his teeth.

They stared at each other.

Frank pointed a finger.

Archy pointed a finger.

"You—" said Frank.

"You—" said Archy.

"—bastard!" they finished together, and burst out laughing.

Len Stanton's homestead, Tharfield, was, no doubt about it, a good place to be after the lake crossing. Old Len (he was at least fifty) wasn't short of a quid, as they say; his daughter Mary, just twenty, was a bit of all right; his wife, Laura, was a charming woman of perhaps forty-two or three who had not let the life and the loneliness of the outback abrade her soul; and Len's mother, Gran Hannah, nudging eighty, was a touch waspish, as old ladies can be, but not a bad sort.

These, at least, were Frank Dunne's thoughts as he stood rather awkwardly in the Stanton dining room, trying nonchalantly to rest his elbow on the mantelpiece of the fireplace, and twirl a non-existent moustache, and introduce into the genteel room a jangle of cavalryman's spurs and panache while Mrs Stanton and Mary laid the table and Archy, on familiar territory, discussed crops and stock with Mr Stanton. Frank sipped his sherry delicately and repressed a shudder. Sherry! What the hell would they think in Platt Street, or in the Standard Hotel? But he looked at Mary and smiled smoothly.

Mrs Stanton, setting out the table napkins, remarked generally: "I think you are both very brave to venture to cross that dreadful place without even a compass."

"Not really," said Frank authoritatively. "Not really, Mrs Stanton. All one needs is one's watch, and one can find one's way anywhere."

Archy, stunned, could only nod, keeping his eyes on Mary the while. And Frank, to his chagrin, saw that Mary was less interested in his learned dissertation on desert navigation than she was in Archy's obvious admiration.

"And why are you going to Perth?" asked Mrs Hamilton during the soup.

"I'm going to join the Light Horse," said Archy, not without a trace of malice.

"Could've joined in Figtree Crossing, couldn't you?" said Mr Stanton. He squinted at Archy knowingly. "You're not of age, are you?" He held up his hand. "Don't tell me, don't tell me. Not my business, boy. I'm not your father."

Old Gran Hannah averted an embarrassing silence by looking up from her soup and saying with vehemence:

"Good! I like a lad with spirit!" And she nodded and shook until her various ornaments jingled. "I like a lad with spirit."

She sighed.

"The Boer War! Ah yes, they learned about us Australians then, didn't they! Our boys could shoot, and ride—" and she broke off, her old face suffused with anger "—and then those British shot our Breaker Morant—our man. Now! Tell me! Did they get him over there to fight, or not? That's what I want to know! And then they shot him!"

"The old lady's quite keen on war," murmured Mr Stanton.

His wife, to get away from Majuba and Spion Kop, asked Frank whether he was joining the Light Horse too.

"Well, not actually," said Frank. "I've got some business interests to attend to in Perth first. After that, I might—well, perhaps—"

Old Hannah snorted—positively snorted—and glared at him.

"Huh! Business—while the Huns crucify kittens—or it may be children, for all I know, the news takes so long to get here—on church doors in Belgium! Business! Pah!"

And the old lady took up her soup aggressively.

Somehow they got through the rest of the meal—a good one, with fish, roast, sweet, tea and port—without further incident; although Hannah, in between taking on, as though she were an empty freighter sailing to the other side of the world, enormous quantities of fish, beef, potatoes, cabbage, carrots and gravy, continued to glare at Frank and mutter about kittens and bayonets and babies.

After dinner Mrs Stanton broached the tender subject again, quite innocently. Mary and Archy were turning over the pages of a new book devoted to highly-coloured prints of heroic figures wearing "Uniforms of the Empire", when Mrs Stanton remarked: "I love the Light Horse uniform."

Mary dimpled and looked at Archy. "Most of the boys around here are joining the Light Horse," she said.

Her father (probably inflamed by the port and a burst of patriotic fervour) looked at Archy's earnest face, poured himself another port and cried: "And if I'd had a son, instead of Mary here, that's what he'd have joined too—the Light Horse! Let's drink a toast to our gallant young friend here—to him and the Light Horse!"

More port was poured; more toasts drunk; and Frank glowered, while Mary gave Archy a special smile.

He was still brooding about the unfair advantage a uniform—or even the prospect of one—gave a man as they lay on their bunks in the otherwise deserted bunkhouse after dinner. It was a quiet time of the year on Tharfield, and the few stockmen Stanton had held on to were in town, so Archy and Frank had the place to themselves.

They chatted idly for a while, avoiding, by unspoken mutual consent, the topic which lay uppermost in both their minds: the charms of Mary Stanton.

At length Archy said, almost too casually: "Business interests in Perth, eh?"

Frank grunted.

"Mmm. Business interests."

"You told me you were broke."

Frank laughed shortly. "I am, thanks to you."

"What would you have done with the money, if you'd won?"

"Started a bike shop—pushbikes first, then motorbikes. I'd have it made then."

They lay in silence for a while. In the big house the lights went out one by one. A small upper window stayed aglow longest. They both watched it, wondering if Mary lay behind those prim lace curtains.

"The Light Horse," said Frank after a while, "they only take toffs and farmers' sons, don't they?"

Archy raised himself on one elbow, staring at him in amazement.

"No, that's not true—are you thinking of joining?"

Frank shrugged.

"Look, there's no way you'd get me near the infantry—and I still don't hold with this blasted war—but the Light Horse has got a bit of class."

Archy sat bolt upright, hugging his knees. Excitedly, he said: "Hey, Frank—we could join up together, mate! Go overseas together! If you can ride, the Light Horse'll take you."

Frank lifted a hand to slow him.

"Whoa, whoa, Archy. There's one problem, mate."

"What's that?"

Frank hesitated.

"Well . . ." he scratched his nose. "Well . . . you know I told you I could ride . . .?"

Archy stared at him, a slow grin forming.

"Well, it was a lie," snapped Frank. "I can't bloody ride. Don't know one end of a horse from the other." Archy forced himself to stop grinning. He knew how touchy Frank could be.

"Look," he said. "Maybe I can give you a few lessons tomorrow. Mr Stanton will lend us a horse."

Frank hesitated.

"Do you think—"

Archy nodded vigorously.

"Course. Athletic chap like you, why, you'll pick it up in a couple of minutes. Nothing to it."

"If you're sure—"

"Old Stanton won't mind. Probably got a few tame horses in the paddock behind the house—"

Frank flared at him:

"You mean broken-down, pensioned-off old nags, eh? I'll look a bloody fool!"

"Frank, be reasonable. Look, I can't ride a motor-bike. I'd have to learn, wouldn't I? If I were in your neck of the woods, would you laugh at me for trying to learn to ride a motor-bike? Well, you're in my neck of the woods now, and I won't laugh at you for learning to ride a horse."

"Hmmm," said Frank, unconvinced. He lay back, thinking. There was no doubt that the Light Horse uniform was pretty all right. And it was a real silvertail outfit, after all, the sort of outfit in which one met influential people, or at any rate the sons of influential people. Now that the bike shop plan was temporarily scotched because of lack of funds, the Light Horse might not be a bad idea. And—hey, hey—he might get commissioned. Lieutenant Frank Dunne! This was war time. People got commissioned quicker in war time. Everybody said so. He closed his eyes and saw himself, commissioned, belted, booted, spurred, possibly even jingling a medal or two, leading his column through Perth on their return from a victorious campaign. And among the cheering crowds, on a discreet balcony, was a face remarkably like . . . he fell asleep and dreamed he was galloping effortlessly along a sweeping moonlit beach on a huge white horse.

"Learning to ride, at his age!" snorted old Hannah, watching the events in the back paddock through the kitchen window, where she was taking tea and bread and butter aboard to get her through the desert between breakfast and mid-morning tea. "Hmmph! He should be learning to shoot, that's what!"

"Take another cup of tea, dear," said Mrs Stanton.

Out in the paddock, Frank was being introduced to Mittens, and wishing heartily that he was back in Perth. Mittens was fifteen, and long retired. She spent all day doing nothing and liked it that way. The Stanton family treated her as they did their other pets, for that is what she was now, her working days a long way behind her. Mittens loved being fed tidbits, and patted on the head by visiting children; she liked being groomed and having her mane brushed by Mary. She even allowed the odd favoured child to be held on her back by its father while she ambled slowly around the paddock.

But, after all these years, to have a saddle slapped on her! And a bridle! And to obviously be expected to carry this great man about! Mittens rolled her eyes and arched her neck and blew noisily through her nostrils.

"Come on, please, Mittens," said Mary, patting and coaxing her. "There's a good girl. Just for a little while, Mittens, and I'll give you some sugar."

Reluctantly, Mittens suffered herself to be led to where Frank stood waiting, his face frozen in a horrible smile of false confidence.

Mary handed the reins to Frank, and Mittens, with an impatient shake of her head, jerked them out of his hands. Frank blushed. Mary retrieved the reins and handed them back to Frank. Mittens repeated the manoeuvre. This time Archy picked up the reins.

"Here," he said, before handing them to Frank again, "watch me. Hold them like this. Pull her head down. Show her who's boss. Keep a good tight pull on 'em—"

Mittens, sensing that Archy was no beginner, eyed him balefully.

"If they sense you're scared, they'll take advantage of you," warned Archy.

"Who's scared?" asked Frank uncertainly.

Mary turned her face away, and tactfully went back to the house.

About an hour later, and probably because she realised that Archy wouldn't stand any nonsense, Mittens seemed to develop a sort of weary tolerance for Frank. So Archy took her up from a walk to a trot to a gallop. Later in the morning Mary, unable to stay in the house any longer, saddled up a horse for Archy and herself, and they all three went for a ride. Mittens got two pieces of sugar at the end of the lesson and retired to the other side of the paddock. Archy helped Frank back to the bunkhouse.

Safely on his bunk, he groaned.

"I feel's though my backbone's been driven up into my skull."

"First few days are always the worst," said Archy.

"Ow, bloody hell! My legs! The skin's torn raw!"

"You'll get over it," said Archy.

Some time later Frank said, thoughtfully:

"You know, Archy, I never realised horses were so bloody high! Fair dinkum, you know, sitting up there—the bloody ground seemed miles away!"

Archy laughed. "Wait till you see some of those bloody great big Light Horse gallopers."

Next day another lesson. Mary was waiting for them in the paddock, which made Frank feel a little better. So was Mittens, rolling a warning eye.

He mounted carefully, still stiff and sore from the previous day. Mittens snorted, and got her own back by trotting so stiff-legged that each step sent shock waves of pain through Frank.

He stuck it out, though, and it was worth it, because he got a smile of approval from Mary—though not as warm, he noticed bitterly, as the smiles she bestowed on Archy.

"Archy and I are going for a ride, Frank," said Mary when the lesson was over. "You coming?"

Frank grimaced. "No thanks! I think I'll just go and, er, stand around for a while."

Mary laughed.

"The first few days are the worst. Come on, Archy." He watched them canter away. Even when they were out of sight behind a line of wind-warped gums he could hear their high clear laughter. He shrugged. Just a pair of kids, Frank, just a pair of kids. But it was with a strange feeling of emptiness that he hobbled back to the kitchen where that redoubtable old lady, Hannah, was drinking tea and eating bread and butter.

The next day Mrs Stanton, Mary and Hannah walked down to the yard gate to say goodbye. Mr Stanton was driving the boys to the station.

"Goodbye, Frank," Mary said. "Good luck with the bike shop—or whatever you decide to do."

She put her hand lightly on Archy's arm. "Don't forget, now, Archy—you promised to write!"

"I will," he said. "I promise."

They touched hands, lightly, and he was gone: the cart rattled away, raising a fine cloud of dust which blew across the scrub.

The older women waved and went inside. Mary stood by the gate until the cart was out of sight and the dust had settled on the bushes.

Archy and Frank, tired, broke and hungry, arrived in Perth station on a gritty, windy, late winter's afternoon. Frank, still stiff and blistered from his horseriding, groaned as they stepped down on to the platform.

"My gawd. Bloody horses!"

Archy picked up both bags.

"How far do we have to walk?"

Frank groaned again.

"Bloody miles. Oh, gawd!"

But they found they had enough small change between them to afford a tram ride for part of the way. It amused Archy to see how, subtly, Frank's demeanour changed as they drew nearer his home territory. When they got off the tram he stood appreciably taller, held his shoulders straighter, and generally assumed the air of a man who know's what's what, thank you very much; and as they drew near Platt Street, and excited urchins and lounging lairs on street corners whistled and shouted surprised greetings, Frank positively swaggered, and put his hat at a rakish angle, eyeing Archy knowingly as though to say: "See, mate? I'm a bloke they know about, around here." And he became almost patronisingly informative to Archy, as "bit of all right, that pub there," or, "see if I can find us a couple of girls to take to the pictures, eh, Archy? When we've got some money, that is."

It took a long time getting down Platt Street, because as they got nearer home Frank knew more and more people, until their passage became a sort of triumphal procession. Frequently, though, Frank's inquiries about an old friend whose face he missed met with the response, "Oh, 'im, 'es orf to th' war, Frank. Guess yer've come back ter join up too, eh?" To which Frank grunted a noncommittal reply and set his new bush hat (picked up with almost his last two bob just before boarding the train to Perth) at an even jauntier angle, and increased his swagger a little.

They reached Number 16 at last, its paint flaking in the pale winter sun. Archy, seeing Frank's home for the first time, suddenly understood a lot of things about

Frank. But before he had time to ponder his fresh insight, the door of Number 16 burst open with a bang, and the house spilled people—Frank's mother, still in her dressing gown, hair in curlers; old Patrick, in blue-and-white striped pyjama bottoms and sweaty singlet; and what seemed to Archy like a hundred children, although there were only eight of them, all laughing and crying and whooping at once, hugging and kissing Frank and making such a fuss of him that it was several minutes before Frank could pull Archy forward and present him to Maureen and Patrick Dunne with the simple introduction: "This is my mate, Archy."

And after that it all became a bit blurred for Archy: one of the older boys was despatched to the Royal Standard for a bottle of whisky on the slate; and later sent back to buy another bottle, on the same terms. Old Patrick had the day off, it seemed, because the war—"th' bluidy English whar!"—was keeping the docks so busy that Patrick was working extra shifts, and had earned a mid-week day off.

Archy got the impression, before falling asleep with his back against the leg of the kitchen table, that old Patrick disliked both the English and the war, so he wisely refrained from talking about the plans he and Frank had jointly made to seek adventure abroad.

Snowy burst through the front door with a whoop of joy.

"Mum! Frank Dunne's back in town! Perhaps we'll get him to change his mind about joining up!"

His mother sighed.

"I wish you'd change your mind, Dennis."

Snowy sighed. He put his arm around his mother's thin shoulders.

"Mum, we've been through that. I've got to go."

His mother kissed his tanned cheek with her pale lips, dry as autumn leaves.

"I can't stop you. You're over twenty-one. But do one thing for me, Dennis—"

"Yes?" Warily, suspecting a tender trap, a demand for a promise that he wouldn't "do anything silly", or a promise that he would try for a cushy job behind the lines.

"You've been away in the bush two years, Dennis, and you've been back only a few days. Don't run off again so soon. Stay home for a while, please. That's not much to ask, is it?"

Snowy looked at the pale tired face. He hesitated.

"We—we were going to join up tomorrow, Mum, Barney and Billy and I."

"Give me a week," said his mother. "That's not long to ask. You're my only son, Dennis."

He kissed her.

"All right, Mum. The war may be over by then."

"I hope so," his mother said fervently. "Dear Lord, I hope so."

It wasn't hard to get hold of an empty birth certificate in Platt Street. People kept a few around in case of accident, so to speak.

Which is how, the following night, still extremely hung-over, Archy and Frank were poring over the official form spread out on Mrs Dunne's kitchen table and working out a new identity for Archy.

Frank picked up a pen.

"What name?"

"Hamilton."

"You can't use your own name, Archy. They'll be able to trace you. One letter from your folks to the army and that's it! So what do you want to call yourself?"

Archy considered this for a moment. Then he said:

"Lasalles. Archy Lasalles."

Frank grinned. "Fancy yourself, don't you? All

right. Archy Lasalles." He filled in the form and waved it about to dry. Then he handed it to Archy with a flourish.

"There you are, Mr Lasalles."

Archy examined it critically.

"It's a bit—new, isn't it? I mean, I'm supposed to be twenty—this form's so new the ink's still wet!"

Frank frowned. "You're right. Give us it—I'll fix it."

He folded the certificate across and across and rubbed the folded paper across the crumb-strewn, gravy-spotted table. When he unfolded it it looked appreciably older: the cheap paper had cracked in places along the folds, and was stained and speckled.

"Leave that out in the sun for a couple of hours tomorrow," said Frank, returning the certificate to Archy, "and the ink'll fade so nobody'll know that isn't a real, genuine Platt Street birth certificate."

"What I can't understand," said Patrick, "is why the hell ye are after joinin' up? I c'n understand him, he's got bluidy English blood in his veins! But ye—you're a Dunne! You're Irish! And now fer Jasus' sweet sake you're joinin' the English army! Why, your grandfather, God bless his soul, he'll be turnin' in his grave at this very moment, I tell ye—"

Frank had just announced his intention of joining the Light Horse with Archy, and he could not have caused a greater stir at Number 16 if he had told his parents that he was joining the Orange Lodge. His mother had instantly resorted to tears and his father to abuse, but Frank was unmoved, and Patrick tried another tack:

"Why, I remember, as though 'twere yesterday," he said, "the murtherin' English soldiers murtherin' your very own grandfather! Hung him with his own belt, they did—"

"—at the crossroads, five miles from Dublin," sighed Frank, completing the story he had heard scores of times.

"An' those murtherin' bastards," shouted Patrick, his face purple with whisky and rage, "those are the murtherin' bastards ye'll be soldierin' with! Wearin' the same uniform as them what killed your own flesh and blood grandfather!"

"Look, Dad," said Frank, "I'm not going over there to fight for the British Empire. I'm going over there to do myself a bit of good! I'm going to keep my head down, learn a trick or two, and come back an officer. I don't want to be pushed around the rest of my life!"

Patrick subsided, rumbling.

"Well," he said, "an' I'll tell ye somethin', me boy. Ye don't come into this house with no bloody murtherin' English uniform, officer or no!"

And that, for the time being, was that.

Almost a year at Blackboy Camp had burned the last civilian softness out of Major Barton. He was no longer a weekend soldier, playing at war and hoping it would never come. It had come, and Major Barton realised that the games were over and the real thing was about to begin, for him and the hundreds of keen young Light Horsemen he had helped to train over the past year. Now he was in Perth, his last stop before going overseas, recruiting reinforcements for the Light Horse.

The recruiting depot was full this morning, long lines of men inching forward, faces hopeful, eager as puppies.

Major Barton lifed his eyes from the stained, creased birth certificate he had been studying and examined the tall, good-looking youth in front of him. Archy stood at attention and tried to look older. He was sweating slightly.

"Lasalles," said Major Barton thoughtfully.

"Hmm. Any relation to the famous runner, Harry Lasalles?"

Archy felt himself blushing.

"No sir."

"Can you ride?"

"Yessir."

"Shoot?"

"Yessir."

"With what?"

"Three oh three, sir. Shotgun, too."

"And you're keen on the Light Horse, eh?"

"Yessir."

The major examined the birth certificate again and Archy swallowed. In daylight the forgery looked impossibly crude.

"Very well, Lasalles," said Major Barton. "Step over there—see the doctor. Next."

Frank Dunne got over the first hurdle, too, but, being Frank, couldn't resist gilding the lily a bit. When asked whether he'd had any military experience (the question was almost a private joke with the major because he knew perfectly well that it was just as likely that these boys had been to the moon), Frank stuck out his chest, pulled in his chin, and snapped:

"Yessir. Five years, sir. Melbourne Horse Cadets."

"Never heard of 'em," said the major, and a youth in the line tittered. A bantam-cock of a corporal bellowed for silence in the line there at once you're not a bunch of bloody schoolboys any more.

When silence had been restored the major mused again: "No, never heard of 'em."

"No sir," said Frank. "They've never had the recognition they deserve, sir."

"Is that so?" asked the major, eyeing Frank narrowly as he stamped the form. "Next!"

After the doctor there was the riding test, and the sour-faced lieutenant could not fault Archy's riding. Almost with reluctance he stamped Archy's form. "All right," he said ungraciously. "I suppose you'll do. Report to the D.O. Dunne, mount up."

Archy whispered out of the corner of his mouth as he marched away to find the D.O.:

"Keep those reins firm."

Muttering the talismanic phrase to himself, Frank approached the horse, an immensely solid chestnut animal which regarded him with indifference. Reaching for the reins, Frank leaned forward towards the animal's ear. "G'day, mate. Meet your Uncle Frank. I'm tough but fair, so don't give me any bloody nonsense, eh?"

"Hurry up, Dunne," roared Lieutenant Gray, "or the bloody war'll be over before you get there."

Frank mounted. The chestnut seemed solid as a rock, and he felt heartened. He picked up the reins, made encouraging sounds with his tongue, and touched the broad barrel-like flanks with his heels.

Nothing happened.

He gave the beast a slap on the withers. It twitched as though irritated by a fly.

A recruit tittered and a sergeant bellowed for silence.

Frank dug his heels into the chestnut's flanks again. It still remained immobile as a statue, gazing into the distance.

Frank cajoled, coaxed, clucked, clapped, flapped the reins, dug in his heels. Lieutenant Gray almost smiled.

The chestnut relieved itself, noisily.

Frank Dunne was not recruited as a member of the Australian Light Horse.

For Archy Hamilton the next few weeks were a blur. Even later he could not remember individual events with any clarity. The day started at dawn with a bugle call and ended in exhausted sleep late at night. In between the recruits gave themselves over, body and soul, to a succession of apparently tireless instructors.

They learned rifle drill, mounted and unmounted. They were taught how to clean, strip and reassemble their rifles. They learned the trumpet and bugle calls of the Australian Army. They had lectures on horse and stable management, how to care for their animals' feet (and their own). Men with lungs like leather instructed them in squad drill, platoon drill and company drill. They learned bayonet fighting, military courtesy and how to write field messages.

They rode and shot and marched and did physical jerks and when they were handed back to Major Barton they were fit as fiddles, tanned and lean and absolutely bursting to go.

Frank, hurt and angry, sulked in his back room at Number 16 for several days, emerging only by night to walk the cold windy streets.

One evening, as he turned the corner into Platt Street on his way home, three figures left the shadows across the road and walked swiftly towards him. Half apprehensive but too miserable to really care, he prepared for trouble.

Then a familiar voice said: "Frank, you old bastard, if you're not going to fight, you can at least buy us a drink."

And another familiar voice chimed in: "It's our last night."

Then Snowy and Barney and Billy stepped into the light and seconds later they were all leaping around and slapping backs and laughing and yelling and bursting into the saloon bar of the Standard and doing serious damage to the ten bob Frank had borrowed from his mother.

"Would've been on our way," said Snowy, "but

my Mum asked me to put off so I said sure—I mean, what could I do?"

"So we're signing up tomorrow!" crowed Billy.

"The infantry," said Barney proudly.

"Still feel the same way about the war, Frank?" asked Barney quietly.

Frank shrugged. "Well—I've been thinking—"

"If you want a fancy outfit," said Billy, "I hear the Light Horse's recruiting."

Frank snorted.

"That bunch of bloody silvertails. No thanks."

"Well, what're you going to do, then?" asked Barney. Frank shrugged.

"Well, look around for a bit, you know. See what turns up."

"Let's have another beer," said Billy. "I mean, this time tomorrow we'll be in barracks."

"It might be an experience," said Frank thoughtfully a few beers later. "A chance to see the world—"

"At the Government's expense," Snowy chimed in.

"—and, when it's over, you don't want to be the only bloke on the street who didn't go," said Billy.

"I'm not joining the infantry," said Frank, wavering.

"Your teeth aren't too good," said the army doctor to Snowy.

"We're supposed to shoot the enemy, mate, not bite them," said Frank, sitting with Billy and Barney on a hard bench in the infantry recruiting depot and nursing a cruel hangover.

The doctor glanced at him.

"A clever one, eh? Well, we'll look at you next." He turned to Snowy. "We'll have to do something about your teeth, lad."

"The army wants soldiers, doesn't it?" asked Frank. "If you knock him back, you've lost the lot of us."

The others nodded enthusiastically. The doctor tapped his teeth with his pen.

"Let's finish the medical first, eh, gentlemen, shall we?" he said. Briskly he checked their feet, lungs, hearts, blood pressure and eyesight. He examined their mouths with special care, probing and digging and pursing his lips. When they were all dressed and sitting on the bench again, the doctor said:

"So you're really keen to join the army, eh?"

"You bet," said Barney, and the others nodded.

"Well, you're all pretty fit—but your mouths are in a shocking state. Shocking! I don't know why Australians have such bad mouths, upon my word I don't. Never find a man with a good mouth, never!" He sighed and pulled a pad of forms towards him.

"However, as you're otherwise fit, and keen to be heroes, I'll pass you. But those mouths must be attended to." He filled out four forms.

"Here. Take these over to the dental pavilion—the sergeant out in the hall will give you the address. The regimental dentist will fix you up."

"Thanks, doc," said Frank. "Don't be down in the mouth about it, ha ha."

"I won't," said the doctor.

As they filed out the doctor remarked, with a friendly smile at Frank:

"Do you know what they call the dental pavilion?"

"No," said Frank.

"The Chamber of Horrors," said the doctor. "Good day."

Snowy Lane, exhausted, cooled his blistered feet in a basin of water and wrote his mother:

Dear Mum,

Are they giving us a time! Makes work on the railway seem like a picnic. Up at dawn. Physical jerks. Squad drill. Rifle drill. Bayonet drill. Signalling. Then more squad drill and more rifle drill, with a little more bayonet drill thrown in for good measure. Our sergeant, Sergeant Sayers, is a real tartar. I don't know how he keeps going, because he exhausts us—and yet every morning there he is, fresh as a daisy. The army food is quite good—at least there is plenty of it—and we are all "fighting fit". Just hope the war isn't over before we get there! Had musketry practice on the shooting range today. I am turning out to be quite a good shot with the S.M.L.E. (the Short Magazine Lee-Enfield) or so the musketry sergeant says. Billy and Frank are managing all right too but Barney, poor Barney, is having a hard time. He is not very good at squad drill (Sergeant Sayers says he must have two left feet) and he is even worse at shooting. At the butts today he missed his own target and got mine instead!

Luckily we four have managed to stick together so far. We're very glad that Frank changed his mind and joined us. What times we will have "over there".

Your affectionate son,
Dennis

12

The Light Horse was embarking, and most of Perth, or so it seemed, had turned out to see them off. The troopship lay at the wharf, steam up and ready to sail, the Blue Peter at its masthead, and long lines of horsemen wound through town towards it. The crowds cheered, the women wept, and the children waved Union Jacks by the hundred.

Harness creaked, equipment jingled, buckles and buttons winked and twinkled in the brilliant sunshine as the Light Horse went aboard. Alongside the ship itself sweating, swearing farriers stepped in piles of steaming horse dung as they fitted broad canvas slings to nervous animals so the cranes could lift them aboard.

When the last horse had been slung aboard, and the last young Light Horseman had passed up the gangplank, Major Barton still stood with his wife and young son among the horse dung, the streamers, the weeping wives and girlfriends and the wet-eyed old men. He forced himself to give his son a last kiss, to embrace his wife for the last time for—God knows how long, he thought.

"Well," he said. "I'll be off then, Anne dear."

The ship's whistle bellowed warning of departure, sending the dockside gulls wheeling away in sudden alarm.

"I packed this for you," said Anne Barton, the tears trickling down her face. She handed him the small wickerwork basket she had carried all morning.

"It's got extra pairs of socks—you must look after your feet—and some singlets—a fresh one every day, mind! And Eno's for your stomach . . . and a bottle of champagne, dear, for you to drink over—wherever you are, on our anniversary."

And then she was gone, almost running through the crowd, clutching the little boy to her.

Slowly Major Barton mounted the gangway. He

must have got grit in his eyes, because they watered dreadfully and the whole troopship, lined with thousands of youthful faces, swam and wavered before him.

Then a pipe band on the quay struck up, the crowds cheered, the lines were cast off and the streamers pulled taut and snapped as the great ship moved slowly away across the sunlit water, surrounded by tooting tugs and headed for the Indian Ocean.

Archy was seasick before dinner. So were several score other Light Horsemen.

Major Barton sat in his shirtsleeves in his tiny, hot cabin and played *Madame Butterfly* on his gramophone.

"It's no bloody pleasure cruise, is it?" said Trooper Harris wearily to Archy. Harris was a tall thin young man from Kalgoorlie, usually referred to by his troop sergeant as "that streak of dysentery". He had a well-deserved reputation as a moaner, but on this occasion Archy had to agree with him. Life aboard the troopship *Geelong* was certainly no pleasure cruise.

Archy had always loved horses: now he came close to hating them. The trumpet blew stables almost continuously: the horses required non-stop attendance. And the manure! It steamed and smelled in piles which seemed to renew themselves as soon as they had been shovelled away. The whole ship reeked of raw dung.

"If I live to be a hundred," said Archy to Trooper Harris, "I'll never forget the smell of manure."

"You'll never make a hundred." said Trooper Harris. "I been readin' the papers. Won't make bloody twenty, most of us won't, let alone a bloomin' hundred."

The trumpeter blew stables again. And so it went all day. Shovelling manure. Stables. Feed. Water. Fall in. Fall out.

"Lasalles, keep those horses moving."

"What the hell are you doing there, Harris? Call that rubbing? I bloody don't."

"And why aren't you hand-rubbing, Smith?"

"Keep those horses *moving*, Lasalles. You're supposed to be exercising 'em."

And yet there were compensations. The sea was a glorious peacock blue, ruffled by a warm breeze. Flying fish lifted off the swells like shimmering locusts. Sometimes, standing alone in the bows, watching the endless sapphire meadows of the sea, Archy felt a strange ache in him that was almost painful.

He wrote to Mary Stanton and mailed the letter at Colombo. A poetic man would have told her of the sea and the sky, of the flying fish and the brilliant sunsets, all gold and green and purple; but Archy was no poet. So he wrote an awkward, stilted letter, which Mary wept over when she received it, months later, and kept between sheets of tissue paper in her album.

> *Dear Mary,*
>
> *Well, we are sailing at last. They are certainly keeping us busy. We work with the horses most of the day, and when we're not doing that we have classes in bayonet fighting, or are made to do physical jerks. It is very hot and we are crowded below decks. I sleep in a hammock like a sailor—quite comfortable once you get used to it. We are quite a mixed bag of men but in general we get on well—of course we have a few grumblers and moaners, and several are already wishing they had not joined up (as I do, sometimes!) but that is to be expected.*

Then he ran out of steam. He wanted to tell her how he felt about her, to remind her of those lightly touching hands, those glances between them. He wanted to tell her how the full moon rising out of the Indian Ocean and the glittering stars aroused a deep longing in him for—something, he couldn't explain it to himself or her. So he finished lamely:

Please thank your father and mother and grandmother for being so kind to Frank and me. I shall write you from Egypt and I hope you will write me as should really love to hear from you.

Then, daringly, he ended it: *With love, Archy,* and rather spoiled the effect, in his critical eyes, by adding a

PS: Poor Frank failed the riding test for the Light Horse. He was very disappointed and so was I, because I would have liked to have him with me on this great adventure. I hope he tries to get into some other unit. The army needs men like Frank.

He longed to write to his parents, too, but he knew that the postmark would give him away. A letter with a postmark from somewhere in the Middle East would set Bindana into a turmoil. His mother would insist that his father do something; his father would ride into Figtree Crossing, cables would be sent, he would be tracked down and sent home in disgrace. No, it would be too much to bear.

Sister Cooley wrote in her diary:

Egypt at last! We have been posted to the Mena House Hospital, a large pleasant building—and surrounded by Australian gumtrees! It makes one feel almost *at home. The hospital is full, or almost so—but not with wounded. We have influenza, scarlet fever, a perfect regiment of sore throats, sunstroke, badly upset stomachs (the local food!), enteric fever, a few broken bones and sprained ankles (the soldiers* will *persist in climbing*

*the pyramids). We have been into Cairo several
times—the place, rather seedy to tell the truth, is
absolutely thick with soldiers. Some of them, I am
afraid, behave rather badly towards the locals. But
it is just youthful high spirits, not malice. Wish I
had brought my water colours—the sunrises and
sunsets are absolutely marvellous. Notes for
painting from memory: sunset—the sands turn
golden, then red, and seem to become suffused with
the colours of the sky: blue, iris, indigo, violet,
pink, apple green. Morning—the pyramids seem to
float in a pale blue mist rising from the desert.*

Snowy wrote to his mother:

*Nothing much happened today. Bayonet
practice, then typhoid inoculations. My arm is very
sore! I hate needles—but then so does everyone. I
have lost count now of all the inoculations we have
had. "They" certainly don't want us to catch
anything. We have two chaplains and a priest
aboard, and there are regular religious services, so
you needn't worry on that score, Mum. We have all
been pretty seasick—poor Barney especially—
"feeding the fishes", they call it, but now that we
have entered the Red Sea it is very calm and
everyone feels tip-top and is dying to get ashore
and off this hot and crowded ship.*

Chapter 5

EGYPT
July 1915

1

"When you arrive at Mena Camp," Major Barton had admonished his men, "I want you to remember that you're not just any soldiers. You're Australian soldiers! And you're not just any Australian soldiers! You're the Light Horse, right!"

And, to Major Barton's immense gratification, they did make a fine sight as they trotted into Mena, emu feathers fluttering, backs straight, equipment gleaming and horses shining like thoroughbreds.

"The cream of our youth," he said proudly to Lieutenant Gray. "The cream!"

"Hmmm," said Lieutenant Gray stolidly. "Pick up your dressing, you sloppy lot!"

"However, I can't help feeling," remarked Major Barton

later, "that playing football in the very shadow of the pyramids is, well, almost sacrilegious."

Lieutenant Gray shrugged. "The infantry, sir. Not our boys."

The two officers were trotting past a rowdy group of Australian soldiers kicking a ball about the hot sand, shouting, laughing, tackling each other with gusto despite the searing heat, and generally amazing the watching crowd of fruit-sellers, water-sellers, postcard-pedlars, beggars, camel men, donkey men and children of all shapes and sizes. The huge camp at Mena, a few miles north-east of Cairo, whose domes and minarets trembled through the desert haze, had attracted a peripheral population of the local people, who seemed to spend their entire day and much of the night trying to sell things to the big strangers. Oranges, hardboiled eggs ("eggs a cook! eggs a cook!" became a catchphrase for thousands of soldiers), melons, chickens, rugs, carvings, beads, girls, boys, taxis, guides, tours, maps, dates, drugs, cheap jewellery—the list of wares was endless, and the sellers indefatigable.

Lieutenant Gray glanced at the sweating men. "I certainly envy them their energy."

"They'll need it," said Major Barton. "I've just seen some photographs of Anzac Cove."

"Rough, is it, sir?"

"Cliffs. Gullies. Ravines. Bush. The men living in little dugouts on the slopes like swifts nesting on a precipice."

"Doesn't sound too healthy."

"It isn't. But we must keep things in perspective. Look at that old fellow there."

The Sphinx crouched like a lion in the desert.

"Almost five thousand years he's sat there, guarding the tombs in the pyramids from evil spirits. Imagine what he's seen in his time! Egyptian armies marching down the Nile to establish forts for various pharaohs in Upper Egypt. The armies of Ethiopia, the Persian invaders. Alexander the Great's Macedonians and Greeks marched by under his nose, and he saw the Romans conquer Egypt in 50 BC. Look at him, and think of the centuries passing him in a great cavalcade of ambition and avarice and power. Think of the great men who have looked on that impassive face.

"He's seen thirty dynasties come and go and watched the Nile rise and fall, regular as the sun. Mohammedan warrior-fanatics, Byzantines, Mamelukes, Turks—he's seen them all come and go. Napoleon himself marched by here in 1798, you know—it was French soldiers who blew the old fellow's nose off with a cannonball, the vandals. Then he saw the British chase the French out in 1802—and now he's looking at yet another army, the Australian and New Zealand Army Corps. And what does he make of us, I wonder? We must seem pretty small beer after Alexander and Napoleon, eh? And after us there'll be another army and another and another down until the very end of time, and the Sphinx will sit there and watch them all, until the sands of the desert cover him and let him rest at last."

He stopped, smiling shyly.

"Sorry, Gray. Got carried away. Lecture over."

"Fascinating, sir."

"Hmmph," grunted Major Barton, and they rode on back to camp in silence.

The horse lines were busy: "Feed" had just been blown, and the air was full of barked commands and rebukes and neighs and whinnys.

"Pick up your dressing, you sloppy lot."

"Stand to your nosebags."

"Files left. Walk, march, trot. Sit up, you sloppy blighter."

"Trumpeter, blow feed."

"In rear of your horses, stand!"

"Call that horse brushed? Don't you know how to hold a flaming brush?"

"Cast off for water."

"Trumpeter, blow cookhouse."

The brazen notes seemed to slice the hot air, to hang, vibrating, over the tents and men and horses and steaming piles of dung and buzzing blue-green flies. It was confusion, but it was ordered confusion. Major Barton and Lieutenant Gray strode up and down the lines looking hard, and what they saw pleased them.

"Fittest crowd I've ever seen," said the major. "Eh, Gray?"

Lieutenant Gray nodded.

"They've created quite an impression on our allies, sir. An English officer—the Lancashires, I think—got quite lyrical. Said they reminded him of, ah, young gods."

Major Barton smiled.

"Sounds like a bally poet."

"He looked rather that sort, sir. Had longish hair."

The major looked along the lines.

"Young gods, eh. Well, I pray we bring most of them home. That's the cream of Australia there; the very cream. The country can't afford to lose them."

"It can't go on much longer, sir. We've been hammering at the Turks for almost four months now. They must crack soon."

"I hope you're right," said the major.

Frank Dunne burst into the tent he shared with Snowy, Barney and Billy.

They're turning us loose!" he shouted. "Tomorrow! We're going to be allowed into town—into Cairo!"

Billy grinned.

"Well, it's about bloody time! Been here two weeks

and all we've had is drill and lectures, drill and lectures. I'm exhausted—"

"Bet you won't be too exhausted to enjoy yourself in Cairo," said Barney with a wink.

"Up the Wasser!" shouted Frank.

"The Haret el Wazir," said Snowy primly, "is a vile place, Frank. I've read about it. It's full of dens and—and—"

"—and women!" Billy finished for him. "Yep. Hundreds of 'em. Big ones, little ones, pink ones, brown ones, yellow ones—choice wares from all over the East, gentlemen, just step up and take your choice."

"You wouldn't—" said Snowy, shocked.

"Too bloody true," said Billy. "Eh, mates?"

"Too bloody true," chorused Frank and Barney.

"Anyway," said Frank, when the excitement had died down, "anyway, there's going to be a lecture first—"

"Not another lecture," groaned Billy.

"This one's especially for you, Snow," said Frank, with a heavy wink at the others.

"Oh yes," said Snowy suspiciously, suspecting a trap.

"Yes," said Frank. He nudged Snowy in the ribs and gave a suggestive leer.

"Yes, heard Sergeant Sayers and the doc discussing it. Right up your alley, Snowy. It's about Keeping Yourself Pure."

The 11th Battalion, washed, shaved, in their best walking out uniforms, stood at ease on the hard-packed earth of the parade ground and tried to hide expectant grins as Sergeant Sayers marched briskly out.

"Stand easy, men," said Sergeant Sayers, "and if I hear any more giggling—you're not a bunch of school-girls—I'll cancel your leave, right?"

Quelled, the ranks fell silent.

"You are shortly to be let loose on the local inhabitants of the capital city, that is to say Cairo, of this land," said the sergeant, who rather fancied himself as a speaker and a wit.

"You'll have noticed, from the members of the local community who loiter about the perimeter of this camp, that the Arabs and Egyptians don't look much like you, a fact for which they are no doubt eternally grateful—"

He paused to let the appreciative snigger die away.

"Now I'll give you a few tips. Beware of the local eggs, which are distinguished only by their antiquity. Be careful of the local liquor, which is poisonous and could be used to strip paint, and stick to beer." He paused and settled his sweating neck more comfortably in his collar.

"However, Cairo has, as you have probably heard, other ah, dangers . . ."

Winks and leers in the ranks.

". . . so," continued the sergeant, "for those of you unwise enough to be contemplating a little horizontal refreshment—"

"Too bloody true, sport," shouted a tough-looking rifleman in the rear rank, and the rest of the battalion bellowed its approval.

Sergeant Sayers looked pained.

"Another outburst like that," he said, "and the lot of you'll be doing a different sort of exercise—a ten mile route march in full battle order!"

The laughter stopped as though a tap had been turned off.

"All right," said the sergeant. "Now, be warned. A few minutes of pleasure are likely—very likely—to leave you with a legacy which is most painful, difficult to cure, and may get you sent home to face embarrassing questions from your girlfriend or wife. However, I have known you long enough, to my sorrow, to know that nothing I can say is going to deter at least some of you from making dangerous experiments. So I'll leave the stage to Doc Morgan, who will show you some pictures which may be more convincing than my poor words. The doctor will also tell you how to reduce the risks I know some of you are bound to take.''

The doctor, Captain Morgan, a slight, gentlemanly man with a perpetually harassed air, scurried up with a blackboard and easel under his arm. The men cheered. Facing the ranks, his spectacles catching the sunlight and winking like a heliograph, he talked very earnestly for twenty minutes.

He warned them that the army took a very dim view of soldiers who became the recipients of sexually transmitted disease. He told them of the special hospital camps established for soldiers with venereal disease—camps in which the discipline was so fierce that they were little better than the penal battalions. He touched, none too lightly, on the currently favoured treatment for the condition, and brought several of the more sensitive members of his audience close to fainting. He rounded off his talk with a collection of lurid pictures which showed, in harrowing detail, what happened to men who caught syphilis.

It was a rather subdued battalion which forced its way through the importunate mob at the camp gate and headed for the shimmering towers of Cairo.

Gharris, carts and almost springless, crowded lorries and ancient trams took them to the city: and the city reached out in the warm yellow afternoon and embraced them with sights and sounds and scents such as they had never dreamed of. They split up into groups and wandered around the hot noisy streets in the afternoon and purple evening, drinking it all in: the cries of the muezzin, the touts; the beggars, some unbelievably horrible, blind, footless, handless, leprous; the money changers chinking coins and counting piles of greasy notes; fortune-tellers; bootblacks; circumcision booths with garish posters; barbers with their chairs in the narrow streets; silk and ivory merchants; black Sudanese and pale Syrians; Turks, Jews, Greeks, Arabs, Cypriots, Lebanese; a swirling stew of flesh and colour, noise, incense, spices, coffee; cafes full of people eating and drinking and staring at the crowds; camels stalking high-footed and disdainful through the mob; naptha flares spluttering outside stalls, women shouting from first-floor windows, balancing huge bosoms on the sills; the muddy smell of the great river sliding silently by. Frank, Snowy, Billy and Barney walked as though in a dream, sucking it all in, soaking it up like sponges.

"It's not much like Perth," said Frank after a while.

"No," said Barney thoughtfully. And they walked on in silence, keeping their hands on their money and declining requests to buy cheap glass necklaces and expensive Persian carpets.

They ate in a small cafe—a fish which tasted faintly muddy, and stringy chicken—and drank warm beer and felt very dashing and cosmopolitan. Almost unconsciously they wore their hats at rakish angles, and swaggered as though spurred and booted.

The city was full of their allies: stout, serious New Zealanders, Englishmen from regiments with famous names (Frank thought they looked pale and puny), swarthy Frenchmen, Zouaves from France's North African colonies in short jackets, baggy red trousers and tasselled caps; enormous Senegalese soldiers, their coal-black faces shining with sweat; turbanned Sikhs, stocky Gurkhas.

In a narrow lane, Frank was haggling over the hire of three donkeys when Bill nudged him: "Look, here's some Pommies coming. Let's introduce ourselves. We might be fighting alongside them before long."

Frank stopped his haggling and glanced at the five soldiers approaching. He snorted.

"Look at 'em."

The two groups eyed each other as cautiously as tomcats meeting on a neutral fence.

The Englishmen all looked the same to the Australians: small and pink-cheeked with thin hair showing beneath their caps. The smallest and pinkest of them, whose cap-badge and shoulder tabs identified him as a member of the Lancashire Fusiliers, spoke first. At least he opened his mouth and uttered words at first quite incomprehensible to the Australians.

"Pardon?" said Frank.

"Ask them if they speak English," said Billy, and the English soldier said with some irritation:

"Ah sed av ee go'a fag then, choom?"

"Sure," said Frank, and offered his packet.

"Ta," said the Englishman, and lit up.

Another fusilier, larger but quite as pale and pink as his comrade, asked:

"Missin' the kangaroos are ye then, lads?"

"No," said Frank. "They can look after themselves—it's me emu I'm worried about."

"What, you keep them as pets, then?" said another fusilier, startled.

"Nah, 'e's 'avin you on, you stupid booger," said the small pink soldier.

Suddenly the Lancashiremen stiffened. Their hands flew to their cap brims as they snapped off respectful salutes.

Frank, Archy, Billy and Snow turned. Two immaculate young English officers—a lieutenant and a captain, all tailored uniform, sparkling brass and creaking leather—were passing.

The Australians knew that they were supposed to salute the officers of the army of any allied nation. It must have been the heat, or the noise, or the strange sights and smells which made them forget. True, Snowy's right arm crept reluctantly upward until Frank kicked him on the shin, causing him to yelp and rub the injured member while the English officers, hands frozen halfway to their caps, looked icily on.

For a moment they seemed about to rebuke the four Australians; but perhaps the glint in Frank's eye, or the glitter in Barney's, or the width of the boys' shoulders—well, something made them hastily acknowledge the salutes of the Lancashiremen and march briskly away, Sam Brownes squeaking.

2

Of course it was Frank who dreamed up the Charge of the Donkey Brigade. They were in the bazaar one day when some evil *djinn* (and legend says they abound in Egypt) placed in the boys' way almost simultaneously a string of donkeys for hire and two English officers. Two young lieutenants, they were a credit to Sandhurst and Eton: beautifully spoken, their uniforms by Gieves of London, their leather gleaming and their boots like mirrors, they had been expensively educated and knew exactly where to go and what to see in Cairo. To parade them before Frank Dunne was like trailing a red rag across the path of a short-spleened bull.

One of the English officers had an especially rich public school voice. He drew level just as Frank, with the hire of the donkeys completed, was about to mount.

The Englishman looked at his expensive watch.

"We've got about twenty minutes," he said. "As I see it, old man, we can either go on and take a look at this bally mosque, or pack it up and go and meet Dickie and the chaps at Shepheards, eh?"

It was too much for Frank. He whipped a penny from his pocket and screwed it into his left eye-socket and warbled in a falsetto voice:

"Righto, chaps. Mount up, you blightahs, and prepare to charge!"

The Englishmen turned, rigid with disapproval, as the four Australians scrambled aboard their mounts. Poor beasts! The boys' legs were so long, and the donkeys so small, that they almost touched the ground.

Frank screwed his surrogate monocle tighter and nodded approval at Billy.

"Jolly fine-looking steed you have there, Carruthers."

"You Australians," said the most gorgeous of the two officers, "are the most crude, undisciplined and ill-mannered soldiers I have ever encountered."

Frank grinned and lapsed, for a moment, into his native tongue.

"If you think that, mate," he said, "wait till you meet the bloody New Zealanders."

The Englishmen blanched, and Frank turned to his troop, adjusting his monocle again.

"Righto, troop. Tally ho! Give the bounders hell, what!"

They spurred their mounts and were away, with yells and whoops and war cries, scattering beggars, hawkers, bootblacks, touts, mangy dogs, fortune-tellers, water-sellers, letter-writers, bowling over tables and stalls, scattering mounds of oranges, and evoking wails and cries and shrieks of protest which echoed around the square.

The English officers, outraged, retreated to

Shepheards Hotel, where they repaired their ravaged feelings with gin and tonic; the *djinn* or genie, satisfied, departed; and the military police arrived.

Sergeant Sayers gave them a severe dressing down, and they were confined to camp for a week.

3

The 10th Light Horse spent two days on dismounted exercises in the desert.

"Tell you what, mate," said Trooper Harris gloomily as he inexpertly dug in beside Archy with his entrenching tool. "Tell you what, mate, they're turning us into bloody infantry, that's what!"

Archy glanced back to the foot of the long dune they were supposed to be holding, at the long patient lines of horses and their holders.

"Nonsense. We've been trained as a mounted force."

Trooper Harris blew sand from the action of his Lee-Enfield, cursing wearily.

"Bloody sand. Gets everywhere. No, mate, I'm tellin' you. That's why we're doing all this dismounted action stuff. You wait and see."

"I'm sure you're wrong," said Archy.

Trooper Harris shrugged.

"You'll see, mate."

Sister Cooley wrote in her diary:

> *Another trainload of sick and wounded from Gallipoli via Alexandria. On my feet (but so was*

everyone else on the ward) for eighteen hours.
Many dysentery cases—and the ones we get are the
really *ill ones. Colonel Bates, our chief, says that*
on the peninsula our brave soldiers do not report
sick with dysentery until they are almost too weak
to stand.

As yet I have not had to deal with too
many wounded—our ward being mainly medical,
and not surgical. Most of the wounded men we
receive are not too badly off—although some of
their wounds are frightful enough. But by the time
they arrive they have been treated at a casualty
clearing station "on the beach". (The treatment is
very basic, because the battle surgeons are so
terribly busy. Usually it consists of simply stopping
any severe bleeding, splinting a broken limb,
putting a field dressing over the wound, and giving
an anti-tetanus injection.) Then the wounded are
taken by lighter to the hospital ships, where some
more "tidying up" is done, and, when the hospital
ship is full, brought to Alexandria and then sent on
to us. I am told that it does not take long to fill a
hospital ship.

Snowy wrote to his mother:

Well, we have been into Cairo again. As I told
you it is very different to Australia. Life is very cheap
here and I am very glad that I was born an
Australian. It is all very interesting but some of the
sights would shock you and any decent person I am
sure. Some of the picture postcards offered for sale
and on public display are really crude but the police
don't seem to do anything about it. I am afraid
that the general atmosphere is having a very bad
effect on some of our chaps who are behaving in a
manner that they never would at home.

Which was a very restrained letter considering the trying day that Snowy had just spent in Cairo with Frank, Billy, and Barney.

It began at a postcard-seller's stall. The postcards were explicit, to say the least. Snowy appealed to Frank, as a fellow Australian:

"How could they do it, Frank? I mean, those are actual *photographs*. I mean, those people must have *posed* for them!"

Frank laughed. "Don't get upset, Snow. Life's cheap out here and these women have no self-respect."

"Nor do the men, by the look of it," said Snowy with a shudder.

"Why," asked Barney, examining a postcard, "do the blokes always keep their socks on?"

"In a hurry, I expect," said Billy.

"Don't worry, Snow," said Frank. "You'll see a lot worse before you get home. It's the same in most foreign places." He winked at Billy and picked up a particularly gross card. "Think I'll send this one home to the old folks, Snow."

"Frank!" Snowy yelped. "You wouldn't!"

4

Then there was the embarrassing affair of the hookah. They had become separated, briefly, while examining the stalls around a large square.

When they met up again, Barney and Billy, who had wandered into different alleys off the square, each carried hookahs—gaudy affairs of brass and tassels and carved wood.

Barney was elated with his purchase.

"A thousand years old, the gyppo who sold it said. Last in the shop. A bloody antique. Sell it for a fortune back home."

"How much did you give for it, Barney?" asked Frank.

"I beat him down to two quid," said Barney proudly. Billy held out his hookah for Barney to look at. It was identical to Barney's.

"Five bob," said Billy.

"The bastard," said Barney.

Snowy shook his head.

"See. No morals. They're all a pack of thieves."

Frank squared his shoulders.

"All right. Show us the shop, Barney."

Grim-faced, they shouldered their way through the crowd.

"That one, I think," said Barney, pointing. "They all look the same to me."

The shopkeeper, middle-aged and hawk-faced, greeted the four soldiers politely.

"Yes, gentlemen," he said expectantly.

Billy clicked his heels and stood to attention at the counter.

"Sir," he said, "we are Australian soldiers."

"Australians my good friends," said the shopkeeper hastily.

"We have come to your country as guests," said Billy.

The shopkeeper nodded enthusiastically.

"Egypt is an old civilisation—"

"Very old," murmured the shopkeeper. "Very old."

"Australia is a new one—"

The shopkeeper smiled sympathetically. Snowy grew impatient. He nudged Billy in the ribs.

"Skip the history lesson and tell him to cough up Barney's two quid," he hissed.

Billy frowned at Snowy.

"We're not just soldiers, Snow. We're diplomats for our country."

Snowy pushed Billy aside.

"Look," he said to the shopkeeper, "give me mate back his two quid or I'll flatten you!"

The shopkeeper retreated hastily behind the counter.

"Take it easy, Snow," said Frank.

But Snowy, still smarting about the postcards, would not be baulked.

"They're all bloody thieves," he snapped. "Thieves and—and perverts."

Billy tried again. He smiled at the shopkeeper. "Look, Mr, er," he said. "I bought this hookah at a shop down the road there, and I paid five shillings for it. But my friend, Private Betts there, well, he bought one exactly the same—show it to him, Barn—from you for *two quid*. And you told him it was a thousand years old, whereas we know that there's a big factory out near the pyramids which turns the things out by the thousand, so we were wondering if you'd mind taking your hookah back—"

"You bludging bastard," interposed Snowy.

"— and give Mr Betts back his two quid," concluded Billy.

The shopkeeper became agitated. He backed away from the proffered hookah as though afraid it would bite him.

"No, no. That not mine. That yours."

"Listen, mate," bellowed Snowy, "if you tried to pull something like this where I come from, you'd last as long as a snowflake in summer. Now give us the cash."

The shopkeeper folded his arms and shook his head.

Frank stepped forward. He smiled warmly at the nervous shopkeeper.

"Look, mate," he said reasonably, "I understand your attitude. I mean, a sale is a sale, eh?—oh gawd, I'm so sorry!"

The shelf he had casually leaned against had collapsed in a shower of pots and pans and cheap souvenirs. With cries of grief the shopkeeper fell upon the wreckage.

"What I was saying was, a bargain is a bargain after all, and if you can't see your way—oh, hell, I've done it again. I'm so sorry, mate. Rotten cheap shelves you've got—"

A second shelf collapsed, adding its load to the goods on the floor.

With a despairing wail, the shopkeeper scrambled to his feet, pulled a dented tin cash box from beneath the counter, scrabbled through a pile of crumpled notes and flung two pounds at Frank.

"Here. Take. Go!"

"Short and sweet," said Frank. He gave the notes to Barney. "Thanks, mate," he said to the shopkeeper. "Pleasure to do business with you. Goodbye."

Elated, they left the shop. Their jubilation received a sharp check a few yards away, however, when Barney grabbed Frank's sleeve and, pointing to a stall, said in an agonised whisper:

"Frank—that—that wasn't the shop. That's it over there. I remember it now—"

Frank detached Barney's clutching hand and stared at him. Dispassionately, he said:

"Barney, you are a flaming idiot, aren't you?"

But worse was to come. Night found them, despite all

Snowy's protests, in the Haret el Wazir. They drifted in a sea of soldiery. Strange smells and sounds. Weird music floated from the high narrow houses. Women called to them from doorways and windows. Soldiers tramped in and out of the cafes, bars, and brothels. Snowy was offered services which made him blush.

They had almost reached the end of the street—much to Snowy's relief—when Billy approached a woman leaning against a doorpost.

"Billy—" said Snowy warningly.

"Er, excuse me, miss," stammered Billy, "but er, may I ask—I mean—"

"Twenty piastres," said the prostitute. "Good time."

"I'll bet," said Frank approvingly. The woman had fine eyes and a good skin and wide hips.

"Remember what the doc said," muttered Snowy, and the woman flashed him a venomous glance.

"Doctor? What doctor? What you mean?"

"Never mind him," said Billy soothingly. "He just worries a lot."

Billy patted Snowy on the shoulder.

"Snow, mate, this is war time. We might all be dead in a month."

Snowy was not convinced. He took Billy aside while Frank and Barney watched, grinning.

"Billy, she's common. Cheap," said Snowy.

"I don't call twenty piastres all that cheap," said Billy.

Another woman, equally attractive, joined the first in the doorway.

"Hell," said Barney, "this beats antique bloody pipes! I'm going in."

"So am I," said Frank. "You wait here, Snow—" he winked. "Won't be long."

"I'm disgusted," said Snowy. "Disgusted. What're

you going to say to your wives on your wedding night?"

"Snow, if you want to look good on a thoroughbred, you've got to learn to ride on a nag," said Frank. "Come on, fellas."

"Bye, Snow," said Barney. "I'll think of you."

Furious, Snowy went back to camp alone.

"What I don't understand," said Lieutenant Gray plaintively, "is *why* we are in Gallipoli? I mean, it's not a major theatre of the war. I just don't see its importance to the overall scheme of things."

Major Barton shrugged and lit his pipe.

"Ours not to reason why, my boy," he murmured.

"Ours but to do or die, eh?"

"Something like that." Major Barton puffed on his pipe.

"Whose hare-brained idea was it, anyway?" asked Lieutenant Gray.

Major Barton removed the pipe from his mouth and sighed.

"Mr Churchill's, I believe."

"The First Sea Lord?"

"The same. Reading between the lines, I get the impression that he felt frustrated beause the German Navy—the High Seas Fleet, I think the Huns call it—wouldn't come out and face the Royal Navy. So when the Russians asked for a demonstration against the Turks, who were giving them a hard time in the Caucasus, Mr Churchill got the bright idea of using the Royal Navy to force a passage through the Dardanelles by knocking out the forts the Turks have got guarding the straits. With the guns out of action, the Allies could get through to the Black Sea and help Russia." He replaced his pipe and smoked in silence for a minute. Then he exhaled a cloud of blue smoke and grunted appreciatively.

"Trouble is, Mr Churchill hadn't counted on the

forts being such tough nuts to crack. Or of the cunning Turks sowing the straits with mines. As you know, the British—and the French, who were also in the operation—took a fearful clobbering. Lost a lot of ships and men. The powers that be should have called the thing off there and then, but oh no. The idea of forcing the straits was well and truly fixed in the official mind, and so they persevered. If the navy couldn't silence the guns, why then, the army would. And that's why the British and the Australians and the New Zealanders and the French are there now, and that's why we're going to join our brothers in arms very shortly.''

"And the guns haven't been silenced yet," said Lieutenant Gray bitterly.

"No," said Major Barton, "they haven't. But a lot of our men have been.''

Lieutenant Gray sat musing for a while. Suddenly he said: "And after a monstrous error of judgment like that, what's to become of Mr Churchill?''

Major Barton sucked on his pipe.

"Get a knighthood, I shouldn't wonder," he said.

6

Company C of the 11th Australian Infantry Battalion fell in under the critical eye of Sergeant Sayers and sweated quietly as he inspected them. They were in full battle order.

"I suppose you'll do," he said at last with a sigh. He turned and pointed to a low sand ridge a few hundred yards away.

"That ridge, for the purpose of today's exercise,

which is a frontal assault, is being held by the enemy. And the enemy—'' he paused for effect, ''the enemy, you'll be glad to hear, is the 10th Australian Light Horse—''

He waited for the boos and catcalls to subside.

''—and any more outbursts like that and we'll be doing some doubling up and down the bloody desert in full battle kit *with* rifle and full pack! Right? Now, as I was saying, the gentlemen we'll be frontally assaulting will be the 10th Light Horse—these gentlemen, presumably because their arses are usually higher off the ground than ours, tend to assume airs of superiority—''

Like a true artist, he waited for the roar of approval to die down before continuing.

''— but they won't have their horses with 'em today. They're doing a dismounted action. So I want you lot to get out there and take that hill—and, short of actually killing the bastards, which might lead to some awkward questions, I want you to show them what the infantry is made of.''

He smiled slightly at the resultant uproar. When the men had quieted, he said: ''Right. On the command—wait for it, Dunne!—on the command, fix bayonets—but with scabbards on—*on*, I said. Don't want any of you bastards spearing any of those bastards, all right!''

Company C fixed bayonets with a rattle and clash and cast eager eyes on the ridge, where a few plumed hats could be seen.

''We'll murder the bastards,'' whispered Barney.

''Don't underestimate those country boys,'' said Frank, thinking of Archy and the race at Figtree Crossing.

''Shuddup, you lot,'' bawled Sergeant Sayers.

Colonel Robinson looked at the infantry through his field glasses. With Major Barton, Lieutenant Gray, and other Light Horse officers, he stood on a small pebbly hill to the right of the Light Horse position.

"A rough-looking lot," said Colonel Robinson, lowering his glasses. He looked at Major Barton with some distaste. Colonel Robinson was tall, thin, cold, immaculate; Major Barton was rather portly, his manner avuncular rather than military, and his uniform was never quite, well, Savile Row or Gieves.

"I expect they'll do," Major Barton said mildly. "All volunteers, sir, you know."

"I'm aware of that, Barton," said Colonel Robinson acidly. "But that doesn't excuse sloppiness or gross insubordination, does it?"

"Insubordination?" murmured Major Barton, watching the infantry assemble.

Colonel Robinson snorted. "Some of them don't seem to have the vaguest idea of military etiquette—why, they salute an officer with the greatest reluctance."

Major Barton suppressed a lurking smile.

"It's only a few weeks since some of them were civilians, sir."

The colonel snorted again.

"Exactly! Civilians at heart. You'll never make soldiers of them."

"They might surprise you, sir," said Major Barton quietly.

"I doubt it," said the colonel icily. Major Barton turned to Lieutenant Gray, who wore a brassard indicating that he was an umpire in the coming conflict—he and other officers with similar brassards would decide who among the attacking force had been killed or wounded in the action.

"Yes, sir," said Lieutenant Gray. "I'll just have a word with the lads first, sir."

"I say, is that right?" said the colonel testily. "I mean, the man's an umpire—"

But Lieutenant Gray was gone. A few seconds later he was striding down the Light Horse line.

"Any minute now, lads. Just remember—keep calm. Steady. Aim carefully. Shots fired in panic are wasted shots. Lasalles, keep your head down—"

"Yessir," said Archy, squinting through his sights at the infantry.

"And for God's sake remember," said Lieutenant Gray, "that although you're using blanks, a .303 blank can kill at several feet—blow the wadding halfway through a man's body. So when the ceasefire whistle sounds, you cease fire—*cease* fire—and defend yourselves with the bayonet—with the scabbard on, Lasalles, do you hear me—"

"Yessir," said Archy.

"Very well," said Lieutenant Gray. "Time for me to get out of the way. Sergeant, they're all yours."

A red Very flare looped into the blue sky and the infantry charged. Their bloodthirsty shrieks floated up to the Light Horsemen.

"One round volley," said the sergeant. "Pick your target. Aim, fire!"

The Lee-Enfields lashed the air. Ejected cartridge cases tinkled and rolled down the slope, glinting in the sun.

"Aim. Fire."

"Independent fire. Fire at will."

The infantry toiled up the slope, sinking in the hot loose sand, sweating and cursing.

"Cease fire. Cease fire." The sergeant blew his whistle. The infantry were only fifty feet away.

"Cease fire. Fix bayonets. Fix bayonets. Scabbards on—scabbards *on*!"

With joyous cries, the infantry and the Light Horse closed. Feet and fists flew: scabbarded bayonets thumped painfully into chests and stomachs. Fighting figures locked in close embrace rolled back down the sand dune. Someone tore his knuckles on the sergeant's teeth and was rewarded with a kick in the groin. Archy bayoneted two infantrymen who unsportingly refused to fall down as they had been instructed to do (ignoring the cries of Lieutenant Gray, hovering on the edge of the melee, to "fall down, you blokes, fair go") and was about to bayonet a third when his legs were swept from under him by a foul kick and he sprawled ingloriously on his back in the sand. The next second a scabbarded infantry bayonet was at his throat, and the second after that the bayonet and the rifle to which it was attached had been thrown carelessly aside and he and Frank Dunne were slapping each other on the back and shaking hands and jumping around like schoolboys and generally behaving in such an unmilitary manner that Colonel Robinson, watching disapprovingly through his field glasses, turned to Major Barton and said, with considerable exasperation, "I say—what the devil are those men playing at?"

Major Barton shrugged.

"Looks like two old cobbers just met, sir."

The colonel was speechless.

Lieutenant Gray and the other umpires stalked among the combatants. Whistles were blown until the blowers were purple in the face.

"You're dead," said Lieutenant Gray, "and you, and you, and you're wounded, and you're dead—" He stopped, appalled, at the sight of a Light Horseman—that Archy Lasalles, no less!—and an infantryman apparently sitting down and having a friendly chat. Lieutenant Gray was speechless, but not for long.

"What the hell," he said, "what the bloody hell do you two think you're doing?"

Frank Dunne gave him his best smile and even sketched a salute.

"We're mates, sir," Frank said. "Old mates."

"There's supposed to be a war on," said Lieutenant Gray wearily. "And you're the enemy. And you're dead!"

"Who shot me, sir?" asked Frank.

Lieutenant Gray looked around wildly. Everywhere was chaos.

"I bloody did," he said desperately.

"No sir," said Frank politely. "You can't have shot me, sir. You're an umpire."

"I'd like to bloody well shoot you, you bastard!" yelled Lieutenant Gray. "You're dead, and that's an order!"

Frank looked at Archy, shrugged, and obediently flopped on to the sand. Lieutenant Gray exhaled noisily and blew his whistle again.

"Right," he shouted. "Right, you lot. Survivors—dress wounded and carry them back to the casualty clearing station. Smartly, now!"

The wounded grinned. The survivors gazed around at the hot sand without enthusiasm.

"Come on now," said Lieutenant Gray. "Lift those wou—" he broke off, momentarily lost for words. As though felled by a single machine gun burst, every standing man, every survivor had fallen.

"Carry 'em your bloody self, sport!" shouted someone and Lieutenant Gray's defeat was complete. He glanced at Colonel Robinson's command post, where binocular lenses winked inquiringly in the sun.

"Oh my God," he said.

"*Well*," said Colonel Robinson; and even Major Barton had to admit he had reason to be annoyed.

Sister Cooley wrote in her diary:

Transferred to the Heliopolis Palace *Hospital. It seems it really was a palace. Now it is an Australian hospital. Very full of wounded and ill men. A horrible amount of armless or legless men. Most of them amazingly cheerful. I have become rather depressed. It all seemed such an* adventure *when I left home. It is still an adventure, but a very sad one. I had no idea war would be so—so brutal! What a silly remark—but it is true. I think the artists who paint those glorious pictures which show the last stand of some regiment or other at some exotic place—soldiers with no wounds but a neat bandage (showing only a spot of red) bound around their foreheads as they defend the flag—well, I think those artists have a lot to answer for.* They *have never been present at an amputation;* they *have never seen major stomach wounds;* they *have never had to hold down on his bed a twenty-year-old boy who has had his skull laid open like a hardboiled egg so that you can see the grey-pink pulse of his brain.*

7

It was hard to get very drunk on an Australian army private's pay in 1915; but Archy and Frank did their best. Did so well, in fact, that they had no money left to pay for transport back to the camp. This would not normally have been much of a problem: the Australians had been known to commandeer trams, *gharris*, carts or wagons as they required them. But this night it was late, there were few Allied troops about, and Archy and Frank had fallen, via the Egyptian beer they had been drinking, into a mood of retrospection. So they staggered into the night, supporting each other, and by the time they had walked a few miles they were almost sober—the desert night was cold, the stars sparkling, the pyramids brooding over all.

At that stage, near dawn, they had an argument. About running, of course: they had been back to Figtree Crossing and the Kimberley Gift race, over and over again.

"Your main problem," said Archy to Frank, "is the way you start."

"You're wrong, Arch," said Frank. "Dead wrong."

"I'm bloody not," said Archy. "Harry Lasalles proved that crouching down for the start makes all the difference—sort of gives you a spring, a leap—like, well, like a leopard—"

"Archy," said Frank, "look, mate, if you crouch, you've got to straighten up again, eh? So you lose time. Stands to bloody reason, mate, whatever your Harry bloody Lasalles says!"

The first yellow light touched the very top of Cheops's Great Pyramid.

Archy stepped off the road, holding Frank's arm. He scratched a line in the sand with his boot.

"All right, mate. First to the pyramid."

They were off: shouting, staggering in the warm sand. They reached the base of the Great Pyramid together and collapsed, panting and laughing, on the ancient stones.

When they had got their breath back they sat up and looked about them. Dawn was creeping across the desert, the sky flushed a deep pink. Above them towered the old stones. They glanced at each other, and with one accord started to climb.

It took a lot of pulling and hauling and some desperate scrabbling for handholds and footholds, but they made it to the top and stood, sucking in the cooler air, awed by the view: the desert lay at their feet and unrolled, yellow and brown, shadowed by dunes, to the horizon. On the crest of a long low dune to the south a camel caravan undulated towards the canal; to the north Cairo rose from the mists. And the Nile slid by, a great green snake.

"Look at this," said Archy, pointing. There were names scratched into the stones: P. Joubert, F. Dufour, S. de Sivray, R. Almeras. Grand Armee de Napoleon.

"Froggies," said Frank.

"Yes," said Archy. He traced the marks with a finger, " 'Armee' must be army, and we know who Napoleon was—look at that—" he blew away some rockdust "—1798! Fancy that—these blokes must have been soldiers in Napoleon's army."

"Well," said Frank, "if the Frogs can immortalise themselves, so bloody well can we! Let's leave a sign for future generations, eh? Got anything we can scrape with?"

Like all bushmen, Archy never went anywhere without a knife: a heavy affair with a wide blade and a spike for removing stones from horses' hooves.

"Beauty," said Frank. "That's spike thing's just the ticket."

They took it in turns to carve their names into the stone. When they had finished they stood back to admire their work. Next to the names of Napoleon's soldiers was now inscribed: Archy Hamilton. Frank Dunne. A.I.F. April 1915.

"Glad to see you used your real name," said Frank. "But you'll cop it if one of your officers sees it."

"I don't think that's likely," said Archy.

"I don't believe it," said Archy. "I just don't bloody believe it. It's just another furphy."

"It's true, mate," said Trooper Harris with gloomy satisfaction. "Bloody official. We go to join the blokes on Gallipoli—but the horses stay here! We fight as infantry. Like I was telling you, Archy—remember all those dismounted actions?"

"I'm going to find out for myself," said Archy, and stormed out of the tent.

Archy found Lieutenant Gray casting a cynical eye over a horse-watering party.

"It's true, I'm afraid, Lasalles," he said when Archy had gasped out his question. "I don't like it either, but there it is. Seems that Gallipoli's so mountainous goats would be more use than horses. Pity."

"Well, thanks, sir," said Archy despondently, and turned to go.

"Ah, Lasalles," said Lieutenant Gray.

"Yes, sir?" said Archy, stopping.

"Just once, Lasalles," said Lieutenant Gray, "just once, I thought, you might salute an officer? Eh? It wouldn't hurt much, you know."

"Oh, sorry, sir," said Archy, and snapped off a salute that made the watering party whistle in admiration.

Trudging back to his tent he had an idea. It was with whoops of delight he ran through the camp, tripping over guy-ropes, startling horses, darting around and through work parties, asking every few yards if anyone knew where the 11th Battalion was bivouacked.

Barging around a tent, he cannoned into another soldier, running just as fast in the opposite direction. They both fell sprawling.

"You clumsy bas—" shouted Archy.

"Can't you look where you're bloody going—" snarled the other, spitting out sand, and removing the hat which had been knocked over his eyes.

"It's you," they cried together. Frank got up and dusted himself off and pulled Archy to his feet.

"I was coming to find you—" he said.

"And I was coming to find you," said Archy.

"Because I've just heard," said Frank.

"Because I've just been told—" said Archy. They stopped, laughing.

"You first," said Archy politely.

"Well," said Frank, "I've just heard that you blokes won't be taking your horses to Gallipoli because it's not exactly horse country—so I thought—as I've always wanted to join the Light Horse—"

"—that you might be able to get a transfer to the Light Horse," shouted Archy. "That's exactly what I was coming to suggest to you!"

"Think we'll pull it off?" asked Frank more soberly.

"We'll have a good try," said Archy. "Let's think of a good yarn to tell the major. Convince him the Light Horse can't do without Frank Dunne."

The truth is, mused Frank as he and Archy strolled among the tents working out their plan of campaign, the truth is Frank Dunne can't do without the Light Horse. Not if he wants to get out of Platt Street and move up in the world. A commission in a classy regiment such as the Light Horse would be a great boot up the ladder. Besides, he liked Archy. And Archy was bloody near top-drawer quality, wasn't he? Sure, Snowy and Barney and Billy were great blokes, and great mates. But they didn't want what he wanted. They'd be quite happy to go back to Platt Street, to the old life.

"I'll try and get us an interview with Major Barton tomorrow," said Archy as they parted. "See you, then."

"See you," said Frank, and strolled thoughtfully away, wondering how he would break the news to the others.

Barney Betts lay on his bunk and sweated with sheer naked terror. In the extremity of his anguish he moaned.

Frank Dunne, the only other occupant of the tent, was dozing. He stirred and sat up, looking at Barney accusingly.

"Was that noise you, mate?" he said. "Can't a bloke catch forty winks in peace?" He lay back again.

Barney cleared his throat.

"Frank."

Frank sighed. "Oh gawd. Yes, Barn?"

Barney swallowed. His sweating face was a bright pink.

"You feeling crook, mate?" asked Frank.

"Yes. No. Well, not actually—" stammered Barney, turning pinker.

"You see, Frank, well—"

"For gawd's sake get on with it!" shouted Frank.

"Well, this morning, Frank, when I went to have a pee, you know—well, it hurt like hell, Frank."

Frank sat bolt upright.

"Jesus Mary and Joseph, Barney, you're having me on!"

Frank shook his head dolefully.

"Fair dinkum, mate. I'm worried out of me flaming mind!" A thought struck him. "Hey, Frank—are you all right? I mean, you were there too, weren't you?"

"I'm all right, thank gawd," said Frank. "Different lady, see, sport. Luck of the draw." He let out his breath with a whoosh. "Hell. My lucky day—or night."

"But what am I going to do, Frank?"

"Have you told the doc?" asked Frank.

"I can't," wailed Barney. "I just can't. You know what they do with blokes with VD, Frank? They send them to a special camp, and they put a special stamp in their pay book—and they send 'em home, Frank!"

"I know all that, Barn—but it's an offence to know you've got it and not report it."

"I tell you I can't, Frank."

"Barney, you saw those pictures of the doc's. If

you don't have it treated, well, it sort of rots you away until your old man falls off. So don't be a bloody fool. Go and see the doc.''

Barney lay in a gloomy reverie for another hour. Then, reluctantly, he got up, put on his shirt, put on his boots, and said to Frank:

"Right. I'm off to the doc."

"Good on you," said Frank. "Good luck. Don't look so down in the bloody mouth! You look as though you're going to be shot!''

"Bloody feels like it," said Barney, and left.

8

Major Barton frowned at the two young men standing at attention before him. From his gramophone came a scratchy rendering of *Il Trovatore*.

"It's quite impossible, I'm afraid," said Major Barton. "If you were brothers, maybe. But as it is—"

He grimaced in vexation as the gramophone emitted a particularly discordant note. He got up, switched it off and examined the record.

"Ruined. This blasted sand—"

He looked at Archy and Frank.

"That's it, lads. I'm sorry. But there's a war on, you know. Where would we be if everyone wanted to change units?"

"If we're not taking horses, sir," said Archy pleadingly, "it doesn't matter if Frank—Private Dunne, sir—can't ride."

"That's not the point," said the major irritably. He turned to Frank.

"Look, Dunne, your own blokes will be going over very soon. Why on earth do you want to transfer?"

"Archy—Trooper Ham—Lasalles and I are great mates, sir. Met years ago. We've ah, trained together."

"That's not a good enough reason—" began the major. He stopped. "Trained? For what?"

Archy held his breath.

"We're runners, sir," said Frank.

"Sprinters, or distance?"

"Sprinters, sir."

"What's your best time for the hundred?"

"We're both under ten, sir."

Major Barton whistled.

"Hmm. Pretty good. Look, I'll see what I can do. A fast pair of legs in a troop is never a drawback—especially when the troop's been dismounted, as we have. Yes, a phone line gets .cut, and you're isolated without a good despatch runner. Very well. Leave it with me."

Archy and Frank gave him their best salutes.

"You don't salute an officer when he's not wearing his cap," said Major Barton. He waved his hand wearily. "Dismiss."

They dismissed, and bottled up their yells of jubilation until they were outside the officers' lines.

Major Barton put another record on his gramophone.

Snowy wrote his mother:

> We went into Cairo again today. It is full of soldiers. We have noticed lately a lot of wounded men "taking the air" sometimes in the company of nurses. You can tell the wounded because they wear

*sky-blue uniforms with white lapels and red
neckties. Some of them have been pretty badly
knocked about—we have seen several with sticks,
and others on crutches. They all seem very cheerful,
perhaps because for most of them the war is over
and their wound is a "ticket home". We had some
bad news today. Frank Dunne has been transferred
to the Australian Light Horse. We don't know how
he wangled it, because he can't ride. I must say we
are all pretty annoyed with Frank. Breaking up the
Four Musketeers at this late hour must be bad luck!
But Frank knows what he wants in life and I
suppose it is his business and nobody else's after
all. But we shall miss him. He was always good for
a laugh and a bit of a skylark.*

"You're a bloody young fool," said Captain Morgan. The
little doctor was hot, tired and angry.

"This army has enough problems with men who are
really sick without having to waste its time on fools like
you with self-inflicted injuries."

"Yessir," said Barney, his face purple. It had been
an embarrassing and humiliating interview. He had been
probed and prodded in the most intimate places, and it
hurt like hell. He had stood around naked in front of
doctors, orderlies, and other patients. Medical
consultations about him had been held as though he wasn't
there. It was no consolation to know that it was all part of
the treatment, part of the punishment.

"What will they think of you back home if we
discharge you, eh?" asked the doctor. "What sort of
reception will you get back in Australia? What will your
girl, if you have one, think of a man who bought it from a
prostitute, eh?"

"Dunno, sir," said Barney miserably.

The little doctor raised himself on his toes and
brought his angry pink face closer to Barney's.

"Or," he hissed, "did you disobey orders deliberately—did you deliberately try to get a dose—so you would be sent home—so you wouldn't have to fight?"

Barney was really shocked.

"Oh, no sir, no. I mean, sir, all my mates are here, sir, we joined up together, sir—"

"All right, all right," said the doctor wearily. "Put on your clothes. Report back tomorrow. Get a move on, man. Plenty of others waiting."

Shamefacedly, Barney scrambled into his uniform and left the hospital tent.

The captain's assistant, a lieutenant, watched him go, and raised an eyebrow inquiringly.

The captain shook his head.

"Don't think so. Just one of those irritating infections of the urinary tract. Didn't think it would do any harm to keep him stewing for a day or two. Give him a fright. Silly young fool." But he added with a grin which changed his whole face, "Still, I was young once, too."

"Indeed, sir," said the lieutenant, and they both laughed.

Sister Cooley, at the end of another exhausting day, sat in her room and fought off sleep as she tried to read *Surgical Experiences in South Africa, 1899–1900*. The writer, G. H. Makins, had been a surgeon with the British Army in the Boer War, and had quite a lot to say about modern weapons and the treatment of the wounds they inflicted. The introduction of the small-calibre, cone-shaped bullet, fired at very high velocity, noted Mr Makins, had relieved the military surgeon of some problems, but given him plenty of others.

The new bullet, said Mr Makins, seldom carried foreign bodies—bits of strap, uniform, or other equipment—into the wound it created; whereas the old, slow, spherical large-calibre musket ball often did so, and greatly increased the chances of wounds becoming infected or gangrenous. But the new bullets frequently inflicted multiple wounds—"one bullet may damage the lungs, liver, kidneys, or viscera; another might shatter both thighs and the pelvis, depending on the position of the victim when shot."

Sister Cooley fell asleep over Mr Makins: when she awoke, cramped and still tired, the dawn was creeping over the roofs and domes of Cairo.

9

Despite Major Barton's influence, it took a lot of fast talking and mountains of paper work to get Frank Dunne transferred from the infantry to the Light Horse. But Barton's argument, that as the Light Horse had been dismounted, and thus deprived of rapid communications should telephone lines be cut or flag-signallers shot, he needed as many speedy runners as he could get, was a cogent one.

So Frank was transferred, and exchanged his rather drab infantryman's uniform for a Light Horseman's plumed finery. He swaggered back from the quarter-master's stores, his hat rakishly cocked, admiring himself in sundry shaving mirrors hanging from tent-poles.

He was hastily stowing his gear into his kit bag when Barney, Snowy and Billy arrived, hot and sweating, from rifle drill. They filed in silently.

"G'day," said Frank, busy with his gear.

"G'day," they grunted, taking off their boots.

Frank decided to brazen it out. He preened himself.

"Well, how do you like it? What do you think of the new uniform?"

They looked at him disapprovingly, wiping the sweat of honest infantrymen from their faces.

"S'alright," said Barney.

The others said nothing. There was an awkward silence.

"Look," said Frank, "what's the matter with you blokes, eh?"

"Nothing," said Snowy.

"Nothing," said Billy.

"Look, I've always wanted to join the Light Horse," said Frank, defensively. "Snow, you know that. I even tried to join it in Perth, but they knocked me back."

"Infantry not good enough for you, Frank?" asked Snowy quietly.

"Obviously not," said Billy. Barney looked distressed.

"All right," said Frank, angrily. "All right. If that's how you're going to be, well then—see you when I see you, eh?" and he stalked out of the tent, emu feather waving.

"Well," said Snow. "What about that then, eh?"

Billy shrugged.

"Ah, come off the boil, Snow. You know Frank."

"Yes," said Barney. "Sell his grandmother for tuppence, and still talk his way into heaven."

Snowy shook his head sombrely.

"It's no joke, Billy. It's bad luck for mates to split up. At a time like this, too." He got up. "I'm going for a walk."

Snowy walked out of the comparative shade of the tent into the glare of an Egyptian afternoon.

The orders for Alexandria were posted that night.

Chapter 6

THE AEGEAN
July 1915

1

The troopship *Hindoo* was awaiting them at Alexandria. The old harbour was stiff with shipping: cruisers, small gunboats, destroyers, hospital ships, tugs, Egyptian *dhows* with huge leg-of-mutton sails swelling in the warm offshore breeze; *caiques* from Greece and the Levant; even a few ancient three-masted *xebecs*; slim torpedo boats from France; and a long low British submarine lurking alongside the sea wall.

The Light Horse sailed first, with a sprinkling of New Zealand reinforcements, both pakeha and Maori, and some lightly wounded men, Australian, New Zealand, French, and British, who had been patched and repaired in Egypt and were now considered fit enough to return to the front. They did not seem too happy about it.

The bulk of the infantry were left in Alexandria to

await the next ship. Snowy, Billy and Barney, with several hundred other young men, spent a hot, gritty and thirsty day sitting on their kit bags, watching the shipping and spitting into the harbour. In the evening, a hospital ship arrived, lit from stem to stern—"like a bloody Christmas tree," said Barney—its great blood-red cross floodlit. The ship was expected: the waiting ambulances lined the quay, bumper to bumper, and the waiting soldiers fell silent as the stretchers were carried down: so many stretchers, scores and scores and scores of them, the nurses flitting around them like great moths in the harsh glare of the floodlamps.

"Doesn't look like it's going to be a picnic," said Snowy quietly.

"No," said Billy.

"We three stick together, hey?" said Barney. "What a pity Frank—"

"Barney, shut up!" said Snowy savagely.

The last of the ambulances was filled. The big lights went out one by one. They could hear the water lapping against the quay. Somewhere out beyond the sea wall a bird cried, a strange haunting tremolo in the night.

"You know," said Billy, thoughtfully, "I was talking to a Kiwi the other day, bloke who was with the First Canterbury Battalion when the Turks tried to take the Canal in February. Tells me the Turks got hell shot out of 'em—lot of 'em just ran, even took off their boots, dropped their guns, chucked away tons of gear. Reckons they didn't put up much of a fight at all."

"Well, they've obviously got a different lot of blokes over where we're going," said Snowy. "Unless all those blokes we saw coming off the ship were just feeling crook and decided to have a break."

"Lot of dysentery over there, I've heard," said Barney. Billy looked at him.

"There is, Barn. And with luck you'll cop it as soon as you get off the boat."

"Let's get some sleep," said Snowy.

"Dysentery can kill you too, you know, Billy," Barney protested.

"Yes. But it can't blow a bloody arm or leg off," replied Billy. "Now go to bloody sleep and stop worrying."

Barney slept, and had only a few vaguely anxious dreams. Captain Doc Morgan and his staff worked late, checking their stores of morphine, chloroform, lysol, carbolic acid, iodine, quinine, lint, bandages, chlorodyne, scalpels, needles, probes, extractors, retractors, rib-spreaders, amputation knives, bone-saws and tourniquets. When Captain Morgan finally dropped into a shallow, uneasy sleep he dreamed of dysentery, cholera, smallpox, malaria, typhus, typhoid, diphtheria, pneumonia, dengue, enteric, pleurisy, meningitis, plague, bilharzia, sleeping sickness, psoriasis and septicemia.

2

The troopship *Hindoo* dropped anchor in Mudros, the main harbour of Lemnos Island. Major Barton, trailing clouds of pipe-smoke and Lieutenant Gray, strode impatiently around the crowded decks.

"Too bad, this delay, you know," he said, indicating the milling soldiery. "Takes the edge off the men. Gives them too much time to think. And listen to rumours."

"There are certainly plenty of furphys around," agreed Lieutenant Gray. "I've heard several new ones today. That Turkey is suing for peace. That the Italians are going to land thirty-five thousand troops to create a diversion at Suvla Bay—"

"There is talk of a big show at Suvla," said Major Barton, "but I don't think it's the Italians. They've got their hands full with the Austro-Hungarians, by all accounts." He shrugged. "Anyway, Gray, forget the rumours—enjoy the view!" He waved his hand toward the crowded harbour—more crowded even than Alexandria's had been—its sparkling blue waters constantly churned into white foam by bustling picket boats taking messages between the grey warships.

"An historical arena, Gray. A classic arena. Over there is Lemnos! Lemnos, Gray, and on those very mountains you're looking at now, why, more than two thousand years ago King Agamemnon lit a chain of fires to signal to his queen, Clytemnestra, news of his victory over Troy. Think of the mighty warriors who have fought in this arena—Achilles, Nestor, Ulysses, Hector!"

"And we're still fighting here in 1915," murmured Lieutenant Gray. "We haven't learned much, have we, sir?"

But Major Barton, the war forgotten, his kindly face alight with enthusiasm, was soaring away into his own world, where warriors were noble, and wore shining armour, and never got drunk or insolent or suffered from distressing diseases.

"There," he said, pointing with his pipe into the blue Aegean, "there, south of us—we passed it in the night, more's the pity—is the island of Rhodes. You know what happened there, Gray, of course?"

"Can't say I do, sir," said Gray.

Major Barton looked disappointed.

"On Rhodes, Gray, in, ah, 1522, the Knights of St

John of Jerusalem were besieged by a huge force of Ottomans—Turks, in fact—for months!"

"And did they win, sir?" asked Lieutenant Gray, watching a Sopwith Navy Pup from the carrier *Ark Royal* drift over the blue sea.

"Well, no," admitted Major Barton. "But they put up a damn good fight."

"Not the sort of thing we can boast about to the men, though, sir," said Lieutenant Gray, rather spitefully. "Might think it a bad omen. Well, sir, if you'll excuse me, I've got a kit inspection." He saluted and left, and Major Barton plunged back into his historical reverie.

That evening Colonel Robinson held a meeting with his officers. One bulkhead of his stifling cabin was almost entirely covered by a sectional map of the Gallipoli Peninsula, and the junior officers saw their future field of battle in total for the first time, saw all the now-familiar names and their relationship to one another: Anzac, Gaba Tepe, Ari Burnu, Suvla Bay, Cape Helles, Y Beach, Old Y Beach, Morto Bay and, inland, the names of minor geographical features unknown, often unnamed, before the landings of April 25: Rhododendron Ridge, The Nek, Hill Q, Hill 60, Table Top, Shrapnel Gully, Lone Pine, Chocolate Hill, Sari Bair, Chunuk Bair, A Beach, B Beach, C Beach, W Beach, a perfect alphabet of beaches.

The senior officers murmured amongst themselves, while Colonel Robinson droned on.

"Hear the Kiwis' Otago Battalion was almost wiped out on Baby 700."

"And Abdul nearly finished the job when the remains of the Otagos joined the Wellingtons and the Aucklands on the push towards Krithia."

"See all those bloody ravines—what do they call 'em?—*nullahs*?—hear Abdul's got every bloody one of them enfiladed with machine guns."

"Hear the Aussies killed seven thousand Turks on Plugges Plateau."

"Bayonet actions only—that's what Robbie's keen on."

"The Munster and Dublin Fusiliers took such a hiding along Krithia Nullah that they've formed the survivors into a unit called the Dubster Fusiliers."

Colonel Robinson raised his voice and tapped the map sharply.

"And in conclusion, gentlemen, if I may have your attention, I'll remind you again of the field combat principles laid down by the General Officer Commanding the Australian and New Zealand Army Corps—"

Colonel Robinson paused, and raised his baton as though about to conduct an orchestra—"principles the G.O.C., Lieutenant-General Birdwood, laid down just before the first landings, and which still apply. I call them the 'five Cs', gentlemen. They are—" a sweep of the baton—"concealment whenever possible. If the enemy can't see you he can't shoot you, eh?"

Another sweep of the baton.

"Covering fire. Always try to give advancing men covering fire."

The baton again.

"Control your fire. There must be no random firing. And this brings me to the next C—control of your men. You must control your men's natural urge to blaze away. And, lastly, but not least, communications. You *must* keep your lines of communications open. Do not become isolated or cut off. If your telephone lines are cut, don't hesitate to use runners. Very well. Any questions?"

"What about C for casualties?" murmured a young captain sitting next to Major Barton.

And so the meeting dragged on, going into details of landing craft, covering fire from the artillery and the navy, cooking facilities, unloading of stores, siting of brigade and divisional headquarters, ammunition supply and sanitary arrangements.

Major Barton finally got to bed, after a late drink with Lieutenant Gray, at midnight. During the night he was awakened by a rattle and splash as *Hindoo* weighed anchor. Soon the deep thudding of her engines changed note and he lay and listened to the swash and ripple of the Aegean against the hull as the troopship headed northeast, towards Imbros and Gallipoli.

3

Archy stood on the deck and watched the lights of Lemnos slide astern into the dark Aegean. The wind of *Hindoo*'s passage was pleasantly cool after the oven-heat of below decks, where the metal bulkheads sweated with condensation and the cockroaches scattered by the hundred.

There were soldiers sleeping all around: they huddled in their greatcoats. Like the dead, Archy thought, and shuddered. The ship was running dark, since German submarines were known to be hunting in the western approaches to the Dardanelles. Within the last couple of months two British battleships, *Triumph* and *Majestic*, had been sunk, and the brass hats were taking no chances with *Hindoo* and her cargo of desperately needed soldiers.

A few hundred yards abeam of *Hindoo* Archy could just make out a long dark shape: one of *Hindoo*'s escorts, the British destroyer *Chelmer*. With deadlights screwed down over all scuttles, showing no navigation lights, and with her bridge lights shrouded, *Chelmer* was almost invisible, betrayed only by the shimmering phosphorescent foam as her forefoot ploughed the warm black sea. Once Archy saw the brief, guarded flicker of a signal lamp as the destroyer spoke to another silent sentinel somewhere on the dark waters astern.

A shape appeared at the rail beside Archy. By the sudden red glow of a cigarette he saw it was Frank.

"Couldn't sleep? Neither could I."

"No," said Frank. "Too bloody hot. And too much on my mind."

"You'll be all right," said Archy.

"I hope so, Archy. I hope so."

They stood in silence, staring at the brilliant stars.

"I used to know most of the stars," said Archy, at length. "My Uncle Jack—"

"The old bloke at the races that day?"

"Yes. He knew all the stars. Used to point them out to me. I can still remember a lot of star names. Sirius, Canopus, Rigel. Vega, Capella, Aldebaran. Proxima Centauri—and Alpha Centauri, its twin, they're the pointers to the Southern Cross—"

Frank peered at the sky.

"Can't even see the old Cross tonight, Archy."

"We're in the Northern Hemisphere, remember? You can only see the Cross in the Southern Hemisphere."

"Hmmm. Don't like that, Arch. Makes a bloke feel sort of—lost, you know. I mean, I've never known much about the stars—nothing, come to that, but everyone back home knows the Southern Cross. It's, well, it's always there, isn't it?"

"I know. You know, I used to look at the old cemetery back on the station, where my grandad and grandma are buried, and my sister Julia, and look up at the old Cross turning slowly above them all the night, and I often thought I wouldn't want to be buried where I couldn't have the Cross above me."

Frank threw his cigarette end overboard, in direct

contravention of the notices all over the ship forbidding soldiers to throw anything overboard. He watched the small trail of sparks whirl away in the ship's slipstream.

"Jesus, Mary and Joseph, Archy, don't talk like that. Why, you'll probably die a rich, old grazier with a million acres, while I'm—" he broke off to light another cigarette, the match cupped in his hand to protect it from the wind, and squinted at Archy over the yellow flame: "You got the wind up, Archy?" he asked quietly.

Archy nodded.

"A bit. I'll get over it."

Frank inhaled deeply and blew out a fragrant cloud of smoke. "Me too. My feet are so cold, they—" Abruptly he turned, striding away into the dark. "Got to get some sleep. See you."

"Not if I see you first," returned Archy automatically, and turned back to his observation of the sea and the stars and the watchful destroyer.

Sister Cooley wrote in her diary:

July 20: Aboard Hospital Ship Gascon *off Mudros Island. Have got badly behind with my diary lately. We were given less than twelve hours' notice that we were being sent to the Dardanelles. Came off duty exhausted at 11 p.m. to be told by a harassed staff nurse a few minutes later (I had not yet gone to bed) that we (that is me and some of my nurses) were to be ready to leave the hospital at 7 a.m. to catch the* Gascon *at Alexandria. Spent much of the night packing and making sure my case notes were up to date for my successor. Managed a few hours' sleep and caught the 8.30 a.m. train to Alexandria. Hot and stuffy. An ambulance was waiting to take us to the* Gascon. *Met the C.O. of the medical detachment aboard. He seems a popular man although he has a reputation as a "hard driver". Well, none of my people are afraid of hard work. NB: Am sharing a cabin with another Australian nurse. Very pleasant woman. Everyone seems very nice.*

July 27: Aboard hospital ship Gascon, *off the "Anzac Beach" just opposite the hill called Gaba Tepe. We can also see the high peak the troops have called "The Sphinx". What a frightful landscape—all rocky and barren, pitted and scarred, like an artist's impression of the moon. Although we carry big Red Crosses on the side of the ship, and are well lit up with strings of electric bulbs at nights, and although the Turks are said to be very good about respecting the Red Cross, the escorting destroyers continually worry and fuss around us like anxious mothers. Two of them seem to have kept an eye on us all day—*Pincher *and* Bulldog, *long thin boats puffing columns of black smoke and threshing the sea to froth.*

July 29: Two dreadfully trying and depressing days. So many boatloads of badly wounded men. Mostly stretcher cases. They just kept coming. They are always exhausted, poor fellows, but so patient, lying there in their filthy uniforms, the khaki black with blood and mud, and crawling with vermin. And the flies! They come out in the boats with the wounded, thousands of them; you have to shoo them off the wounds. So many terrible abdominal cases, and these cases are so depressing, because most of them die.

July 30: Almost constant gunfire from the land: a low, slow grumble, all day and night, with a sort of counterpoint, a dry crackling, which the soldiers say is rifle fire. We have had aeroplanes—ours, or rather British, of the Royal Naval Air Service—flying over us all day, "spotting" for the big battleships lying further out in the bay. I fear I almost disgraced myself and my uniform today: it was a frightfully busy time. The C.O. and his operating team were so busy that I was called in to help. I shall never forget it. The soldiers to be operated on lay on their stretchers—or on the deck—outside the operating theatre; we cleaned them up as best we could right there; no time for all the careful scrubbing and shaving one does in civilian life. I had just helped lift one poor boy with a dreadful leg wound on to the operating table; I stepped back and almost fell over something. I looked down and almost screamed: it was a pile of arms and legs, all warm and bloody and horrible. I had to bite my tongue to stop crying out, or being sick. I caught a flash of the C.O.'s exhausted eyes above his mask, and I pulled myself together, and went out to prepare the next patient.

4

There was a ghostly mist on the sea that night: it swirled across the beams of the escorting destroyers' searchlight, settled clammily on the metal decks and soldiers' faces and hid the land.

"Listen," said Archy. He and Frank were at the rail at their disembarkation station in full kit—weighted down by pack, greatcoat, groundsheet, entrenching tool, rifle, bayonet, emergency rations, water bottle, ammunition, first aid kit, wire-cutters—everything they owned, and everything the army had given them. "Listen," said

Archy, and they all heard it: the slow deep thudding grumble out there in the darkness.

A sigh, almost of relief, rustled over the crowded men, like a breeze through a cornfield. So that was what a battle sounded like.

Clanking and snorting, a picket boat towing several whalers nudged *Hindoo*'s side. Quiet voices gave orders: ropes rattled on decks, seamen swarmed down swaying ladders.

"Steady now, lads," said Major Barton. "Go down fast but carefully. Don't want anyone falling into the sea."

Strong sailors posted in the whalers helped the laden soldiers make the precarious transition from vertical ladder to heaving boat.

Lieutenant Gray, more officious and agitated than usual, spotted Archy and Frank about to go over the side.

"I say," he said, putting a hand on Frank's shoulder and turning him so that he could examine his face by one of the shaded disembarkation lamps, "I say, aren't you an infantryman? Didn't I see you at—"

"No sir," said Frank hastily. "No sir. Horseman through and through, sir—"

Still Lieutenant Gray paused. He shook his head.

"No. Something funny going on here—"

Just then Major Barton called testily: "Keep those men moving, Lieutenant Gray, or we'll be caught out here on the water like sitting ducks at daylight."

Irritably, Gray waved Frank on.

"Right. Get over, get over."

Starshells burst twinkling almost overhead. The destroyers snapped off their searchlights and withdrew to safer waters.

The picket boat cast off and went ahead, putt-putting through the mist which suddenly lifted to reveal an amazing sight: a black rampart sparkling with a thousand tiny, flickering lights. Starshells arched above the dark line of the cliffs, and somewhere to the right a big gun was emitting a regular crump. The soldiers were transfixed by the weirdness, the sheer unexpectedness, of the scene.

"Told you they were living in the cliffs like birds," grunted Major Barton to Lieutenant Gray. "Those lights are the candles in the dugouts. Abdul can't see them, of course—"

"But he can bloody see us," said Lieutenant Gray, as something passed overhead with a whoofing roar and exploded noisily behind them.

"Yes, he knows something's up," said Major Barton, imperturbably. "But we'll be ashore before he gets our range."

"I hope so, sir."

In the first whaler, Frank glanced at Archy. By the last light of a fading starshell Archy's face glowed, rapt, as he stared at the looming cliffs. Frank shook his head, silently.

More starshells rushed skyward: three, four, five, scattering brilliant flakes of white light. A large-calibre shrapnel shell burst a hundred yards astern of the little flotilla: they saw its lethal load whip the black water to foam.

"Thank God we weren't under that lot," murmured Frank, his stomach tightening, and a sergeant bellowed to him to shut up.

"There's a bit of a show on," said Major Barton. "This can't be just a reception for us."

"It's not, sir," said the Royal Navy midshipman conning the picket boat. "They have a couple of shows like this a week. Keeps the blighters happy, I suppose, but, my word, don't our chaps make a mess of 'em when they get too close."

Major Barton leaned nearer to get a glimpse of the young man's face by the dim light of the binnacle lamp.

"How old are you, my boy?"

The midshipman paused to allow an echoing explosion on the right to rumble away across the sea.

"Sixteen, sir, last birthday."

"Been doing this job long?"

"Since the landing, sir, I mean the April 25 landing, sir."

"My God," said Major Barton, shaken.

"You new to this sort of thing, sir?" asked the midshipman after a while.

"Rather," said Major Barton.

"You get used to it, sir. We had a round dozen middies on picket boat duty to begin with, sir. Now we've six left. But I expect we shall manage." He paused. "Hear that deep bang, sir? That's a Turkish bomb. My word! They are coming on strong tonight. And that—that's a machine gun. One of ours, I think. Well, here we are, sir. Good luck."

The lines were slipped, the picket went astern, gears whining, and the whalers nudged the gravelly sand. The midshipman gave a cheery wave, Major Barton waved back, and the soldiers splashed ashore in the growing light.

The wounded were waiting on the water's edge, on the new timber jetties, everywhere: lying, sitting, standing, staring hopefully at the sea, smoking, chatting quietly. Harassed medical orderlies moved among them, giving sips of water, lighting cigarettes for men who could not use their hands, adjusting bloody bandages. The long lines moved slowly toward the lighters and whalers taking them out to the hospital ships which had moved closer inshore and now waited, a blaze of lights from stem to stern, a few hundred yards off shore.

Frank took in the scene and winced. He bit his lip and looked at Archy, but Archy scarcely seemed to notice the wounded. He walked, his face aglow, looking at the heights towering above the beach.

They were fallen in at last. The roll was called, and

called again. They were checked and checked again. Sergeants bellowed, corporals shouted themselves hoarse, the half-dozen horses which had been brought over from Egypt for despatch-riding duties reared and whinnied, upset by the noise and milling soldiery and the boom of the guns.

At last, with the sun well up, they were ready to move into their positions. Major Barton gave them one last bit of advice:

"Keep your heads down, boys—and remember the advice given by the Commander in Chief of the Middle East Expeditionary Force, General Sir Ian Hamilton. And that advice is dig, dig, dig. Sink into that hillside so the Turk can't see enough of you to shoot at, right? Carry on. And good luck!"

They hurled themselves up the cliff towards their allotted positions, and dug: in their shirtsleeves and then shirtless, they dug like startled moles, and when the sun was rising on Anzac Beach, the 10th Light Horse had melted into the torn and ravaged hillside. And there, all day, they slept, undisturbed by passing aeroplanes, or the constant duels between Turkish guns beyond the ridges and the battleships out in the bay.

Archy and Frank, sweating and swearing, had made themselves a passable home between two huge slabs of rock, split asunder by some primeval extreme of heat or cold: their groundsheets made a roof of sorts and provided a patch of shade, essential in that broiling Aegean summer.

They slept off their exertions, and in the comparative cool of the violet evening sat on the doorstep of their dugout and watched the sun slide into the indigo sea. The grey battleships turned black and Samothrace and Imbros squatted, darker shapes on the darkening water.

Major Barton and Lieutenant Gray came around on a tour of inspection, stumbling and grunting on the rough ground. They told the men where the nearest field kitchen was, pointed out the medical tent on the beach and the nearest latrines, and left them to their own devices, with a parting injunction from Lieutenant Gray to "look smart, boys", and from the major to "look after yourselves, boys. Keep your heads down!"

5

The next day the reinforcements were absorbed into the established forces. Archy and Frank began to understand—and very quickly, for their lives depended upon it—the network of trenches which criss-crossed the slopes. They learned the difference between a fire trench and a communications trench, between a parapet and a parados. They learned very quickly that when a crudely-painted sign at the entrance to a sunken path warned "night road only!" it meant just that—and they learned it by seeing Trooper Harris lying dead in the dust with flies on his face a few seconds after he had decided to "chance it" and use the path during daylight.

They spent a night in Quinn's Post, the very mention of which was enough to make braver riflemen shudder. They came around the easy way to Quinn's for a night's garrison duty—that is, round by Anzac Cove and up Shrapnel Gully, and were shot at only a few times on the way; from Shrapnel Gully they alternately crawled and dashed up Monash Gully (where a Turkish sniper was especially active that day), then past Russell's Top and Pope's Hill, and so at last, drenched with sweat, because they were each carrying, as well as their rifles and two hundred rounds of .303 ammunition, two petrol-cans of water, safe to Quinn's Post.

Quinn's Post was a place out of a nightmare. It clung to the edge of the cliff like an eagle's eyrie. One direct hit by a large shell or mortar bomb would have sent it sliding down the hillside. Luckily it was tucked so close to the summit that the Turks had no gun with a trajectory high enough to reach it. Quinn's Post was so close to the Turkish lines that the enemy's front trenches were about twenty feet away, and at one point a listening post had been dug to within six feet of the Turkish line. Men went mad at Quinn's Post: Australians and New Zealanders had died by the dozen in Quinn's Post: the fleas lived on their blood in the dust of the trench floors, and when they tired of the dead, they leaped on to the living.

Everything had to be carried up the hill to Quinn's Post—food, water, firewood, first aid dressings, guns, ammunition, mail, bombs. The relieving garrison arrived every morning, exhausted before their one-night tour of duty began.

Part of the terror of Quinn's Post—apart from the constant bombing—was the strain of listening for the muffled chink of pick on stone, which would signal a Turkish attempt to run a sap under the position, pack it with gun cotton, and blow Quinn's Post and everyone in it into the Aegean.

Archy and Frank got through their night there and got away alive, which is more than many soldiers before them had done; but the strain of a night in Quinn's Post almost cost them their lives, nevertheless. They were staggering back, down the slopes and gullies, eyes glazed with fatigue, thinking only of getting back to their dugout and sleeping, when a hoarse voice bellowed: "Hey, watch it, you bloody idiots!"

They stopped, trembling with the strain of the steep

descent and weariness, and saw a grizzled, suntanned infantryman, clad only in a pair of torn khaki shorts, glaring at them from a firestep.

"Yes," said Archy shortly, "what's up?"

The infantryman snorted.

"What's up? What's bloody up? You nearly were, mate. Can't you bloody read?" He pointed.

Immediately in front of them the trench ended, running down into an open gully, twenty feet wide, before the next piece of trench started. At the end of the trench they were in, a sign whitewashed on a flat stone warned: "Danger. Busy sniper."

They gazed at it dully, almost too tired to comprehend. An infantryman further down the firestep noticed their hats and laughed.

"The bloody Light Horse. Can't you get used to walking, boys?"

"Here," said the first soldier. "Look at this." He picked up a long stick with an empty jam tin on the end.

"Watch Abdul," he said, and thrust the stick out beyond the parapet, into the gully.

There was a sharp crack and a rattle, and the tin had two neat holes punched in it, in one side and out the other.

"See what I mean?" asked the infantryman with a grin. Archy had a sudden memory of Uncle Jack and his readings around the fire on winter nights.

"The flying bullet down the pass, that whistles clear, all flesh is grass," he recited softly, but not softly enough: the infantryman gave a whoop: "Aye, aye! A bloody poet, eh?"

"Yes," said Archy with dignity. "Kipling. You like Kipling?"

"Dunno, mate, I've never kippled," said the infantryman, and laughter resounded up and down the trench. Archy and Frank fled to their dugout, but by a safer route.

6

The mornings were beautiful. The Aegean stretched flat and impossibly blue to the horizon. Imbros and Samothrace floated like dark green clouds on the sea that Ulysses had sailed. But the soft blue sea lost much of its charm inshore, where the bodies of transport mules and sometimes men rolled in the lacy ripples washing against the shore; barbed wire rusted, tilted ships leaked oil and petrol into the clear water, and the *River Clyde*, hard aground, marked the last landfall for hundreds of Englishmen. But small gulls still flew, and sandpipers picked their delicate ways among the rusting wire, and on the hills and gullies now, in high summer, the flowers grew—yellow daisies, poppies, ilex, pink oleander, and wild thyme which scented the air when crushed by heavy army boots.

From their dugout Archy and Frank, when not in the line, would watch the spotting planes come and go—Sopwiths, Maurice Farmans, Nieuports, Short seaplanes, flying from British and French aircraft carriers, and from landing strips at Cape Helles and Tenedos Island. The little planes seemed very frail as they clattered overhead, swaying and rocking in the gusty airs over the peninsula. Then little white puffballs would blossom around them and the faint crack-crack of air-bursting shells would drift downwind. They saw enemy aircraft, too; Taubes and Rumplers and Albatros, and once a small bomb fell near their dugout; but no one seemed to take the enemy flyers seriously.

Some days there were balloon ships off shore—strange sights with their bloated gasbags like over-ripe marrows, and oddly unwarlike. On windy days the balloons bobbed and dived and twisted at the end of their cables and were hurriedly winched down, with sailors running all over the decks like ants to secure them.

The men had to go to the beach most days when out of the line, to fetch water or draw rations (tea, Fray Bentos corned beef, jam and hard biscuits). The trip to the beach was hot and tiring, but there was always the chance of a swim at the end of it, if Beachy Bill was not too active. Beachy Bill was a large-calibre Turkish gun, dug in somewhere on the reverse slopes of the highest ridge and had so far evaded every effort of the Royal Naval Air Service to find him. Beachy Bill fired pure shrapnel, fused to explode over the beach: the big shells exploded with a distinctive crack-boom, and sprayed a deadly cone of leaden balls.

They swam despite Beachy's attentions, however, laughing and skylarking as though swimming off an Australian beach with nothing but sharks to worry about. Beachy Bill fired on a high trajectory, and could often be heard coming, which was the signal for shouted warnings and a deep dive. The explosion shook the water, and the shrapnel ripped up a foamy swathe before sinking, harmless, to the bottom.

Men got wounded swimming, and sometimes killed. But more often Beachy confined his attention to the crowded beach itself, searching out the troop concentrations, the stores, the water-condensors, the ammunition dumps. Often shrapnel killed wounded men lying at the water's edge or on the jetties, waiting for lighters.

They saw a man hit with shrapnel on the beach: a

tall muscular man, tanned almost black, he was loading an artillery mule when a shell burst almost above him. The mule reared and snorted, but was unharmed: for a moment the soldier himself stood as though untouched while the balls tore up the sand around him; then he fell, heavily, on his belly, and a shining fountain of bright blood pulsed a foot out of a dark hole in his broad brown back. He lay quite still: once he groped for his pipe, but it had been broken by his fall, and he frowned, and closed his eyes.

"Must have hit the aorta," said a doctor who had run from the dressing station. "To go that fast. Pumped it all out of him in a minute or two."

The blood soaked quickly into the sand and the flies buzzed irritably.

7

Like most men from the bush, Archy regarded himself as a fair cook, and Frank was quite happy to let him take over the housekeeping. To be sure, Archy's culinary scope was limited by the ingredients available, but he could whip up quite edible stew from Fray Bentos, Bovril extract and biscuits. Washed down with thick, sweet, much-stewed tea, it built a man up for the day ahead. At least, Archy said so.

This beautiful morning, with a day off ahead of him and a good night's sleep behind, Archy whistled happily as he stirred the savoury mess bubbling in the smoke-blackened billy balanced precariously over a tiny fire: wood was precious on Gallipoli, and fires were made just big enough to do the job required.

In the corner of the dugout, Frank stirred, awoke, groaned and lifted a sleep-bleared face.

"Thing I can't stand about you, mate," he said, 'is that you're always so bloody cheerful in the morning."

"Best time of day," said Archy, stirring and tasting. "Ummm! Best yet."

"What's for breakfast?" asked Frank.

"What do you think?"

"Oh gawd."

"Well, if you'd get the bacon you've been talking about—"

"Archy, I can't work bloody miracles."

"You keep saying there's some around."

"There is, and I'll get some, don't worry."

"We're out of rum, too."

"I've got a deal today with one of the Kiwis. A Turkish officer's cap-badge for a bottle of rum."

In the ten days they had been on the peninsula Frank had built up a thriving barter and exchange business. Equipped with a sharp eye and a knack of knowing just the sort of souvenirs that would appeal to the people back home, Frank frequently risked his life by crawling along the parapets of front line trenches at dawn and evening, sifting the debris of war.

He was scornful about bent, spent bullets.

"A penny a dozen, Archy," he said. "Everyone's got half a dozen. Now if you could get me a bullet embedded in a Bible that someone had in his breast-pocket! Bits of shell? No, not unless you can say, 'They took this out of Uncle Fred's lung or leg or head!' Same with shrapnel. Now a Turk bayonet—that's something. That's more personal. I mean, it belonged to someone, didn't it? Or a water-bottle with a hole in it. No, a trench periscope with a hole in it's no bloody good. Hell, every trench periscope has a hole in it—you can't stick one over the parapet without Johnny Turk putting a round through it. Fact, I reckon some of these officers stick their periscopes up just to give Abdul a chance to put several holes in 'em, so they can skite how brave they are, watching the savage Turk under fire and all that." He paused, shovelling corned beef into his mouth.

"I tell you, Arch," he said, after swallowing and taking a gulp of tea, "the Turks've got some German officers, well, you get one of those German officer's revolvers, that big Mauser pistol they use, and that'll get you bacon, my lad."

"Thanks for the tip," said Archy drily. "Soon as I've tidied up here I'll just nip over to the Turkish trenches, ask to see a Hun officer, knock him down and bag his pistol, eh?"

Frank grunted, drinking tea.

"Don't be smart. I mean just keep your eye skinned for a dead Hun. They're all officers, anyway, the Huns, so you can't go wrong if you see a dead one. Just grab his pistol before anyone does, and give it to me. I'll get you bacon for a month."

"I hope we won't be here that long. There's talk of a big show—a drive to push the Turks back to Constantinople."

"There's always talk of a push, Archy, you know that. Look, they'd be mad to try anything silly—"

"Of course they would. Every time they've rushed our lines we've massacred them."

Frank sighed.

"Not the Turks, Archy, I mean us. Our top brass. Why should they try a push, and risk heavy casualties, when we're dug well in here? We're tying up thousands of Turkish troops just by being here. When the Huns have been cleaned up in Europe, and that can't be long now, then the British and the French move around with the Russians and take Turkey from the north, we hold him here, and that's it. He's chased like game into the guns."

"I don't think they're going to let us sit here until the end of the war, Frank."

"Well I hope they do. I've got no great desire to make a hero of myself."

"Be awful to go home without actually being in action," said Archy.

"Not as far as I'm concerned," said Frank. "The fewer bullets that are shot in my direction during this war, the *better*." Frank got up. "I'm going down to the beach. Got some business to do. See you."

"See you, Frank," said Archy. He washed out the billy with a few drops of precious water and a dirty rag, and then set about stripping and cleaning his rifle, checking the action, feeling the edge of his bayonet, emptying and reloading the magazine.

With the dugout to himself, he decided to write another letter to Mary Stanton. He was not sure how to begin. He scratched, and thought, and scratched his head. He had to get it right—paper was valuable on Gallipoli. Archy had managed to bring across a small pad with him, but once that was finished (and he had already given several sheets to Frank and other less foresighted Light Horsemen) he would not be able to get another. So he sharpened his pencil carefully and thought, and as he did so a fly alighted on his nose. He slapped it away wearily, automatically, and began:

Dear Mary,

Well, here we are in Gallipoli, which is just about all I can tell you about military matters or the censor will put his black pencil through this letter.

A lot has happened since I last wrote to you (I hope you received my letter) but before I go into details I must tell you about our biggest enemy here. The fly! Yes. I know we think we have flies in Australia, but you should see these—

Ah, the Gallipoli flies. They scalded themselves to death in boiling tea, and floated in shimmering scabs on the stew. They crawled into noses, ears, mouths. They covered the dead and rose in humming clouds when disturbed by burial parties. They laid their eggs and hatched their soft white maggots in dead men's bellies or living men's wounds. They flew from gangrenous stumps to corned beef sandwiches, with a stop at the ripening latrines on the way. They were carriers of disease and death, and, unlike the Turks, who stopped for a breather between attacks, the flies kept coming. They thrived and grew fat in the ghastly fields of No Man's Land, and the rifles and machine guns of both sides made sure that the fields always had a harvest for the flies.

Archy told Mary that the flies were pretty bad, and went on to other things: the reunion with Frank, the beauties of the pyramids (daringly inserting a reference to moonlight) and the dishonesty of the Egyptians. He ended it by saying: *Looking forward to seeing you again* very *much* (he underlined the very so heavily that his pencil point broke), *please give my regards to your parents and grandmother, love, Archy.*

Then he went down to the beach for a swim. (And, although it was not the sort of thing you mentioned to a young lady like Mary Stanton, a chance to drown a few lice. Archy, like every other soldier, was lousy, crawling with the things. Itching heads were shaved bare—and the lice retreated to the seams of the soldiers' uniforms. When Archy went for a swim, he would usually strip naked—everyone else did, to the horror of some British officers—and sink his uniform with the aid of a heavy rock. The lice would desert the sinking shirt by the score. The trouble was that the lice had seemingly inexhaustible reserve battalions waiting back in the dugout.)

"Stand to, boys," said Lieutenant Gray quietly. "They're coming." The word whispered down the trench: "Stand to. Stand to."

"Watch the moon," said Lieutenant Gray. He looked at his watch. "She'll be setting any minute now."

The moon set. Silence. The night wind sighed across No Man's Land, blew dust across their faces as they waited.

There was a sudden flicker behind the hills, like summer lightning.

"Here it comes," said Lieutenant Gray. "Keep your heads down."

The first shells arrived with a whistle and crash. They fell short, exploding in a ragged line of smoke and flame in No Man's Land. The earth shook. Sandbags shuddered and dribbled sand into the trench. Archy and Frank crouched below the parapet, hugging the earth.

The next salvo was over, crashing away into the dark. Obviously the Turkish spotters were finding it hard to pinpoint the trenches.

Now the lightning-flickers beyond the hills were continuous. The noise was one long roll. Thick cordite smoke rolled into the trenches, making the Australians choke and cough. In the brief lulls between shells they could hear the steady rattle of rifles from the Turkish trenches, and the patter of bullets against the parados behind them. Ceaselessly the cry rang up and down the line: "Any casualties? Any damage? Any casualties? Anyone wounded there?"

Lieutenant Gray cranked the field telephone and crouching on his knees in the trench, bellowed into the instrument.

"Stand by with starshell. Starshell! Any minute now."

Archy wiped the dust from his face.

"Not very good shots, are they?" he said, with only the slightest quaver in his voice.

"They're just tryin' to put the wind up us, mate," said a grimy rifleman. "Kick up a row with the shells, see, and while we're hidin' they'll rush us. You'll see—" His voice was drowned in a shattering roar as another salvo exploded just ahead of the trench, showering them with sand and stones. "Jesus," said Frank.

Then, with startling suddenness, the guns stopped. It was suddenly deathly quiet. Rifle-bolts snicked along the trench.

"Starshell," shouted Lieutenant Gray into the telephone. "Starshell now!"

From across No Man's Land came a long ululating wail.

"Here they come," shouted someone. "Up you go, lads." A howitzer banged behind them and seconds later a starshell cracked overhead, shedding its brilliant white light over No Man's Land, and hundreds of running Turks.

"Jesus, Mary and Joseph," gasped Frank.

"Open fire," shouted an angry sergeant somewhere. "Open fire. Fire at will, independent fire. Open fire." The Australian line flamed, and Turks began falling. The fading starshell was reflected from their bayonet points.

All along the line, the Australians were scrambling up to sit on the parapet and fire, aiming as steadily as though at the shooting range. Along to Archy's left a big belt-fed Vickers machine gun began its metallic stammer, and the Turks fell, thick as scythed grass.

Cartridge cases tinkled into the trench. Archy fired

until his shoulder ached, forcing himself to make each shot count as he had been taught: "Pick your target. Squeeze, don't pull. Reload. Squeeze."

Frank leaned against the parapet beside him, his face grim, muttering steadily under his breath, giving a little grunt each time he fired.

The Turks kept up a steady wailing cry. Sometimes Archy thought they were chanting a prayer. The starshells twittered overhead. Men fell back into the trench, knocked down on to the firestep by Turkish bullets.

"Oh God."

"Take it easy, Blue."

"Jesus, mate, watch that leg."

"Stretcher bearer! Stretcher bearer! Where are those bloody stretcher bearers?"

"Take it easy, mate."

A Turkish Maxim-gun team manhandled their weapon over the parapet of their trench. They staggered halfway across No Man's Land with it, and set it up as methodically as though on manoeuvres.

"Get that gun," shouted Lieutenant Gray. He banged futilely at it with his revolver.

The Turkish machine-gunner sat behind the weapon and grasped the firing handles. His loading number seemed to be having trouble with the belt feed.

"Get that gun," screamed Lieutenant Gray. "For God's sake, get that gun!"

"The Vickers is coming round now, sir," said a sergeant.

"About ti-" said Gray, peevishly, and stopped. The Vickers had fired, hesitated, and then delivered a long burst. The hundreds of jacketed .303 bullets, travelling at maximum speed and flat trajectory at a range of fifty yards, swept the Turkish gunners away in a storm of lead. The loader and the ammunition carrier jerked upright and then seemed to dance, to quiver, to wriggle, as the bullets tore into them and threw them aside. The gunner was knocked flat on his back. Seconds later, unbelievably, he hauled himself back to his firing position, his face a gaping hole in the livid light of the starshells. His hands tightened on the firing handles and the Maxim loosed a futile burst at the stars: then the gunner fell forward on to the breech.

The starshells whimpered away and darkness returned. Men cried out in the bloody blackness of No Man's Land and the stretcher bearers worked until the rose-pink dawn brought the snipers back to their posts.

More than ninety Australians died that night. Colonel Robinson raged at Major Barton. "Most of those men were outside their trenches. *Outside* their trenches, for God's sake! Sitting on the parapet as though they were at a shooting gallery! Why the hell couldn't you keep them on the firestep, Barton?"

"The men are keen, sir, and they're good shots. They reckon that just peeping over the parapet, using loopholes, that sort of thing, well, it inhibits their accuracy and rate of fire. Some of them do get rather carried away."

"Carried away! My God, I can't believe my ears! Carried away! Disobeying orders! Major, exactly what sort of soldier do we have out there?"

Major Barton drew himself up and looked the colonel hard in the eye.

"Bloody good ones, sir," he said. "Now, if you'll excuse me—"

9

After that they had two blessed days out of the line. When they went back the brave Turkish gunner was still there.

His gun had been captured by a night bombing party, and was now being used by the New Zealanders on the left flank, but rigor mortis had frozen the gunner in the position in which he had died: he sat in No Man's Land as though at his gun still, his clenched hands thrust out before him.

As the days passed he grew black in the face—or what was left of it—and swelled like a balloon: his uniform strained across his bloated belly. The sun seared him and the flies laid their eggs on him and he fed maggots by the thousand. No Man's Land was full of Turkish bodies, some bloated, some flattened as though melting into the earth, but the gunner was something special.

They went into the line and out of it and into it again and still the machine-gunner remained. The skin drew back from his ruined face and exposed his shattered teeth in a demoniac grin.

One windy night his body, now reduced to sun-dried skin stretched across bone, was blown over: in the morning he was still there, but lying on his back, his clenched hands pointing to the sky as though in supplication.

10

Archy and Frank were on the beach getting water supplies after two days in the line when Frank suddenly gave a shout and ran to Watson's Pier, where a cutter was discharging reinforcements from a troopship which had arrived that morning.

As Archy watched in surprise, Frank hurled himself at three heavily kitted young infantrymen who had just stepped from the pier to the beach. Then, while other soldiers smiled tolerantly, Frank and the newcomers fell into an orgy of back-slapping and hair-ruffling and hand-shaking.

"Arch," bellowed Frank, "come and meet my mates."

Archy approached, rather slowly. He had heard about the coolness Frank's departure from the infantry had provoked.

It was still there, too, at least as far as he was concerned. He felt rather like a man meeting the former husband of the woman he has stolen. The three newcomers nodded coolly, and said "g'day", equally coolly. But the coolness couldn't last and it melted rapidly in the warmth of Frank's pleasure at seeing his mates again. And it was hard not to like Archy. Soon they were chatting like old friends.

"Seen any action yet, Frank?" asked Billy.

Frank looked at Archy.

"Yes. A bit," he said slowly. "Don't worry, Billy, the war's not over yet." He looked at Barney. "You're still with us, Barn—how's your, er, problem?"

Barney blushed.

"Not what I thought it was, thank gawd. All cleared up. But it'll be a long time before I go near that sort of woman again—"

Frank laughed.

"That's what they all say, Barn. Wait till you've been here a few weeks."

Barney shook his head.

"No, mate, fair dinkum. Once was enough for me. Gave me a helluva scare, I can tell you."

"Thought his donger was going to drop off," said Billy with a grin. "Didn't you, Barn?"

Barney flashed him an appealing look.

Snowy tactfully asked Archy:

"Where you from, mate?"

"Up the bush," said Archy. "Good to meet you all at last."

"Been talking about us, has he?"

"You know Frank. Likes talking," said Archy.

"Likes the sound of his own voice, all right," agreed Snowy with a nod.

"I reckon I know more about you lot than your mothers do," said Archy.

"Let's hope so," said Barney fervently, and everyone laughed.

"What's this, a bloody picnic?" bellowed an irate voice behind them. "You've come here to fight, not natter away like a bloody flock of galahs! Now *get fell in*!"

Sergeant Sayers, hoarse and purple-faced, stopped in mid-bellow.

"Dear me," he said. "Dear me! I do apologise. It's Dunne of the Light Horse."

Frank smiled his best smile.

"Good morning, sergeant. Good to see you again."

Sergeant Sayers almost smiled. At least, his face twitched; but that could have been the flies.

"How're you doing, Dunne?" he asked. "All right?"

"Fine, thanks, sergeant."

"Mind if I have me men back then? *Right! Carry on you lot! Fall in! At the double!*"

"See you, boys," said Frank. They plodded away through the sand to join the platoon Sergeant Sayers was abusing at the top of his considerable voice.

Archy and Frank watched them go.

"They seem a good mob," said Archy.

"The best," said Frank.

Sister Cooley forced herself to write in her diary:

Hospital ship Gascon *off Mudros, August 1, 1915: Back to Alexandria tomorrow, with a full ship. Everyone quite exhausted. Endless boatloads of wounded. There was a big Turkish attack in the hills the other night—have lost track of the date; and in the morning—a glorious dawn, reminded me of that Greek poem about dawn's "rose-pink fingers in the sky"—in this lovely morning, a cutter full of wounded was hit by shrapnel from the gun they call "Beachy Bill". The shell burst right over the boat. The balls killed many of the wounded and several sailors, and knocked holes in the cutter so that when it was finally brought alongside us it was half-full of water—red water, a horrible sight. To save time the cutter was hooked on to our seaboat's falls and hoisted aboard, and while it hung there, the bloody water ran out from the shrapnel holes in ghastly streams. A sickening sight. But to be fair I don't think the Turks knew there were wounded in the boat; everyone tells me they are most meticulous about respecting Red Crosses and hospital ships and first aid tents. So it was just "the fortune of war", but none the less horrible for that. Oh, I shall be glad to get back to Australia. To think how excited I once was about coming here! What ages ago they seem, those carefree days in Sydney.*

Chapter 7

ANZAC COVE
1915

1

"This," said Frank, "is the bomb factory."

Snowy, Billy and Barney, being given a brief tour of the beach, stared in amazement at the thousands of empty tins spilling across the sand. Jam tins, condensed milk tins, tobacco tins leaked the remains of their contents in sticky streams thick with struggling flies.

"G'day," said the bomb-makers briefly, inured to the heat and the flies and the smell, and went on with their work. A handful of charge, some shrapnel in the form of broken bits of metal, a length of fuse and the bomb was ready.

The nearest bomb-maker noticed the expressions on the newcomers' faces and grinned through grime and sweat.

"What, don't like my bombs, mate?" he said.

"Save your bloody life up there, they will—" He held up a bomb be had just completed. "There's my plum jam special. I'm getting a special order ready for Johnny Turk, see."

"Here's a cracker," said another bomb-maker. "Damson and apple! Guaranteed to blow your head off!"

"Do you mean to say," said Snowy indignantly as they walked away, "that we've got to use home-made bombs? Why, they look bloody dangerous."

"They are, Snow," said Frank. "To both sides. Sometimes those blokes make the bloody fuses so short they explode before you can throw 'em. Other times they make 'em so long that it's still fizzing when it lands in Abdul's trenches, and he's got time to throw it back. Like a bloody game of tennis, sometimes."

"My gawd," said Barney.

"But where are the real bombs?" asked Snowy. "I've seen pictures of them in the training manuals—like the Mills bomb."

Frank shrugged.

"Don't know, sport. None of 'em over here, are there, Archy? We've had to improvise. We're a sort of cut-price bargain-basement do-it-yourself army."

"We are," said Archy. "Look at the periscope rifle—"

"Periscopes? Here?" asked Billy.

"Same idea as with submarines," said Archy. "When the fellows first got here, every time a bloke put his head above the parapet to have a shot at a Turk, another Turk would blow it off. So a bright bloke in the engineers dreamed up a periscope attachment which allows you to stay in the trench and poke only your rifle over the parapet when taking a pot shot at the Turks. Of course, it doesn't work when there's a raid on and you've got to shoot quickly. But the old periscope's saved a lot of lives—"

"Yes," Frank laughed, "and cost the navy a lot of mirrors."

"True," said Archy. "Once the blokes saw how well the periscope worked, every ship in the bay was raided and stripped of mirrors for periscopes. The officers were furious. Had to shave by touch!"

They picked their way along the beach, through the litter of fuel and water drums, shells, ropes, stacks of picks, shovels and axes, medical stores. They stopped to let a tall turbanned Sikh lead a string of mules past, followed by several stocky Gurkhas and a mountain battery.

They passed the hospital, almost empty by Gallipoli standards, which meant that though every bed was occupied, there were, for once, no soldiers lying on the sand floors between the beds, and no rows of bloody stretchers lined up outside. But even in this quiet time the hospital thrummed with activity: the sterilisers hissed and bubbled, orderlies checked stores and instruments and rolled bandages, and on the beach beside the tent an ambulance corpsman was strapping folded stretchers to a patient donkey wearing a Red Cross brassard looped across its forehead.

"Expecting a busy day, mate?" asked Archy as they walked past. The ambulance man grunted.

"Aren't we always?"

Snowy patted the donkey.

"Poor little bugger doesn't look as though he could carry much."

The ambulanceman laughed.

"Him? Why, he's strong as an ox, aren't you Murphy? Murphy's carried bigger blokes than you down that hill, mate, no fear." He strapped another stretcher to the donkey's back and slapped its rump. "Come on, mate, off we go."

Silently the boys watched man and animal trudge

up a rocky defile.

"Hope I never have to ride his donkey," said Snowy after a while.

"Well, it's free," said Barney, but nobody laughed. They walked back up the beach in silence, and separated at Watson's Pier.

"I'll be around to your bivvy later to see if there's any mail for me," said Frank. "It'll all still be addressed to me at the 11th Battalion."

"I'll pick it up for you," said Snowy.

"See you, then."

"See you."

Archy and Frank picked up some water and laboured up to their dugout in silence. Later, as they sat and watched the sun set over the sea, Frank said:

"Notice anything on the beach, Arch?"

"Yes. Suspiciously busy."

"Something coming up, I reckon."

"They've sent most of the wounded blokes away. The hospital's all cleaned up and ready to go. And did you notice those stacks of stretchers?"

"Yep. And the ammo and the engineers bustling around fixing extra telephone wires to divisional and brigade HQ. I don't like the looks of it, Archy."

Frank got up.

"I'll make a cuppa. With a dash, eh?"

"Thanks."

Archy sat watching the sea and the ships until it got dark. As the day died the hospital ships switched their lights on: white floods illuminated the great blood-red crosses on their sides, and strings of white and green bulbs outlined them stem to stern. Beyond them lay the warships occasionally winking at each other with shaded lamps. *Queen Elizabeth* and *Bacchante, Albion, Grafton, Endymion, Colne, Triad, Chatham, Grampus* and *Euryalus*—over the past three weeks he had grown to know them all.

Frank brought the rum-laced sweet tea and they sat drinking it and watching the pallid dugout lights appear all along the cliff. Over towards Steele's Post a green Very flare twinkled, trailing luminous smoke, and a brief spiteful chatter of gunfire ran along the line.

"Some bloody fool putting on a show," said Frank. Somewhere to the north a big gun was firing steadily: a heavy regular cough.

Below them, with much creaking and groaning of timbers, members of a Maori battalion were hauling a water tanker closer to the New Zealanders—the Wellingtons—dug in beneath Chunuk Bair.

"Look at that," said Frank suddenly, pointing at the beach. "Like a bloody ants' nest. I tell you, something's going on."

Even from their height, and despite the gloom of the beach lit only by shielded lanterns, they could see that there was unusual activity: men ran to and fro, boats slipped out of the dark to be unloaded at Watson's Pier, blocks and tackles whined and creaked.

They looked at each other in the starlight, questioningly, but finding no answers.

"Any more rum? asked Archy.

"A bit," said Frank. "But I thought I'd keep it. We might need it tomorrow."

"Yes," said Archy, and turned back to watch the sea again. The moon was up, and laid a brilliant track across the water.

There were several Turks in the cage; unshaven, hollow-cheeked, in cheap, thin uniforms, they sat or squatted in attitudes of profound dejection.

Frank and Archy joined the small inquisitive crowd around the cage.

"Doesn't look too fearsome to me," said Archy, pointing to a particularly woebegone soldier.

"Probably the midget of the family," said Frank.

The Turk, sensing he was being talked about, got up and walked to the wire.

"Here, have a smoke, mate," said a lanky artilleryman, pushing a home-rolled through the wire. "Got a light? Here you are, then."

The Turk drew on the cigarette gratefully. He took it from his mouth and said, loudly:

"Allemain, bad!" and spat noisily, then, with an ingratiating smile, "English, good, very good."

"Allemain's the Huns," said a knowledgeable rifleman. "The Turks don't like the Huns even though they're supposed to be allies. Too bloody cocky, those Hun officers. All that heel-clicking and saluting."

"English good," said the prisoner hopefully.

"Hey, pack it in, mate," shouted a Light Horseman. "We're not the bloody Pommies—we're Aussies."

"Pardon?" said the prisoner, cocking his head like an inquisitive parrot. "Pardon?"

"You watch it, mate," said a gunner. "Call us Pommies and you'll really have a fight on your hands."

2

"Seen a sniper working?" asked Frank that afternoon.

"No," said Archy. He envied the snipers. They were pointed out on the beach. They were men who could *shoot*, really shoot.

"Follow me," said Frank, and they toiled up the cliffs to an Australian fire trench near The Nek, a fearsomely defended saddle of land slung between two peaks. It was a baking hot day: even the flies seemed drowsy.

The sniper and his observer were working despite the heat. As Archy and Frank arrived, the sniper, wearing only shorts and boots, was crouched on the floor of the trench, as though about to begin a race. His observer was looking towards the Turkish lines through a rough boxwood periscope.

"Here he comes," said the observer. "Hang on. Yes. Nearly there. Seventy-five yards . . . ready—"

The sniper adjusted his sights.

"Right. Seventy-five yards, one o'clock—go!" In one bound—helped by a stake driven into the trench wall—the sniper was on the parapet, firing almost as he stopped moving, and swinging back into the trench in one movement. As he landed several bullets thudded into the sandbags he had been squatting on seconds before, sending dribbles of sand down into the trench.

Panting, the sniper ejected the spent cartridge case and jacked another into the breech.

"Get him?" asked Archy.

"Have a look," said the observer, grinning at the sniper.

Archy fumbled awkwardly with the clumsy periscope. At first he could see nothing but a close-up view of their own sandbags. Then, tilting the periscope, he picked up No Man's Land, littered with rotting bodies, equipment, the unidentifiable detritus of war. Then he found the Turkish trenches: a line of sandbags with the occasional flicker of movement behind the loopholes.

Something stirred and raised itself above the enemy parapet: a large piece of flattened tin with a crude target painted on it. As he watched, a long stick rose up beside the target and tapped the inner circle.

The observer, watching through another periscope, grunted appreciatively.

"Inner. Not bad, Norm."

Norm shrugged modestly.

"Not my best, mate."

The observer, reading the boys' faces, explained:

"Just a little fun between fights, lads."

"Keeps my eye in," said the sniper. "Johnny Turk likes his little joke, you know. Course, when he's serious, he's bloody serious—comes over that bloody parapet yelling and screaming, and then we've got to give him a sharp lesson, but generally speaking, he's all right. Knows his place and we know ours, you might say."

"I know where my bloody place is, right enough," said the observer glumly. "It's Cairns, Queensland, and I wish I was there now, mate, my bloody oath I do."

They were stood to late that day, before they had had a decent sleep: marched up to the line—at least it was called marching, but no formation could be held for more than a few feet in that twisted landscape—held in a support trench for hours, and sent down again. When they were halfway to the beach the Turks attacked again, and the Light Horsemen dragged themselves wearily up the gullies and across the shot-swept ridges. There was a lot of bombing in that assault: Archy quickly grew to fear and loathe the vile hissing fizzing things. Soon the support and communications trenches were full of wounded men and sweating ambulancemen, stretcher bearers, and medical corpsmen.

The final assault was turned at bayonet point: the long blades flashed and winked in the late afternoon sun and the Turks retreated. The Australians mounted the parapet and squatted on the sandbags and shot them as they ran.

"Silly buggers," said a young sergeant, while a medical corpsman bound a slight shrapnel wound in his arm.

"In broad bloody daylight, too, with no artillery to soften us up first!"

"Some sector commander wants to impress

Mustafa Kemal, the Turk bigshot, I reckon," said the orderly. "I heard he's hanging around, just over the hill."

"Get on," said the sergeant scornfully. "Mustafa Kemal! And he had the bloody Kaiser with him, I suppose. How would you know? You linseed lancers always reckon you know everything."

The orderly was stung.

"It's fair bloody dinkum, sergeant. We had a wounded officer on the beach only this morning—a bloody brigadier—and I heard him telling our C.O. that one of them aeroplanes from Tenedos had seen this bloody great staff car just over the hill there, and the brigadier said intelligence reckons it was Mustafa Kemal and Von Sanders having a bit of a recce like."

"Von Sanders, the Hun general, helping the Turks?" asked the sergeant sceptically.

The orderly nodded.

"The very one. You mind my words, sergeant, there's big things in the wind."

"Well, at least it'll give you lot something to do," said a private waiting to have a nasty gash on his calf attended to.

"Yes, it bloody well might," said the orderly grimly.

Snowy wrote to his mother:

Well, Mum, I can't say this is a picnic but I am glad I am in it. There is a feeling in the air that we are taking part in something great. It is hard to describe to people at home, but it is real, all right. There is tremendous spirit here. I am proud to be an Australian. We don't mix very much with our Allies, not because we don't want to, but because we are so scattered around the Peninsula. However, we've seen a lot of Englishmen—very pale, some of them, they

don't get much sun in England; and then there are
Gurkhas, strange mountain men who still use a
sword—a strange, thick, pear-shaped thing called a
kukri—and are supposed to be very good fighters.
Then there are Sikhs, who always wear their turbans.
Saw a dead Sikh the other day—his turban fell off as
the burial party picked him up, and beneath it was
this huge coil of long, black, oily hair—long as a
girl's! The Sikhs usually burn their dead, but here on
Gallipoli, with so many to dispose of, and wood so
scarce, they often bury them, on land or sometimes
from ships at sea, if there is time.

But that is enough of morbid things. It is a
lovely day today—I even heard a bird singing! I told
you we all met up again—it was good to see Frank
and meet his mate Archy. It must be a good sign.

You would like the R.C. father here, Father
Dougherty. I have never seen a man work so hard
(except, to be fair, the other chaplains). They visit the
wounded and sick, go right up to the lines, attend
burials, write letters for men too ill to write (and
chivvy the rest of us to write home more frequently),
pray for us a lot, I think, as well as conduct regular
services for those who can attend them, when Johnny
Turk is not keeping us busy, and write to the parents
of men who have been killed. Father Dougherty is
very good friends with the artillery's C. of E.
chaplain, Padre Barrett. I know they have a drink
together (army issue rum!) when they can spare a
moment, which is not often. Padre Barrett is a fine
man, very kind. He has been here from the beginning.
I thought he was an old man but one of the gunners
tells me he is only forty-eight. He has a parish in
Gippsland, Victoria, and a son my own age in the
navy. Must close now, Mum. Your loving son, Dennis.
PS: Mum, I promise—when I come home, I'll paint

*the front room like you're always asking me to do. In
fact, I'll paint the whole house out!*

3

"Any mail for me?" asked Frank.

Sergeant Sayers looked up wearily. "Ah. The Light
Horse, eh? Swag of mail, sport, and a parcel. Like
Christmas. Here." He threw a parcel and a letter to Frank.

"Anything for me?" asked Barney hopefully.
Sergeant Sayers shook his head.

"Sorry, mate."

"None of his family can write," said Billy.

"Don't worry, Barn," said Snowy. "You can read
mine. Most mothers say the same things."

"Jesus," said Frank, looking up from his parcel.
"Cop this lot, will you? 'Your name has been selected at
random by the Ladies' Auxiliary. By the time you receive
this you will probably have seen heroic service in France.
We salute you and all the other brave sons of the Empire
and hope this parcel does its little bit to keep up morale.
God bless you.' "

He grimaced. "Well, let's see what this brave son's
got—oh my gawd! Look at that!" He held up a very badly
knitted sweater in brown wool, with one arm noticeably
longer than the other.

"Well, your name was selected at random, Frank,"
said Billy.

"So were the measurements, too, by the look of
this," retorted Frank. He dived into the package again.
"Violet scented soap, lavender water, Eno's Fruit Salts,

liniment—gawd, the old ducks have sent me half a chemist's shop—and look at this, will you—a bloody cookbook!"

"It's the thought that counts," said Snowy.

"Yes," said Frank. "And it would count a damn sight more if they could bloody well think."

The others roared with laughter.

"All right, all right," he said. "Let's see what else I got. Gawd—that just about finishes it off. A bloke who fixed my bike eighteen months ago has sent me a bill for seven and six!"

"Tell him to come and fetch it," suggested Billy with a grin. He struck a pose. "Dear sir, I regret that circumstances beyond my control prevent me sending you a cheque, but if you would care to present yourself at the six hundred and twentieth dugout from the top of the nasty ridge between Lone Pine and The Nek, I should be happy to oblige you with a cash settlement."

"That'd settle him," agreed Barney. "The rotten bludger." He picked up a square of white cloth and, stripping off his shirt, began stitching the cloth to the right sleeve.

"After you with the needle and thread," said Billy.

"What the hell're you doing?" asked Frank.

Sergeant Sayers came back, his mail delivery completed. He nodded approvingly at Barney. "That's right. Give it a good spread so it can be seen from behind."

"What's going on?" appealed Frank.

"That's a white patch, Light Horseman Dunne, sewn so that when we make the hop over today, our friends in the artillery who'll be giving us a covering barrage, we hope, will be able to see which is us and which is the Turks, and drop their blooming shells among the Turks."

"Hopping over?" said Frank. "When?"

Sergeant Sayers looked at his watch.

"Just after four, mate. Wish you were with us?"

"Jesus," whispered Frank. "What are you attacking?"

"Lone Pine."

A hush in the dugout. Somewhere a single rifle banged. The wind stirred the sparse bushes. The daisies were long dead now.

"We'll be over the ridge by five," said Sergeant Sayers, "and on the road to Constantinople. Lovely on the other side of the ridge, I'm told."

"I met a New Zealander who got almost over, just after the landing," said Snowy. "He said it was great. Mulberry trees and olive groves, streams, old stone houses, grape vines—beautiful, he said."

"Well, he can show us around when we get there," said Sergeant Sayers briskly.

"He can't, I'm afraid," said Snowy. "He's dead."

The sergeant grunted. "Hmmph. Yes. A lot of it about. Now come on, you lot. Get moving with those patches. Don't want to be late. See you later, eh?"

"Sergeant," said Billy.

Sayers stopped.

"Yes?"

Billy held out his hand.

"What's all this then?" said Sayers.

"Just wanted to say good luck, Bob," said Billy. Slowly Sergeant Sayers put out his hand.

"Good luck," he said. "You cheeky bastard." He shook hands with Billy and Snowy and Barney.

"Don't worry, Digs. You'll be all right. We'll have a beer together in Constantinople yet. We're going to make history this afternoon."

He held out his hand to Frank.

"Good luck to you too, Dunne. Don't look so glum. The Light Horse hasn't been forgotten. You're charging The Nek tomorrow morning, I hear. Goodbye." And he was gone.

"My gawd," said Barney, breaking the stunned silence.

"The Nek. The flaming bloody Nek. Turks've got machine guns everywhere up there, Frank."

Frank tried to look unconcerned.

"Ships' guns'll blow them away before we get there. The brass wouldn't charge a position that hadn't been shelled, would they?"

"No," said Billy. "The brass wouldn't. But we're not the brass."

"Reckon we'd better have a drink," said Frank, producing a small flask.

"No thanks," said Snowy quickly.

Frank took a swig and gave the flask to Barney who drank from it and handed it to Billy.

"The Lord's not going to hold it against you today, Snowy. He turns a blind eye an hour before every battle."

"Give it to me," said Snowy. He lifted the flask, coughed and spluttered.

"Goodbye," said Frank, "and good luck."

4

Major Barton's normally placid countenance was flushed. Lieutenant Gray and the two artillery officers attending the conference in Colonel Robinson's dugout exchanged glances.

"The colonel will put him on a fizzer if he's not careful," one of the artillery officers whispered behind his hand to Lieutenant Gray.

"What you're telling me, sir, and please correct me

if I'm wrong," said Major Barton, trying hard to control his fury, "is that the infantry attacks at Lone Pine and our attack at The Nek tomorrow are just—*diversions*?" He spat the last word out.

Colonel Robinson was icily placatory.

"Not just diversions, major. Vitally important diversions to enable the British to get safely ashore up north. We've got to convince Johnny Turk that the main thrust is coming from us down here in the south, so he'll divert all his troops this way and give the British a chance."

"Here—" he tapped the map with his baton, "—here, in Suvla Bay, is where those twenty-five thousand British troops are coming ashore."

"That's General Stopford's IX Corps, sir?" asked an artillery officer.

Robinson nodded. "That's right. Specially assembled for this operation. As soon as they do get ashore, they're going to sweep down south to join us, and together we'll capture the heights and then it's on towards Constantinople."

It's still a long way to Constantinople, thought Major Barton, looking at the map. A bloody long way.

"Now to the diversionary attacks," said Colonel Robinson. He looked at his watch. "Very soon, the Australians will attack at Lone Pine—there—with several battalions of infantry and some units of the Light Horse. A heavy artillery barrage before the assault should cut the wire and clear the Turks out of the trenches—"

"I've heard that one before," muttered a tired-looking artillery officer in Lieutenant Gray's ear.

The colonel tapped the map again. "Major-General Godley will attack Sari Bair and Hill 971 with twenty thousand men—Australians and New Zealanders. I believe he's got a Maori battalion that's just itching to go in with the bayonet—"

The assembled officers murmured approvingly. The colonel frowned. He did not like being interrupted. He tapped the map again and said:

"When you're quite finished, gentlemen. Thank you. Sari Bair, as I was saying, is to be heavily assaulted. By tomorrow morning, we should have the heights, gentlemen. Then, when the Light Horse has cleared and secured The Nek, the new British force and our own lads can move inland in great strides, sweep up the Peninsula and clear the road to Constantinople. Any questions?"

"If we may, sir," said Major Barton, "just go back to the Suvla Bay landings—"

"Yes? You seem to have some doubts, major. I can assure you the operation has been thoroughly planned. The staff work has been excellent. A very heavy naval bombardment will precede the landing. *Bacchante, Endymion, Grafton, Colne, Chelmer, Jonquil, Triad, Theseus* and heaven knows how many more ships are going to give the Turk a jolly pounding, I can assure you."

He paused. The distant rumble of the guns, a steady background to their lives for weeks, had suddenly swelled into a raging crescendo. The canvas roof of the dugout shivered in the hot breath of passing shells.

"That's for Lone Pine, I imagine," said Colonel Robinson, looking at his watch. "Yes." He raised his voice above the raging of the guns. "Major Barton—any more questions?"

"Is it true, sir, that the troops landing at Suvla Bay are all absolutely green? That they've never been into battle before?"

"I believe that is so, major. They are what's called the New Army, I believe. However, they have been very well trained—"

"Yes, in England's 'green and pleasant land', sir," said Major Barton. "The hopfields of Kent can hardly be a good preparation for the salt lake behind Nibrunesi Point, or the country beyond Suvla Plain."

"Don't worry, major, they've got a few experienced Australians with them. The Naval Bridging Team is landing with the English. They'll build pontoons and bridges and things to get the Tommies over the rough spots."

"Well, that's good news," said Major Barton stolidly.

"And now, major, let us get down to your particular share in tomorrow's, ah, business," said the colonel, with a touch of impatience. "You have studied The Nek, of course,"

"Yes. It's a fortress," said Major Barton shortly.

"At least five machine guns," said Lieutenant Gray. "Point blank range."

"We've considered that, major," said Colonel Robinson. "That—" with his thumb he indicated the barrage raving overhead, "—is nothing compared to what our guns are going to do to the Turks at The Nek tomorrow."

"By the time we've finished, major," said a senior artillery officer reassuringly, "there won't be a Turk within miles."

"A walkover," said the colonel. "Major, if you meet any opposition, which is unlikely after the guns have finished with them, take them out with the bayonet. The bayonet's got a great psychological effect. No bullets—just cold steel. That'll put the wind up them in Constantinople."

"Hmmm," said Barton.

"Major Barton," said Colonel Robinson testily, "I cannot impress upon you sufficiently the importance of this whole operation. This new British landing will give us the chance to break out, to take the fight home to the

Turk. If it fails—which it won't—we could be pinned down here for years."

"I appreciate that, sir, and I know my men will do their best," said Major Barton stiffly.

"Their very best, their very best!"

"Of course, sir."

"Now then," said the colonel briskly, turning to the senior artillery officer. "Everything all right at your end?"

"Yes sir. We're in position, ranged and ready to go. For once we have plenty of ammunition. Stacks of HE. So Major Barton needn't worry. We'll pour it into 'em."

Colonel Robinson gave a wintry smile.

"Perhaps you and Major Barton will get together and check times and things, eh? I have another conference in here in a few minutes."

Abruptly the gunfire dwindled to a few spaced shots and then ceased almost completely.

Outside the colonel's dugout Lieutenant Gray listened intently.

"They'll be hopping over now."

"God help them," said Major Barton, looking around for the artillery officers so he could synchronise his watch. They were gone. "What time do you make it, Gray?"

"Four sixteen now," said Lieutenant Gray.

"Accurate?" asked Barton.

"I think so, sir," shouted Gray as the rifles and machine guns began firing. He winced.

"There's a bloody big fight going on somewhere," said Major Barton sombrely. "Let's pray that we're winning it."

He set his watch. On the other side of the hillock the artillery officer stopped in his stride. He'd forgotten to synchronise. "Do it later," he thought and walked on. But he didn't. His watch was six minutes faster than Barton's and it gained another thirty seconds overnight.

Major Barton sat in the Light Horse brigade headquarters and listened with disbelief to the reports coming down from the heights.

"It's a shambles," he said angrily to Lieutenant Gray. "A bloody butchers' picnic!"

"They've taken Lone Pine, anyway," said Lieutenant Gray.

"That's the only good news," said Major Barton.

5

All night the reports dribbled in. The 15th Battalion had taken frightful punishment at Hill 971. The attack on Chunuk Bair had failed, despite superhuman efforts by the Australians, New Zealanders, Gurkhas and Punjabis. The usual trickle of wounded to the beach had become a bloody flood. The gullies and ravines running from the heights to the beach were jammed with dead and dying men. The IX Corps landing at Suvla Bay had bogged down with only a few hundred yards gained.

"I can't understand it," said Colonel Robinson, listening to the reports from Suvla Bay. "Aerial reconnaissance by our aeroplanes and the French couldn't find any big Turkish troop concentrations."

"Well, they're there now," said Major Barton, listening to the roar of battle outside.

"It all makes your attack on The Nek even more vital, major," said the colonel. "You must, absolutely must carry it."

"I've said we'll do our best, sir," said Major Barton.

"Jesus, Mary and Joseph," whispered Frank, awed. "Will you listen to that!"

The noise of battle raged and swelled about the cliffs. Every ridge and crest twinkled with muzzle-flashes. Starshells cracked and flared overhead and Very pistols trailed red and green lights across the sky.

"I've had this," said Frank. "I'm going to see how the boys are doing."

"Don't be a bloody fool, Frank," said Archy. "If you're trapped up there on the line and miss our hop over tomorrow, you'll be done for desertion in the face of the enemy or something. Just try to get some sleep."

"Sleep! With that bloody row going on! I'm going. Don't worry, I'll keep my head down. See you."

And he was gone into the clamorous dark, running and weaving his way upwards through the ravines and gullies through support and communication trenches choked with dead men, wounded men, terrified men; trenches where pale medical orderlies, working by candlelight and torchlight, tried to staunch great gaping wounds, to shut off severed arteries pulsing thick gouts of blood.

"Frank—Frank." He jumped as someone touched him: a livid face in the flickering gloom.

"Billy—Jesus, are you all right?"

Billy, smoke-grimed, sweat-stained, his uniform torn and covered with dirt, clutching a bloody emergency field dressing to his shoulder. Gritting his teeth to stop crying out with pain now that the numbness of shock was wearing off. Frank squatted beside him and put his arm around Billy's good shoulder.

"They got me Frank," Billy panted, his eyes wild. "The bastards got me before I'd even got out of the bloody trench, Frank. They were waiting for us! Oh God, oh God, they were waiting for us, Frank—"

"Take it easy, mate," said Frank. Blood oozed from the field dressing and ran down Billy's chest.

"It was bloody murder, Frank." Billy's chest heaved and he wept silently, the tears cutting through the sweat and grime on his cheeks.

"They got Barney, Frank. Barney's dead. Right beside me, as we got out of the trench. He fell and I thought—I thought he'd tripped, you know how clumsy he is—but he was dead, shot through the chest, bloody stone dead, Frank—" Billy rocked to and fro and Frank hugged him, helplessly.

"Shh shh," he said. "Shh. Take it easy, mate."

"There was one bloke," cried Billy, clutching Frank, "he got something low down in the guts and—his guts fell out. Frank, oh God, they fell out on the ground and he was trying to put them back—oh Jesus!"

"Ssh. Ssh, mate," said Frank desperately. "Take it easy, Billy. You're going to be all right. They'll look after you, mate, don't worry—" and then Frank was crying, too, angrily wiping the tears away with his free hand.

Billy rocked back and forth, clutching the sodden dressing to the wound. His eyes seemed to be fixed on something a long way away.

"They got Snowy, too," he said conversationally.

"Oh Jesus," said Frank.

"Yes. He almost made it to the Turkish lines. But they got him. Oh yes they got him. They got most of us. Barney's dead—did I tell you Barney's dead, Frank?"

"Yes, Billy," said Frank.

"But Snow's not dead. Snow's wounded. He almost made it to the Turks—I saw him, you know, while I was lying there."

"Where's he now, Billy?" asked Frank.

"Barney's dead, Frank. No good asking about Barney."

"Snowy, Billy." said Frank urgently. "Where's

Snow?''

"Snow? Oh, Snowy's down the line. They took him down the line on a stretcher. To Doc Morgan. On a stretcher. I walked, Frank. Someone helped me a bit but I walked.''

"Now just take it easy, Billy, and they'll fix you up. Look, Bill, it's your turn next. They'll patch you up and send you back to Cairo. Give you a decent bed and a bath, and you'll be fine. I've got to leave you now, Billy, and find Snowy. All right? See you—''

"See you, Frank," said Billy.

"Come on, mate," said a bloodstained orderly, "let's have a look at you.''

Frank left and fought his way down the crowded slopes to the beach.

6

The beach casualty clearing station stank of blood and chloroform. Wounded men lay and sat around it in dozens. Orderlies moved among the men, doing what they could, injecting morphine when the agony of torn flesh and shattered bone became too much to bear. Men moaned and cried out and swore, steadily, endlessly, and clenched their teeth and bit their blankets; and in the tent Captain Morgan and his assistants, red to their elbows, their aprons sodden rags, clamped severed veins and arteries, groped in writhing bodies for pieces of metal, closed sucking chest wounds, pushed spilling intestines back into torn bellies, picked pieces of bone from shattered skulls and tried not to the hear the threnody of suffering which made a ghastly undertone to the thunder of the guns.

Frightful vignettes leaped at Frank from the flickering gloom as he searched for Snowy: a lanky rifleman clutching an arm which ended in a bloody tangle of flesh and white tendons: "Trying to throw a bloody Turk bomb back, mate, and the bloody thing exploded in my hand!"

A man with no face, just a bloody mask from which a thick red fluid fell pat pat pat on the sand.

A young soldier with a gaping hole in his head, ripping off his bandage and trying to tear his brains out while two wounded comrades fought to restrain him.

The gasping bubbling breath of men with lung wounds.

Snowy was lying on a stretcher in a corner of the tent. He was horribly pale: all the blood seemed to have drained from his face. He lay quite still, staring at the canvas ceiling. He had been given morphine and an anti-tetanus injection and labelled and then carried aside to await transport to a hospital ship.

Frank knelt beside the blood-soaked stretcher. Snowy smiled, his pale face lighting up briefly.

"Frank."

"How are you, Snow? How are you?"

Snowy moved a hand, very slowly, and touched his belly.

"Something went in there, Frank. Just as I got to the Turk trenches. Felt like I'd been hit with a bloody hammer—"

His voice was thin, reedy. Frank bent closer.

"They won't let me eat or drink, Frank. Why d'you reckon that is?"

"They know what they're doing, Snow," said Frank. "Just leave it to them."

Snowy lay quietly, watching Captain Morgan's distorted shadow on the ceiling. Then he said: "Something's bust inside, Frank. It feels all—funny."

"You'll be good as new soon, Snow."

Snowy moved his head on the rolled-up shirt serving him as a pillow.

"Don't think so, Frank. Don't think so. Frank—I'm cold, freezing. Can you get me a blanket?"

"Sure, Snow. Hang on, I'll find one."

"Take this greatcoat, mate," said an orderly bending over a still figure on the stretcher beside Snowy. "This bloke won't need it any more."

Frank covered Snowy with the greatcoat, flinching as his hands touched something wet and sticky.

"Thanks, Frank," whispered Snow. He fumbled in his shirt pocket and took out a crumpled envelope.

"Post this for me, will you? It's my last letter to Mum. A good long one."

"I'll post it," said Frank. He squeezed Snowy's cold hand.

"Must go. See you, mate."

"See you, Frank," whispered Snowy.

Frank stopped on his way out and spoke to the orderly who had given him the greatcoat.

The orderly, grimy and bloody, looked up in exasperation from the shattered foot he was bandaging.

"How'll he be?" asked Frank, nodding towards Snowy.

The orderly studied Frank's face.

"You mates?"

Frank nodded.

"Joined up together."

"Well, he's got three machine gun bullets in the guts. Nothing we can do for him here. If he gets aboard a hospital ship in time, well, maybe—" the orderly shrugged. "Bad abdominals don't have much of a chance. Sorry, mate, but that's the truth."

He went out into the dark. The lines of wounded

stretched down the beach. Somewhere a man was sobbing, great retching gasps of pain and grief.

They carried Snowy out of the tent and down to a cutter. Two sailors lifted him aboard. He felt the cutter move under him and heard the gentle swash of the little waves. Above him the stars were terribly bright: he had never seen them so bright. He closed his eyes. He was very tired and still cold. Just a little doze. Just a little doze and when he got to the ship he would be able to tell them about this funny feeling in his stomach. All soft and liquid, it felt. Very strange. He'd forgotten to ask Frank about Barney and Billy, that was another strange thing. He tried to sit up but his head swam and a strong hand pushed him gently back.

"Easy, mate," said someone.

"Frank," he whispered, "ask Frank—"

He died before the cutter reached the white ship.

7

"You'd better get some sleep, Frank," said Archy. "It's an early start tomorrow."

Frank stared at him dully. His lips trembled.

"Have some of this," said Archy, passing Frank the rum flask. "A big one. That's right. Now try to get some sleep."

"Yes," said Frank. "All right." He curled up on his greatcoat, staring at the sea beyond the dugout. The noise of the battle rolled down the hills.

Archy sat and looked at the stars and thought of home and Uncle Jack. He opened his kit bag and took out his Kimberley Gift medal. It had grown a little tarnished and he cleaned it with his rifle cleaning kit. Then he hung it on its watered silk ribbon around his neck. The medal awoke memories: he turned to say something to Frank, but Frank was sleeping at last.

By the dim light of a slush lamp he wrote to his parents.

Dear Mum and Dad,

I know you probably still haven't forgiven me for running off, but I'm sure in my own mind that I was right and I'm sure you would think so if you were here now. We're getting ready to make an all-out assault on Johnny Turk and we all know we're going to give a good account of ourselves and our country. I am very sorry if I have made you worried but I am sure that you will end up being very proud of me and the boys with me.

Your loving son,
Archy

He sealed the letter, addressed it and put it in his kit bag. Then he remembered something: retrieving the letter, he wrote:

PS: If anything happens to me and the army sends you my things, please give my Kimberley Gift medal to Uncle Jack.

Chapter 8

THE NEK

5–6 August 1915

1

It was still dark when the Light Horse began assembling in
the gullies below The Nek. Major Barton and Lieutenant
Gray had been up all night, going from dugout to dugout,
trench to trench. Now they stood in the chilly dark and
watched the whirring grindstones squirting showers of
bright yellow sparks as the Light Horsemen put new edges
on their bayonets.

"They're still holding Lone Pine," said Lieutenant
Gray, watching the grindstone.

"At a hell of a price," said Major Barton. "The
Turk trenches were covered, I hear, so our blokes had to
lift off the timber before they could get at 'em. Imagine
dropping down blind into a trench full of Turks. Still,
they've cleared them out, about the only thing in this
whole benighted operation that's gone according to plan."

"How are the English doing at Suvla?"

"Bloody slowly. The whole advance seems to have faltered. Troops scattered all over the place. IX Corps GHQ seems to have lost contact with huge sectors of the line. The Kiwis have made some advances but they're taking shocking casualties."

"And now it's our turn," said Lieutenant Gray softly.

"I'm afraid so," said the major.

Lieutenant Gray was still watching the grindstone. It seemed to fascinate him.

"How do you feel about this bayonet-only business, sir?" he asked.

Major Barton snorted angrily.

"Bloody madness. Oh yes, I know the bayonet has a great psychological effect on the enemy—after all, no sane man wants eighteen inches of steel in his belly—but actually forbidding the men to fire—bloody nonsense. We might as well be back in the Middle Ages using lances and swords."

"Ours not to reason why," murmured Lieutenant Gray, and the major looked at him, surprised, before completing the line: "—ours but to do, and die. Yes, and what a fine gory debacle that poem records. Ah, there's a young man I want to see—I say, Lasalles—"

Archy came up and saluted, and suddenly something about his name and the freshness of his face jolted Barton's memory.

"Sir."

"What'd you say your time was for the hundred?"

"Under ten, sir."

"Your best time, boy."

"Uh, nine and five-sixteenths, sir,"

"You're Archy Hamilton, aren't you?"

"Yes, sir," said Archy.

The major nodded.

"Read about your run in a newspaper in Perth. I know your Uncle Jack."

Archy stood ramrod stiff.

The major lit his pipe, slowly, methodically.

"Don't worry. I'm not going to turn you in. Proud to have you with us." He paused for another puff on his pipe. "I need a runner tomorrow."

Archy swallowed.

"With respect, sir," he said, his voice trembling, "I'd rather fight."

He's not just saying it, either, thought Barton. Stubborn and brave like his uncle.

"Do you know how heavy the casualties have been at Lone Pine?"

"Yessir," said Archy. Inwardly he *was* scared but he was determined not to show it. Now or in the morning. "Am I brave?" he'd once asked his father. "Nobody can tell until they're tested," answered his father gruffly, "but I'd be surprised if you weren't."

Barton injected a note of toughness into his voice.

"I have to have a runner tomorrow, Hamilton. Communications won't last five minutes once the shelling starts."

Archy stared fixedly ahead.

"You could use Dunne, sir."

Barton looked questioningly at Archy.

"He's just as fast as I am. And I'm the one who really got him into this, sir. He wanted to start a bike shop."

Barton looked towards the dugout.

"Is he scared?"

Archy hesitated.

"No, sir—well, just a bit."

Major Barton rubbed his chin thoughtfully.

"Who isn't?" he said. "I'll sleep on it, Hamilton, and make up my mind in the morning."

Archy realised this was probably the best he could do.

"Thank you, sir," he said and retreated.

"It's a bit early, I know," said Major Barton turning to Lieutenant Gray, "but could I interest you in a glass of champagne?"

"It's three in the morning, sir," protested Lieutenant Gray.

"Don't be a stick-in-the-mud," said Major Barton. "This is a special occasion. Come along, man."

"It's a good drop," said the major, filling Lieutenant Gray's chipped enamel mug. "My wife gave it to me the day we sailed. I was keeping it to open on our anniversary next month. Our tenth, it will be. But I thought, well, one never knows what will happen. Cheers."

"Cheers," said Lieutenant Gray.

"Do you like opera?" asked the major, refilling their mugs.

"Don't know much about it," said Lieutenant Gray.

Major Barton busied himself with his gramophone. "You'll like this, I think. From *The Barber of Seville*. Quite rousing stuff."

The rich sounds of "Largo al factotum"—a trifle scratchy—filled the dugout, and passing soldiers grinned.

"Very enjoyable, sir," said Lieutenant Gray. "Those Italians have such—such gusto, don't they?"

"All that spaghetti and red wine," said the major. "And talking of wine, how's your glass—or mug?"

"Well, really, sir, I think—"

"Come on, Gray. Can't leave it. It goes flat, you know. Drink up."

2

In the forward trenches the Light Horse waited for dawn. The gunfire had died during the night: now single shots could be heard, bouncing echoes from crag to crag. Along the heights weary men were digging in for the coming day.

First light: the sky beyond the heights flushed soft pink, then flaming orange. A faint breeze stirred. It was going to be a beautiful day.

As the light crept into the trenches men began writing hurried letters, giving and taking messages for wives, girlfriends, mothers, fathers. The light grew stronger and winked on the newly sharpened bayonets. In shorts and shirtsleeves the 8th and 10th Light Horse regiments steeled themselves for battle. The first wave, pale faced, seized the stakes which had been driven into the trench walls to give them a handhold to haul themselves up by.

Frank stood beside Archy and watched the dawn paint the hills pink and gold.

"Any minute now," said Archy.

Frank swallowed. "Reckon the big guns'll—clear 'em out, Arch?" he asked.

"They'll blow 'em away. Don't worry, Frank. It'll be a walkover."

Lieutenant Gray strode up to them.

"Dunne, report to Major Barton. Quickly now, lad." He smiled suddenly. "You're off the hook. The major needs a runner, and you're the boy. Hop to it, man."

He turned away.

"Half your luck," said Archy. "Good luck, Frank."

Frank held out his hand.

"It's you who'll need the luck, mate. Well, see you when I see you, eh?"

Archy grinned. "Not if I see you first."

He watched Frank edge his way down the crowded trench.

"Ah, there you are, Dunne," said Major Barton. "Stick close to me, boy." He peered through his periscope at the Turkish trenches commanding The Nek: several lines of them, wired and sandbagged, with ominous black holes in the solid line of bags which, Major Barton knew, hid the snouts of Maxim machine guns. He grunted. "Looks solid as the bloody Rock of Gibraltar."

The barrage arrived with a whistling, roaring crash, a deafening shaking of air, rending of earth, smoke and flame and screaming metal shards. The ground beneath their feet shuddered. Smoke and debris rose all along the Turkish line. The Light Horsemen crouched in the trenches and cupped their hands over their ears.

"That's it," muttered the major, watching through his periscope. "Keep it up. Pour it on."

Lieutenant Gray came up with a message.

"Aeroplane from *Ark Royal* says the Turks are retiring from the forward trenches, sir," he shouted above the din. "The guns are lifting to straddle the support trenches." They watched as the shells walked up the slope opposite, seeking out the support trenches, reducing them to piles of rubble. They could smell cordite, lyddite and hot metal.

"Good shooting," said Major Barton appreciatively. "Damn fine shooting, eh, Gray?"

"Yes, sir," said Lieutenant Gray. "Hope they leave something for us, sir."

Major Barton glanced at his watch.

"Should be stopping soon."

"The first wave's ready to go, sir. Keen as mustard."

The first wave mounted the firestep.

Major Barton broke his revolver and checked the cylinder.

He looked at Lieutenant Gray, a smile lighting his face, and said:

"Remember, Gray, he that outlives this fight, and comes safe home—*Henry IV*, wasn't it?"

Lieutenant Gray winced as a flight of shells shrieked overhead.

Major Barton stared at the smoke and flame exploding along the Turkish line.

"They're certainly pouring it on. Sounds like big navy guns amongst them. Our old friend *Queen Elizabeth*, perhaps."

"I hope so," said Lieutenant Gray fervently. "I'm told that every one of her fifteen-inch shrapnel shells holds twenty-four-thousand balls."

They watched the torn earth erupting.

"That's got to clear them out," said Lieutenant Gray.

"Of course it will," said Major Barton. "Nothing could live through that."

Sergeants walked down the trench shouting: "Check your rifles. Nothing up the spout, lads. First wave ready on the firestep. Stand by. Bayonets only. Bayonets only. Check your breeches."

"A few minutes to the end of the barrage, sir," said Lieutenant Gray.

"Stand by, first wave," bellowed the sergeants. "Once you're hopped over, don't hesitate. Don't look back. Keep going. Fast as you can. Use your bayonets."

Major Barton glanced along the crowded trenches. He held out his hand to Lieutenant Gray.

"We'd better get into our positions," he said. "Good luck, Gray."

They shook hands.

"Good luck, sir," said Gray. His face was pale but determined.

The barrage stopped with shocking suddenness: the lifted dust settled and the oily smoke coiled away on the gentle breeze. It was so quiet that the men's breathing could be heard, all up and down the line.

Major Barton stared toward the Turkish trenches, now coming into sight again through the clearing dust and smoke.

Lieutenant Gray grabbed his arm.

"Sir, that bombardment's not over. Seven more minutes to go."

Expectant faces watched Major Barton from the firestep. He looked at his watch.

"You're right. Must be reloading for one last salvo. Lull Abdul into thinking it's over, eh?" He turned to Frank.

"Dunne, get Colonel Robinson on the telephone at Brigade. Ask him what the devil's happening."

In the crowded trenches soldiers stirred.

"What's the hell's happening?" asked a young trooper next to Archy. "Why's the shelling stopped?"

"I don't know," said Archy uneasily.

Frank cranked the telephone desperately.

An angry young captain forced his way through to Major Barton.

"What's happening, sir? My men are ready to go!"

"We're trying to find out now," said the major.

"Sir, we've got to go now. If the Turks get back into the trenches, they'll cut us to ribbons."

"I realise that, captain," said the major. "Dunne—Dunne, have you got Brigade yet?"

"Still trying, sir."

A young lieutenant, surveying the Turkish lines through a periscope, swung around, his face ashen.

"Sir—they're pouring back into the trenches, sir!"

Frank got through to Colonel Robinson. The colonel's voice shook with anger.

"Tell Major Barton I don't care what his blasted watch says. Mine says the Light Horse should've gone over three minutes ago, so tell him to send them now. *Now*, do you understand, *now*!"

"Sir, the Turks are getting back into their trenches," said Frank.

The colonel's voice rose to a shriek.

"Dammit, man, did you hear me? Tell Barton to go!"

He slammed the telephone down.

"Colonel Robinson says go, sir," said Frank.

"My God," said the major. He looked at the Turkish trenches. Bayonets glittered above the parapet now: a gleaming frieze of steel, a giant metallic porcupine preparing itself for battle.

"All right," said the major.

"First wave, advance."

A whistle shrilled.

One hundred and fifty Light Horsemen, yelling and cheering, launched themselves over the parapet.

The Turkish lines exploded in a wavering sheet of flame. One long, ripping, roaring bellow. And the Light Horsemen fell, like puppets whose strings had suddenly been cut, in clumps, singly, some with a cry, some soundlessly, some before they had cleared the parapet. Their useless unloaded rifles clattered, the newly-sharpened bayonets shone in the dirt thirty yards from the Turkish lines. Some of the wounded fell back into the trench. Some fell on top of the second wave taking up positions on the firestep. Others tried to force themselves into the very earth itself to avoid the hailstorm of flying lead.

The firing stopped. Turkish officers could be heard shouting orders. Pale blue cordite smoke drifted above the Turkish positions until it was twitched away by the breeze.

"Jesus, Mary and Joseph," whispered Frank.

The silver whistle trilled again. The second wave went over the parapet, scrambling past the dead and the dying. Running into a storm of gunfire, some of them clutching yellow and red flags to mark the forward limit of the advance. The flags flapped among the bodies ten yards from the Light Horse trenches.

And still sergeants moved down the trenches where the third wave waited on the firestep reciting their litany: "Magazine cut-offs down. Nothing up the spout, lads. Go in with the bayonets."

Stepping carefully among the bloody debris in the trench. Ignoring the frightful noises raging around them, the sobs and gasps and groans, the bloody gurgles.

"Stretcher bearers. Stretcher bearers. Jesus, where are those bloody stretcher bearers!"

The stretcher bearers, bloody enough, worked like mules, and still the cry ran up and down the trenches.

"Stretcher bearers. Stretcher bearers. Jesus, where are those bloody stretcher bearers!"

The firing ceased. Not one Light Horseman had reached the Turkish lines. But one brave boy, still clutching his yellow and red flag in one hand and his shattered rifle in the other, had got within thirty feet of the target before a machine gun had almost severed his legs from his body: he lay on his face and the dry earth sucked the blood pulsing from his ruptured femoral arteries.

Archy leaned against the trench wall, closed his eyes and

tried to close his ears against the frightful sounds of the wounded. His hands were shaking and he forced himself to clutch his rifle more tightly. It can't go on, he told himself. They'll have to stop it. We're being wiped out. Wiped out! There'll be no one left to go home.

"My God," said a voice near Archy. "Just look at that, will you!"

The Turks were climbing out of their trenches, settling themselves on the parapets. Machine guns were manhandled over the sandbags and settled into new positions giving them a bigger field of fire. Ammunition belts were passed up. Some of the Turks were laughing and smoking.

"Like they're in a bloody shooting gallery," said someone in a hushed voice, and another soldier laughed grimly. "They are, mate, an' we're the bloody coconuts!"

3

Lieutenant Gray was on the telephone. He replaced the instrument and said to Major Barton:

"Still little progress at Suvla Bay, sir. Division reports that some of the men are still on the beach."

Major Barton nodded, watching the Turkish lines. "Madness," he muttered. "Madness, madness."

The telephone rang again. Lieutenant Gray snatched it up. Colonel Robinson roared at him:

"What the devil's happening up there, Gray? Why aren't your men attacking?"

"It's pretty confusing at the moment, sir," said Lieutenant Gray. "The timing of the barrage, sir, well, we've had pretty severe casualties. The Turks are back in their trenches—"

"Has it been successful or hasn't it, man?" raged Colonel Robinson over the wire. "Damn this connection. Hullo! Hullo! Can you hear me? Gray—are you there?"

"Yes sir. I'm here."

"Are your men at the objective? Are they in the Turk trenches? Speak up, man!"

Lieutenant Gray hesitated.

"There was a report, sir, we're checking it, that one of our marker flags was seen near the Turkish trench—"

"Well, dammit, why aren't your men moving? Why's the attack stopped? On whose authority. Tell Barton—no, dammit, put Barton on the line."

The phone died. Lieutenant Gray jiggled the receiver.

"Dead, sir," he said to Major Barton. The major finished scribbling a note. He folded the piece of paper and passed it to Frank.

"Get that to the colonel, Dunne. Quickly, now, boy!"

Frank seized the message and ran.

A young trooper beside Archy was trembling, his eyes starting out of his white face.

"Are they—are they going to make us go?" he asked.

"Not much point now," said Archy. "They can't make us go now."

A few yards to his right a soldier who had been shot through both lungs was gasping his life away in bloody froth. A weary stretcher bearer dabbed weakly at his smeared lips with a blood-soaked cloth.

Automatically, Archy began doing the breathing exercises Uncle Jack had taught him. Long, deep breaths. It made him feel calmer. He closed his eyes.

Colonel Robinson ran his eyes hurriedly over Major Barton's scrawled note. He hunched his shoulders in an exasperated shrug.

"Dammit, can't the fool of a man understand? The attack on The Nek *must* go ahead. This whole operation is collapsing on every front! The English have made no progress at Suvla, and the New Zealanders are taking a fearful beating on Chunuk Bair. Everything hinges on The Nek! Tell him—"

"Sir," said Frank. "I don't think you appreciate the position. The Turks are back in their trenches. Major Barton's men are being cut down before they've gone five yards!"

Colonel Robinson glared at him.

"Your marker flags have been seen near the Turkish lines! Lieutenant Gray told me so!"

"Sir, the man who carried those flags is dead. There's not a living Australian within fifty yards of the Turks, sir."

Colonel Robinson lifted the telephone and cranked wildly.

"Still haven't fixed that blasted line. Where the hell are the engineers? Isn't anyone doing his job today?"

"The engineers are helping clear wire on the slopes of Sari Bair, sir," said Frank.

The colonel seized a field signal pad, scribbled a note, and gave it to Frank.

"Get that to Barton. And impress upon him that I mean it. That attack must go on! Do you understand? It must go on! And if Barton doesn't obey this order instantly, he may hand over to his second in command and come back down the line to me, and I'll see that he's damn well sent home!"

Frank took the message and flashed the colonel a look of pure loathing. The colonel narrowed his eyes.

"One moment," he said coldly.

"Sir?" said Frank.

"Have you heard of dumb insolence, private?"

"Yes sir."

"Well, get out of here before you're on a charge."

The major, his expression incredulous, read the colonel's message.

"Who the hell told him we'd got a marker flag at the Turk lines?" he blazed. "Gray?"

"I was told there was one seen well up front, sir," said Lieutenant Gray.

"Yes. And you can still see it, you idiot, Gray! And the man who got it there is lying dead beside it. My God!"

"Excuse me, sir," said Frank. "Why don't you go above Robinson's head, sir?"

Major Barton stared at him.

"Sir, I could get a message to General Gardner—"

"General Gardner?"

Major Barton and Lieutenant Gray exchanged glances.

"General Gardner—you're absolutely right, of course, Dunne!" Major Barton scribbled out a message. "Go like the wind!"

Forcing his way through the waiting third and fourth assault waves, Frank met Archy. They stared at each other, and managed a brief silent handshake. That was all.

General Gardner's headquarters were half a mile beyond Colonel Robinson's—half a mile of thorn scrub, ravine, cliff and gully. For a moment Frank hesitated. The safe route, away from the snipers' rifles—down the gullies, along the beach, and up a ravine directly below General Gardner's headquarters—would take him at least half an hour each way, toiling up and down those narrow passages choked with men and equipment. An hour all together. By then, a thousand men, Archy among them, would have been launched into eternity.

He had no option. He hurled himself out of the trench and across the savage hillside, dodging along "night only" roads, leaping across salients marked with ominous skull and crossbone signs, while snipers' bullets spat and whined around him.

General Gardner, a tall, white-haired man, read Major Barton's signal and frowned.

"Hmmm. It does seem pointless to go on—they really are suffering heavy casualties, are they?"

"They're being slaughtered, sir," said Frank.

"On the other hand, it is a vital position," mused the general. "Absolutely vital—"

An aide handed him a message.

"IX Corps HQ report that 32 Brigade's advancing strongly on Tekke Tepe, sir," he said, "and the 11th Division have already established a Corps HQ inland from East Beach."

"Well, if they're digging in for a long stay," said the general, "it's not really much use throwing away any more men at The Nek. I know that Colonel Robinson wants to continue but I really think the attack should be—"

Gardner hesitated indecisively.

"Cancelled!" said Frank with a finality that made it less a question than a command.

"Yes, cancelled," said Gardner, almost relieved that someone else had said it for him.

"Thank you, sir," said Frank and leaped from the tent.

His lungs burned: his legs quivered as though the muscles had turned to jelly. The tortured landscape wavered before his eyes as he forced his body to keep going. Up this gully.

Over this ridge. Down this ravine where the sniper's bullets whistled and sang. Another half mile. Think of Archy. Something struck his foot a violent blow and he fell heavily, rolling down the slope, clawing at the bushes. He lay gasping, sucking in great gulps of air. He got me, he thought. Bastard sniper got me. Can't feel anything. Funny I can't feel anything. He forced himself to look at his foot. A bullet had ripped the heel off his boot. Carefully he put two fingers into the ragged tear, wincing at the thought of feeling blood and torn flesh, cringing at the thought of the pain to come. Nothing. The bullet had ripped the heel off without touching him. Come on, he told himself, get up. Keep going. They'll be putting Archy over the top any minute now. That bastard Robinson will know Barton's stalling. He'll get that line fixed and order the Light Horse to go. To go on and be killed, all of them, all your mates. Slowly he got to his knees. The sniper saw the movement and fired again. The bullet raised a squirt of dust near Frank's right hand. He snatched it away as though he'd touched a live wire. Then he was up and running again, dodging across the gully with the bullets pattering around him and shrieking away into the sky.

4

Private Ellis whistled as he worked. Private Ellis was a fatalist. He also had very little imagination, which was just as well, because his situation would have been profoundly disturbing to a man with a lively mind. Private Ellis was lying in a shallow scrape in the rocky soil, splicing the telephone line linking the Light Horse with Colonel

Robinson's headquarters. The engineer who had tried to repair the break a little while before was lying dead a few feet from Private Ellis. He had been shot through the top of the head while bending over the break in the wire: the sniper's nine-millimetre jacketed bullet had punched a small hole in the crown of his head and left a great torn gash at its point of exit under his jaw. The bullet, distorted and flattened by the engineer's skull, had sent out massive shock waves as it ploughed through his brain, and these had forced his eyes outwards so they almost burst from their sockets, and the dead man seemed to be watching Private Ellis work with pop-eyed wonder. Private Ellis, for all his fatalism, had no wish to join the dead engineer, so he kept his head down, snuggling deeper into his scrape in the ground, and worked with only his hands exposed. The sniper sent round after round at Private Ellis's busy hands, and peppered them with sand and small rock splinters, but he was shooting downhill at an awkward angle, and none of his Mauser bullets had Private Ellis's name on them that day. The linesman gave the wire a last crimp with his pliers and slid backwards down the gully to comparative safety, and the telephone jangled in Colonel Robinson's dugout. An aide snatched it up.

"Line's back, sir," he said. "Shall I get Major Barton?"

At the colonel's curt nod he whirled the crank furiously, barked, "Hullo! Hullo! Oh, damn. Hullo! Major Barton? Hang on, sir, colonel wants you."

Colonel Robinson snatched the telephone.

"Barton, what the hell are you playing at, man? Didn't you get my message? Those men should have gone, dammit. Marker flags have been seen along the Turkish trenches!"

"The man who carried them there is dead, sir! And so are hundreds of my men!"

"Your orders are to attack, Barton, and to keep on

attacking until those trenches are taken.''

"Sir, with respect, I'm seeking reconfirmation of those orders from General Gardner.''

"You're what? Barton, I'm now giving you a direct order. Do you understand me? A direct order. You understand the implications of that, Barton? Your orders are to attack, and to attack immediately.''

"It's cold-blooded murder, sir.''

"That's an order, Barton. Push on with the attack at once, or hand over to your second in command and come down the line.''

"I'll stay with my men, sir.''

"Then attack with your men, damn you!''

"I intend to, colonel,'' said Major Barton. "I can't ask my men to do something I'm not prepared to do myself.'' He replaced the receiver and turned to Lieutenant Gray.

"I'm going with the third wave, Gray. Then it's you with the fourth, I'm afraid.''

"But, sir, Dunne—''

"May not have got through, Gray. We can't wait.''

Lieutenant Gray watched him draw his revolver and mount the firestep. He turned and looked at the lines of men.

"We're going, lads,'' he said. "I know every one of you will do your utmost. Good luck to you all, and God bless you.'' He turned away and grasped the climbing peg.

Archy slowly took off his Kimberley Gift medal and hung it from one of the climbing pegs. As though in a dream he seemed to hear Uncle Jack's voice again, to see the pepper trees behind the house, the cockatoos in white clouds at sunset, to hear the thunder of rain on the corrugated iron roof. Pictures ran across his mind's eye, fast as summer lightning: Billy Snakeskin. Zac. Stumpy and the camel. Mary Stanton. Frank learning to ride. The images flickered and ran together and he heard himself saying softly: "What are your legs, boy? *Springs. Steel springs*. And what are they going to do, boy? *Hurl me down the track*. How fast can you run, boy?" Tears rained from his eyes and pattered on the bloody dust of the trench floor. "How fast can you run, boy! *Fast as a leopard!* Then let's see you do it!"

The silver whistle shrilled.

Archy was over the parapet and among the dead. For a second it was breathlessly still: cordite smoke from the Turkish guns eddied among the bodies.

Then the gunfire crashed around him. He ran as he had never run before, head high, rifle forgotten. He was alone, at the head of the field. "How fast can you run, boy? *Like a leopard!*"

He was still running with head high, his eyes half-closed, when the nearest Maxim gun team clipped a fresh belt into their weapon, and Archy fell with a roaring in his ears.

Lieutenant Gray, on the firestep, turned irritably as someone seized him by the arm.

"Dunne!"

Frank sank to the floor of the trench, "It's cancelled! General Gardner's orders!" Then he screamed a long cry of anger and rage and was violently sick. Lieutenant Gray slowly holstered his revolver. He looked at the dead and the dying in the trench and the bloody debris in No Man's Land.

"My God," he said. "My God."

Something winked in the early sunlight. Frank looked at it dully, uncomprehending. Then he recognised it, as it twirled on its watered silk ribbon, catching the sun. Archy's Kimberley Gift medal.

Epilogue

They cleaned Billy up aboard the hospital ship, and took chips of splintered bone from his shoulder, and drugged him, and sent him to Alexandria, and from there by train to Cairo, where they operated again, and took his arm off. For weeks Billy floated in a strange half-world of pain and chloroform, and it was a long time before he was well enough to sit on the verandah of the Heliopolis Palace Hospital and watch the jacarandas and oleanders bloom.

Major Barton died with his men at The Nek. He was killed before he had run ten feet, and his revolver was never fired.

Frank Dunne survived Gallipoli, but never got his bike shop in Perth. After the evacuation in December, the tattered remnants of the Light Horse were shipped back to Egypt and combined with the New Zealand Mounted Rifles (most of whom, like the Light Horse, had fought

277

dismounted in Gallipoli) to form the Anzac Mounted Division. Frank's riding ability—or lack of it—drew considerable unfavourable attention from the division's officers and non coms, but probably saved his life. After the first unsuccessful attack on Gaza he was—to his great relief—given more and more administrative work to do. He had a flair for figures and an ability to scrounge almost unobtainable stores which amounted to genius. Frank spent the rest of the war in Egypt, Syria and Palestine, and watched General Allenby's triumphal entry into Jerusalem through the Jaffa Gate in 1917.

He caught dysentery and malaria and yellow jaundice and beat them all to come home a warrant officer in 1918. By that time it was plain that the motor-car had arrived to stay. Frank took night classes in motor mechanics, got transferred to the Transport Corps and later, after being commissioned, to the infant Australian Armoured Corps. He retired a major in 1933, and went into partnership as a Ford motor dealer in Perth with his youngest brother, Mick. During the early years of World War II he became quite famous for his fiery sabre-rattling recruiting speeches at Rotary lunches.

Lieutenant Gray got through the war without a scratch. He fought with the Anzac Mounted Division at Magdhaba, at Rafa, at both attacks on Gaza and at Beersheba, and died in his bed at the age of seventy-four.

Sergeant Sayers was slightly wounded on Gallipoli, during a night attack along Rhododendron Ridge. He was patched up and spent a pleasant two weeks convalescing in Cairo. He was sent back to Gallipoli and mentioned in despatches for his work during the evacuation. After that remarkable operation Sergeant Sayers was posted to France and killed, with several thousand other

Australians, amid the mud and blood of Frommelles. His body was never found.

Colonel Robinson was promoted to brigadier and killed by a German shell while acting as a brigadier-general (non-substantive) near Pozieres in 1916.

Sister Cooley could not bear to open her diary after Lone Pine and The Nek. She was badly run down when she got back to a shore hospital in Egypt, and came down with a fever, malaria or dengue, nobody seemed sure which; and when she recovered she was sent to France, where she was present at sights too horrible to record. She became ill again, this time with enteric fever, and almost died. She was posted to England to convalesce before being shipped home, but before a berth could be found for her on an Australia-bound ship, the Spanish influenza pandemic broke out, and she could not be spared. She finally sailed aboard the *Suevic* in the middle of 1919.

On the voyage back she made the last entry in her diary:

> *September 28, 1919: We have crossed the Equator, and last night I saw the Southern Cross again—for the first time in five years. Now I truly believe that I am going home!*

Many others never went home. The Australians lost 7594 men at Gallipoli; 2431 New Zealanders died with them. The English forces—which included Indians, Gurkhas, and other colonial troops—lost 119,696 men. The French buried 27,004 soldiers from metropolitan and colonial France. The Turkish empire was bled of 55,127 men. These were the known dead. Many thousands of others were simply posted as "missing"; many, many thousands more were wounded. Almost one million men were engaged on the bloody Peninsula: more than 500,000 of them, among all the armies, were casualties in one way or another.

P.S.

Interviews,
features and
insights
included
in a new
section…

The Anzacs at Gallipoli

THE TURKISH port of Gallipoli, at the entrance to the Sea of Marmara, was a strategic position, and here the Allies planned to take control of the Dardanelles, the passage leading to the Black Sea, in order to open it for Allied shipping. In theory, with the Allies anchored in the shadow of Constantinople, the Turks might surrender in terror, leaving Germany and Austria–Hungary exposed, and the sea lanes open to resupply Russia with essential munitions. The Allies could then head directly west to Berlin.

A brief naval battle began on 18 March 1915 — but after losing three key ships and over 700 Allied lives, the Royal Navy's fleet withdrew without clearing a single Turkish mine or destroying a single Turkish gun. It was the turn of the soldiers.

The generals thought the job could be done in three days: land on the Gallipoli Peninsula, clear it of Turks and disable the seaward defences. But they too failed, and at a much greater cost in lives than even the naval assault. For 259 days, from April 1915 to January 1916, the Allied forces — a total of about 500,000 men — hung on to the precarious cliffs and coves of Gallipoli.

The force that landed on 25 April 1915 was mostly made up of soldiers from the British 29th Division and 1st Royal Naval Infantry Division, the French 1st Infantry Division, the 29th Indian Infantry Brigade and of course the Australia New Zealand Army Corps (ANZACs), plus smaller contingents from many different parts of the British empire including the Assyrian Jewish Refugee Mule Corps.

The Anzacs landed in a location now known as Anzac Cove, which bore no resemblance at all to the description and maps given to the commanding officers in their briefings. Instead of a flat beach with gently undulating terrain behind, they were faced with shrub-covered rocky formations and sharp ridges that nearly ran into the sea, with deep valleys and gullies running in between them. Surprisingly, there was much less Turkish resistance than expected — until the Australians and New Zealanders realised they'd been put ashore about 2 kilometres past their assigned beach. The source of the mistake has never been clarified — it may have been human error, although the Navy maintained that an uncharted current pushed them off course.

Despite the chaos and confusion on the beach — with soldiers not sure which direction they were to advance in, getting separated from their battalions, and still more troops landing and adding to the disorder — the Anzacs quickly pushed inland until they met the tough commander of the Turkish 19th Division. Mustapha Kemal was one of the greatest soldiers his country ever produced and one of the best commanders to emerge from the war. His men drove the Anzacs back off the heights of the peninsula and almost back to the beach, where the numbers of wounded were growing.

For the next several months, the Anzacs remained dug into trenches. The sniping rarely stopped and Turkish bombs kept raining down. Unlike their Turkish opponents the Anzacs had not been

> **For the next several months, the Anzacs remained dug into trenches. The sniping rarely stopped and Turkish bombs kept raining down.**

equipped with hand grenades and so could only hope to throw the Turk's projectiles back before they exploded. In the end, the Gallipoli Peninsula never came anywhere near being cleared of Turks. The British never managed to push more than five miles inland, and though the Anzacs fought with great skill they got little further than the heights overlooking the beaches.

On 6 August 1915, hoping to break the deadlock, the commander General Ian Hamilton mounted another landing further north at Suvla Bay — and although the area was lightly defended, the British troops were unsuccessful. In the meantime, the Australians were staging a series of attacks that were designed to draw off Turkish troops that could have been used against Suvla. At the Nek, the 3rd Light Horse were commanded to advance on foot across a very restricted front to attack trenches full of Turkish troops. Three waves went forward, one after the other, each was slaughtered by the Turks, none of the attackers gaining much more than a few yards before they were cut down. The Turks even climbed out of the trenches and perched on the parapets to get better shots. This, and similar failures at Lone Pine and Helles, were massacres made even more bitter by the lack of success of the Suvla landings.

Conditions for the Anzacs and in fact for both sides continued to decline. At least the Allies' troops had ships bringing supplies — the Turkish army were supplied by a single rail line into the peninsula and were often starving. Casualties for both sides were massive, living conditions were poor, the flies were at nightmarish proportions and the stress and monotony of living in the trenches took a heavy toll. The summer heat was blistering, and followed by a stormy, muddy winter. Hamilton wrote, 'The beautiful battalions of April 25th are wasted skeletons', and, eventually, Kitchener recommended withdrawal. Troops — which included 83,000 Anzacs, plus their 5000 donkeys and horses, 2000 vehicles of all kinds and 200 pieces of artillery — were removed slowly and surreptitiously, with the final rearguard being withdrawn silently overnight so that on 8 January 1916, the Turkish troops woke to find themselves alone on the peninsula.

Over 8000 Australians died at Gallipoli, out of an estimated 50,000 Allied deaths (including the French forces). There were approximately 250,000 Allied casualties, and Turkish casualties are estimated at over 300,000. Most are buried at the Ari Burnu Cemetery at Anzac Cove. ■

Visiting Gallipoli

UNTIL RECENTLY, the battlefields of Turkey's Gallipoli Peninsula were not on the usual tourist route, and certainly visiting them was not the backpacker rite of passage it has become today. By 1984, the main dawn service at Lone Pine attracted only 300 people. But over the past 20 years the commemoration of Anzac Day has become a major event on Turkey's tourism calendar. In 2002, the dawn service attracted a crowd of over 15,000 people and again in 2004 up to 15,000 young Australians defied Federal Government terrorism warnings to attend. (In comparison, in the entire year of 1995 the area was visited by 14,000 overseas tourists.) Year round, thousands of Australians visit the area in organised groups and independently. In Australia too, attendances, especially by young people, at Anzac Day events have increased markedly. Hundreds of articles have been written on the phenomenon. The Australian National Museum in Canberra has an exhibition on the "Anzac Pilgrims — recent Australian experiences of Gallipoli," which features journals, letters home, memories and images from young Australians visiting the peninsula. Journalist Tony Wright has written a personal memoir of his trip to the area. Even TV audiences for the ceremonies are growing — the ABC's coverage of the 2002 Anzac Day events was watched by 2.1 million viewers compared with 1.6 million in 2001, for example.

But why this relatively recent upsurge in interest in commemorating Anzac Day? Some credit the release of the film *Gallipoli* with sparking an interest from a new generation of Australians, or at least coinciding with a renewed perspective on Australian history. But perhaps it's that in the rebellious sixties and seventies, young Australians questioned the "sacredness" of Anzac Day, that to the anti-Vietnam War protestors, the day represented a glorification of war and of militarism. Anzac Day belonged to the diggers, so why not let it die along with them? But to their children, young people whose closest connection to war might be a photo of their great-grandfather, Anzac Day has become important once again. Is it an assertion of "Australianness" at a time when Australia's unique identity appears threatened by globalisation? Is it that, as the generation of men and women who experienced World Wars One and Two first-hand die out, more people have become interested in their family history and their country's wartime heritage?

In his official Anzac Day address at Lone Pine in 2003 Treasurer Peter Costello said, "Today there are many young Australians here. Like their great-grandfathers and great-great-grandfathers they have travelled half a world away from their homes to be here today out of love of their country. They want to pay homage and to take something of the ideals that were established here that day in 1915. They want the ideals of Anzac to inspire and nourish them again. And they want the legacy never to be forgotten."

66 Over the past twenty years the commemoration of Anzac Day has become a major event on Turkey's tourism calendar. 99

For many, the journey becomes an almost spiritual experience — a journey to a landscape rich in meaning, with the war graves of the 8709 young Australians nearby causing huge emotional impact. Travellers returning from Gallipoli talk about their desire to say thank you to their ancestors, about the "pilgrimage" to this site where so many lives were lost. There is a search for meaning: why did so many Australians fight and die here? What does that mean for Australians?

But there are other, perhaps less noble reasons too. More young Australians travel overseas now than ever before, and visiting the Australian war graves and other sites of interest at Gallipoli has become part of the recognised tourist itinerary, much like Pamplona's running of the bulls or Munich's beer-drenched Oktoberfest. Package tours combine stops at the war memorial sites with free time in the bars of Chanakkale or Eceabat, or a chance to wind down in Istanbul after the Anzac "experience". Many of the young backpackers don't come directly from Australia, in fact many come from working holidays in London where Anzac Day conveniently falls between Easter and an English Bank Holiday. It has become a ritual, part of their "overseas experience".

Or is the reason, as Manning Clark wrote, simply "something too deep for words"?

Those who visit the battlefields will find a memorial dedicated to the mothers of those soldiers who lost their lives. Written by Mustapha Kemal, the Turkish Commander who went on to be the founder of a Turkish

Republic and who was renamed Kemal Atatürk (Father of the Turks):

"Those heroes that shed their blood and lost their lives … You are now lying in the soil of a friendly country. Therefore, rest in peace. There is no difference between the Johnnies and the Mehmets to us where they lie side by side, here in this country of ours. You, the mothers, who sent their sons from far away countries … Wipe away your tears. Your sons are now lying in our bosom and are in peace. After having lost their lives on this land, they have become our sons as well." ■

Peter Weir
and Gallipoli

IN 1975, after finishing his film *Picnic at Hanging Rock,* Peter Weir began thinking about what his next project should be. "I was thinking of a story set in France, dealing with the big battles of 1916–17, then someone said to me why not make a film about Gallipoli, it's the obvious one", he said in a 1981 interview. "The following year I went to London for the opening of *Picnic* and thought I should take a look at Gallipoli along the way. I went to Istanbul, hired a car and drove to the battlefield, an extraordinary experience. I saw no one in two days of climbing up and down slopes and wandering through the trenches, finding all sorts of scraps left by the armies: buttons and bits of old leather, belts, bones of donkeys, even an unbroken Eno's Fruit Salts bottle. I felt somehow I was really touching history, that's really what it was, and it totally altered my perception of Gallipoli. I decided then and there that I'd make the film.

"I wrote a story outline and gave it to David [Williamson] and that became the first of a series of drafts. Our first approach was to tell the whole story from enlistment in 1914 through to the evacuation of Gallipoli at the end of 1915, but we were not getting at what this thing was, the burning centre that had made Gallipoli a legend. I could never find the answers in any books and it certainly wasn't evolving in any of our drafts, so we put the legend to one side and simply made up a story about two young men, really got to know them, where they came from, what happened to them along the way, spent more time getting to the battle and less time on the battlefield.

"The draft fell into place. By approaching the subject obliquely, I think we had come as close to touching the source of the myth as we could. I think there's a Chinese proverb — it's not the arriving at one's destination but the journey that matters. *Gallipoli* is about two young men on the road to adventure, how they crossed continents and great oceans, climbed the pyramids and walked through the ancient sands of Egypt and the deserts of the outback to their appointment with destiny at Gallipoli. The end of the film is really all about that appointment and how they coped with it. I don't think we could have sat down in the early stages and got this — it took years of talking, writing, arguing, to finally get back to something incredibly simple." Williamson and Weir chose the Light Horse for their character's regiment because "they were the regiment that fought at the Battle of the Nek which we see at the end of the film. You only had to read the official account of the battle by Bean to gain a respect and admiration for the type of man in the 10th Light Horse, a type of Australian largely vanished from the country," says Weir.

Picnic at Hanging Rock producer Patricia Lovell came on board in 1979 and after five years of planning and with a budget of $2.6 million, filming began. Most of the almost five-month shoot took place in Australia from July to October 1980, using locations such as the South Australian town Beltana for Figtree Crossing, Archy's home in WA, and Lake Torrens for the WA desert, while the coastline near Port Lincoln was transformed into Gallipoli. Some filming was also done in a small town near Cairo in Egypt, although Weir says the reason more filming wasn't done in Egypt was that it was "too complex getting Anglo-Saxon extras. We needed large numbers — we finished by using almost 4000 people" in the training and battle scenes.

Weir describes the filming of certain scenes as being "almost like planning a battle — we used 600 or 700 extras in some of the battle scenes. Each day, working with army advisers, we drilled our 'soldiers,' marching, presenting arms, cleaning weapons, etc. For the first couple of days you could see they didn't like it much, then slowly they began to change. Mark Egerton [assistant director] and I used to keep them informed of what the sequence was, reminding them of what the original men went through at that moment. Sometimes we handed them out printed notes so they could get a historical summary of what actually happened. So really they were re-enacting rather than acting. I'll never forget one night addressing the men from the boats, feeling a bit guilty because we'd keep them in the boats and wading through the surf for five hours while we filmed shells whizzing around them. I said: 'I'm sorry it's been five hours, you're released now and you might go home and get a bit of sleep.' And one of the extras said indignantly: 'Don't be sorry. We only spent five hours, the real Anzacs had to go up the hills under fire, march an hour and a half, then try to sleep with only a thin blanket over them.'" ∎

About the screenwriter
David Williamson — Life and Work

DAVID KEITH WILLIAMSON was born in Melbourne in 1942 and grew up in Bairnsdale, Victoria. He studied mechanical engineering and psychology, working as a design engineer and then lecturing in thermodynamics and social psychology before leaving teaching to write full-time. His first full-length play was *The Coming Of Stork* which premiered at the infamous La Mama Theatre in Melbourne's Carlton in 1970. Williamson says, "At that time, there was a really exciting feeling in the air, that at last we were going to get our own stories on stage spoken in our own accents, reflecting our own life, because up to that stage Australian plays had been few and far between. There were no Australian films, no Australian television, and our stories were simply not being told. And so there was an anger about that, but also an excitement and a determination to get the Australian way of life on stage."

The Removalists (1972) was Williamson's first major commercial success as a playwright and won an Australian Writers' Guild Awgie Award as well as the British theatre's George Devine Award. He is regarded as one of Australia's best known and most widely performed playwrights and his plays include *Don's Party* (1971), *The Department* (1974), *The Club* (1977), *Travelling North* (1979), *Emerald City* (1987) and *Money And Friends* (1991) — and many more. Many of his plays have been made into movies, including *Travelling North* and *Emerald City*.

Williamson has written several screenplays, including those for *Gallipoli*, *The Year of Living Dangerously*, *Phar Lap* and *Eliza Fraser*. "Working with Peter Weir," he says, "was the highlight of my life because he's a great director and we had a very strong collaboration through both *Gallipoli* and *The Year of Living Dangerously* … We were both in Australia, we were both doing Australian projects. I certainly have spent lots of mental energy trying to work out why we are as we are and I've always wanted to explore that in my work."

PLAYS

Influence (2005)
Operator (2005)
Amigos (2004)
Charitable Intent (2002)
Soulmates (2002)
A Conversation (2001)
The Great Man (2000)
Up for Grabs (2000)
Corporate Vibes (1999)
Face to Face (1999)
After the Ball (1997)
Third World Blues (1997)
Heretic (1996)
Dead White Males (1995)
Sanctuary (1994)
Brilliant Lies (1993)
Money & Friends (1991)

Siren (1990)
Top Silk (1989)
Emerald City (1987)
Sons of Cain (1985)
The Perfectionist (1982)
Celluloid Heroes (1980)
Travelling North (1979)
The Club (1977)
A Handful of Friends (1976)
The Department (1974)
The Family Man (1973)
What If You Died Tomorrow (1973)
Juggler's Three (1972)
Don's Party (1971)
The Removalists (1971)
The Coming of Stork (1970)

FILMS

Brilliant Lies (1997)
Sanctuary (1995)
Emerald City (1988)
Travelling North (1986)
Phar Lap (1982)
The Year of Living Dangerously (1981)
Partners (1981)
Gallipoli (1981)
The Club (1980)
Don's Party (1976)
Eliza Fraser (1976)
Petersen (1974)
The Removalists (1974)
The Family Man (1972)
Stork (1971)

TELEVISION

On the Beach (miniseries 2000) Adaptation, for Showtime USA. Nominated for Golden Globe Award.

Dogs Head Bay (1999)
The Four-Minute Mile (miniseries 1988)
A Dangerous Life (miniseries 1988)
The Club (1986)
The Perfectionist (telemovie 1985) Writer
The Last Bastion (mini-series 1984)
    Co-produced and co-wrote
The Department (1980)
Certain Women (1975) ■

The film at a glance

CAST

Archy Hamilton (LaSalles) *Mark Lee*
Jack *Bill Kerr*
Les McCann *Harold Hopkins*
Zac *Charles Yunupingu*
Stockman *Heath Harris*
Wallace Hamilton *Ron Graham*
Rose Hamilton *Gerda Nicolson*
Frank Dunne *Mel Gibson*
Bill *Robert Grubb*
Barney *Tim McKenzie*
Snowy *David Argue*
Railway Foreman *Brian Anderson*
Athletics Official 1 *Reg Evans*
Athletics Official 2 *Jack Giddy*
Announcer *Dane Peterson*
Waitress *Jenny Lovell*
Billy Snakeskin *Steve Dodd*
Camel Driver *Harold Baigent*
Mary *Robyn Galwey*
Lionel *Don Quin*
Laura *Phyllis Burford*
Gran *Marjorie Irving*
Frank's Father *John Murphy*
Major Barton *Bill Hunter*
Mrs Barton *Diane Chamberlain*
Lt. Gray *Peter Ford*
Army Doctor *Ian Govett*
Sgt. Sayer *Geoff Parry*
English Officer 1 *Bennington*
English Officer 2 *Giles Holland-Martin*
Egyptian Shopkeeper *Moshe Kedem*
Col. Robinson *John Harris*
N.C.O. at Ball *Don Barker*
Solider at Beach *Kiwi White*
Sniper *Paul Sonkkila*

Observer *Peter Lawless*
Sentry *Saltbush Baldock*
Sgt. Major *Stan Creen*
Col. White *Max Wearing*
General Gardner *Graham Dow*
Radio Officer *Peter R. House*
Australian Soldiers *The Men of Port Lincoln and Adelaide, The 16th Air Defence Regiment*
Cadets *No1 Recruit training unit Edinburgh South Australia.*

CREW

Director *Peter Weir*
Director of Photography *Russell Boyd A.C.S*
Camera Operator *John Seale*
Editor *William Anderson*
Art Director *Herbert Pinter*
Screenplay *David Williamson*
Story by *Peter Weir*
Executive Producer *Francis O'Brien*
Produced by *Robert Stigwood & Patricia Lovell*
Associate Producers *Martin Cooper & Ben Gannon*
Production Manager *Su Armstrong*
Production Manager Egypt *Ahmed Sami*
Original Music *Brian May*
Non-Original Music *Tomaso Albinoni (Adagio in C)*
Georges Bizet (Les Pecheursde Perks)
Jean-Michel Jarre (Oxygene)

FINANCED

Australian Film Commission
South Australian Film Commission

RUNNING TIME

110 Minutes

RELEASE DATES

Australia, United States 1981

AWARDS

1981 Australian Film Institute Awards
Best Film: *Robert Stigwood; Patricia Lovell*
Best Actor in a Lead Role: *Mel Gibson*
Best Actor in a Supporting Role: *Bill Hunter*
Best Director: *Peter Weir*
Best Screenplay, Original or Adapted: *David Williamson*
Best Achievement in Cinematography: *Russell Boyd*
Best Achievement in Editing: *William M. Anderson*
Best Achievement in Sound: *Don Connolly; Greg Bell; Peter Fenton*
1982 Australian Cinematographers Society Awards: Cinematographer of the Year: *Russell Boyd*

AT THE BOX OFFICE

Australia: ranked number 12 of all Australian films at the Australian box office, total sales of $11,740,000

United States: ranked number 31 of Australian films released in US, box office sales of $5,732,587 ∎

The critical eye
Gallipoli

"TO WATCH A Peter Weir film is to step into an otherworldly place," comments Randee Dawn of hollywoodreporter.com. Janet Maslin, writing in the *New York Times* in 1981 when *Gallipoli* was released in the US, agreed. "Mr Weir's work has a delicacy, gentleness, even wispiness that would seem not well suited to the subject. And yet his film has an uncommon beauty, warmth and immediacy, and a touch of the mysterious, too." She also comments that "… the film approaches the subject of war so obliquely that it can't properly be termed a war movie. Besides, it is prettier than any war film has ever been, which makes its emotional power something of a surprise … Much of *Gallipoli* has a full-blown, almost romantic style … There's nothing pointed in Mr Weir's decorous approach, even when the material would seem to call for toughness. But if the lush mood makes *Gallipoli* a less weighty war film than it might be, it also makes it a more airborne adventure." "Weir patiently constructed *Gallipoli* in such a fashion as to enable his audience to become emotionally attached to Archy and Frank," said ozcinema.com. "Their spirited youthfulness, enthusiasm, joy of living, competitive nature and the mateship that they share is used to great effect in highlighting the awful betrayal of war. In doing so, and in the chilling frozen framed conclusion, Weir has shown how quickly and pointlessly young lives can be destroyed. His visual masterwork carries a deep anti-war message that strikes home powerfully in its examination of the futility and tragedy of war."

> **"** Perhaps just once or twice a year you walk out of the darkness of a cinema knowing that you've seen the perfect thing. *Gallipoli* is such a film. **"**
> *Sydney Morning Herald*

"Perhaps just once or twice a year you walk out of the darkness of a cinema knowing that you've seen the perfect thing. *Gallipoli* is such a film" raved the *Sydney Morning Herald.* Brisbane's *Courier Mail* said "To sum it up, superb." And in *The Age*, Phillip Adams praised the film: "*Gallipoli's* qualities would bring honour to any nation, to any film industry. See it and be proud." Overseas, the *New York Post* called it "an awesome epic", and the London *Sun* assured us the film was "a powerful and brilliant film which grips the emotions with its stunning realism."

The release of the DVD version of the film in 2001 allowed reviewers to take another look, and to place the film into context. The BBC's DVD review noted that "Peter Weir's gripping account of the tragic First World War Gallipoli landings makes a welcome addition to DVD. A remarkable epic, this movie takes place in some truly beautiful settings that look great on disc ... *Gallipoli* is an impressive film by any standards, but its sheer scale was incredible for an Australian movie made in 1981 ... With a slew of war epics filling the screens recently, there has never been a better time to revisit this classic that now looks and sounds as grand as comparable films do today."

"*Gallipoli* delivers all the power and explosiveness that the best films of the genre contain ... Director Peter Weir's sense of composition is magnificent. His films are consistently haunting. The camera places his well-developed characters in a superbly realized world," said filmsondisc.com's reviewer, concluding that "Mark Lee is very effective as Archy, but it's Gibson as Frank

> ❝ Weir has shown how quickly and pointlessly young lives can be destroyed. ❞

that the camera can't keep its eyes off".
Movieline magazine agreed: "In 1981's
Gallipoli … Gibson is a genuine life force, a
cynical young rogue caught, unknowingly, in
the gears of history at its most savage … The
magic of Gibson here is in his remarkably
wide-open, guileless face; for a time, he was
one of those rare screen presences who suck
us in with the simple nakedness of their gaze.
This natural rapport with the camera is at
least as vital as things like acting technique or
role research, and Gibson has it in spades …
Then there's the film's throat-grabbing
climax … The image of Gibson reeling out of
control as the whistle blows sticks to you like
a fever. We see in Gibson's desperate,
screaming face signs of the man Frank will
become—haunted, empty, defeated. For that
moment, Gibson tells us all there is to know
about war." ■

Find out
more…

Find out more

ON THE WEB

www.anzacsite.gov.au —
Visit Gallipoli
The Commonwealth
Department of Veterans
Affairs' Anzac
Commemorative site —
with excellent
information, links and
resources

www.nma.gov.au/
exhibitions/community/
anzac_pilgrims
National Museum of
Australia's Anzac Pilgrims
exhibition online.

http://user.glo.be/
~snelders/contents.html
A fascinating Gallipoli
website with
contemporary and
historical information on
locations and events,
pictures, "Gallipoli
Gossip" and much more.

www.peterweircave.com
A website devoted to Peter
Weir and his films

www.nzhistory.net.nz/
Gallery/Anzac/galli-poli/
A New Zealand
perspective on the Anzacs.

http://library.trinity.wa.
edu.au/subjects/sose/
austhist/anzac.htm
Comprehensive collection
of links to more Anzac
resources.

READ

*Turn Right at Istanbul: A Walk on the Gallipoli
Peninsula* by Tony Wright (Allen & Unwin, 2003)

*Gallipoli: Our Last Man Standing: the
extraordinary life of Alec Campbell* by Jonathan
King (John Wiley & Sons, 2004)

Gallipoli by Les Carlyon (Macmillan, 2001)

*The Official History of Australia in the War of
1914–1918* by C.E.W. Bean (first published 1942)

VISIT

Australian War Memorial
Treloar Crescent, (top of ANZAC Parade)
Campbell ACT, 2612
AUSTRALIA
Phone: (02) 6243 4211
www.awm.gov.au

The Gallipoli Peninsula, Turkey
See www.turkeytravelplanner.com

SEE

Australian Story: Carve Their Names with Pride
(ABC TV, screened Nov 4, 1999)
The moving story of North Mackay High
School Students and their epic "Lest We Forget"
project (transcript available at
www.abc.net.au/austory/series4/9937text)

Breaker Morant (1980), a film directed by Bruce
Beresford

The Anzacs (1985), mini-series starring Paul
Hogan and Andrew Clarke. Based on the 1978
book by Patsy Adam-Smith. ■

homecoming

Adib Khan

'Khan's writing is so beautifully polished.
This is a very Australian story, told with a refreshing
simplicity and a convincing self-deprecation'
THE WEEKEND AUSTRALIAN

HOMECOMING
Adib Khan

'a significant novel ... expertly told'
Australian Book Review

Martin Godwin is a man who prefers to live a quiet life alone. But there is the question of his son Frank, and there is also the question of Nora.

Haunted by his memories of Vietnam, Martin takes solace in old friendships, but his marriage is over and his relationship with Frank is often strained. And is he responsible for what happened to Nora? If he'd come home earlier that day, if he'd acted sooner ...

Frank's happiness in a new relationship throws Martin's solitude into even sharper relief. And Frank's partner, Maria, just happens to be Vietnamese. As he gets to know her, Martin begins to see her homeland in a new light. And to look at new ways of living with the past and imagining a future.

'This is not just a saga of war-scarred veterans ... but of
all who have an interest in morality and the ability to look
within ... *Homecoming* bears re-reading on many counts'
The Age

'Khan's writing is so beautifully polished ...
This is a very Australian story, told with a refreshing
simplicity and a convincing self-deprecation'
The Weekend Australian

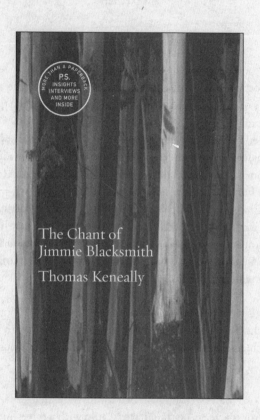

P.S.
MORE THAN A PAPERBACK
INSIGHTS
INTERVIEWS
AND MORE
INSIDE

The Chant of
Jimmie Blacksmith

Thomas Keneally

THE CHANT OF
JIMMIE BLACKSMITH
Thomas Keneally

When Jimmie Blacksmith marries a white woman the backlash from both Jimmie's tribe and white society initiates a series of dramatic events. As Jimmie tries to survive between two cultures, tensions reach a head when the Newbys, Jimmie's white employers, try to break up his marriage. The Newby women are murdered and Jimmie flees, pursued by police and vigilantes. The hunt intensifies as further murders are committed, and concludes with tragic results.

Thomas Keneally's fictionalised account of the 1900 killing spree of half-Aboriginal Jimmy Governor is a powerful story of a black man's revenge against an unjust and intolerant society.

'A lean, spare, menacing novel'
New York Times

'An unforgettable story ... riveting'
Daily Telegraph, London